# Radiance is Blooming

**Other Bella Books by Y. L. Wigman**

*Filigrane*
*Milgrane: Embracing the Sapphire*
*Closeness*

# About the Author

Emerging from a career in research and public service, Y. L. Wigman has turned her skills to the art of telling heartfelt stories. Her passions for studying the human condition, spirituality and astrology are evident in her novels. With extended family nearby, she lives in *Bandicoot Hollow*, a cottage in the hills above Perth, Western Australia. Website: www.ylwigman.com.

# *Radiance is Blooming*

## Y. L. Wigman

BELLA BOOKS

### PUBLISHER'S NOTE

# Acknowledgments

When I told a dear friend I was writing another book, she asked if it got any easier. I had to confess that it doesn't. For me, it's an act of blind faith. When I take a step and write those few first words the path appears, which never ceases to astonish me.

But I don't operate in a vacuum. I'm encouraged by close ones like my sister Annette, and niece-in-law Kerrie. Every book, I rely on intelligent criticism and support from my cousin Christine and her wife, Annelies. With Cath Walker's expertise as editor and Bella Books working their magic to make it so, a fine result does us all justice.

A warm shout-out goes to ancestors who barrack for me from beyond–thanks! Especially great-grandmother "Mags" Mewett, cockney laundress and mother of many who, in another time and place, would have been an author—you live on in lucky me.

# CHAPTER ONE

*January 1996*

Bella barked once—a short, toneless cough that made Nadeen start. She turned from her perch halfway up the stepladder where she was about to attach yet another poster to the wall.

"What's the matter, Bell-bell?" A rhetorical question because the elderly Cavalier King Charles spaniel was as deaf as a post. Still, her barking was rare. "It's not like you to make a fuss about nothing, eh?" The black-and-tan dog sat alert in her padded basket and stared toward the front of the shop. Nadeen followed her line of sight and spotted someone peering through the glass front door.

She tucked a rebellious dark curl behind an ear and sighed. Hot and tired, and with a long list of tasks awaiting her attention before she could open the gift shop, the last thing she needed was some busybody wasting her time. Sorely tempted to ignore the visitor, she dangled the poster she was trying to secure with one hand and felt the ladder shift sharply. Spooked, she clambered down, spread the poster on the cluttered counter and dusted off her faded khaki chinos on the way.

A blast of searing late January air smothered her breath. To the wide-eyed girl fidgeting with her backpack, Nadeen said, "We're not open yet. Should be by Friday."

"Sorry. Are you the owner? Could I have a chat?"

Nadeen took pity on the ethereally pretty, yet awkward young thing who looked to be in her midteens. "Yes, I am. What for? Come in out of this ridiculous heat." She stepped back, let the girl shuffle past her and quickly secured the door and made her way back to the counter. Her visitor took long, loose steps behind, then stalled in front of a large, colourful poster of Sesheta, Egyptian patron goddess of books. The girl put her hands together, as if in prayer, and stared.

Impatient yet amused, Nadeen said, "So, young lady. How can I help?"

Catlike golden eyes caught her attention, then dropped away. "Sorry. I'm looking for work experience in Toodyay village." She spoke in gulped sound bites. "Just until school goes back in February. I don't expect to be paid. Just, I'd love the experience." She glanced around, rhythmically strumming the nails of one hand against the other hand's. "I *love* your shop. There's nothing like it anywhere around here. It's awesome."

With a polite smile, Nadeen nodded. "Thank you. How about you tell me your name and age. And what year you're in."

"Sorry. I'm Melanie Chidlow. Everyone calls me Mel. I'm nearly eighteen and I'll be in year twelve. And I'm honest and reliable."

Nadeen's chocolate eyes glinted and narrowed. "I'll have to take your word for that. Tell you what. How about you come in on Sunday, say nine a.m., and I'll show you around. We can have a chat about how you might fit in. Okay? Now off you go. I've heaps to do before opening."

They walked together to the door. Nadeen said, "Must say, I'm impressed with your initiative. It takes courage to make a cold call at your age. Do your parents know you're doing this?"

"Sort of. My mum told me to find a job or work experience. Anything to get me out of the house for the rest of the holidays, she said."

With a wide grin, Nadeen shooed Mel outside. "Congratulations, job done! I'll see you Sunday."

Dusk deepening into night, it was seven thirty p.m. when Nadeen unlocked the front door to the vintage fibro cottage in Ellery Place. She let Bella trot in ahead, switched on the light and the air-conditioning system, and stooped to detach the dog's lead. It had been a mere seven-minute walk from the shop to home, yet she was too tired to think for very long about anything. Leather wedges off, she relished the cool of the jarrah floorboards.

At the half-round side table in the hall, the phone's answering machine was blinking red. Two messages. She stared at it and exhaled, sore shoulders sagging even lower. One caller was an easy guess, but the other? Against her better judgement, she hit the "play" button.

Her father's cultivated voice held a teasing edge. "Surprise! Yes, I'm checking up on you. And I've some great news. Call me back, asap. Cheers."

Eyebrows arching, she pressed the "play" button again.

"Nadeen? I *have* to talk to you." Greer's usually sonorous voice was commanding, then cracked into wheedling. "Absolutely have to. Don't do this to me. It's not fair. Ring me immediately."

"Not fair. Seriously?" With a gleeful snort, she made a face at the machine storing her ex's voice. "Nope. Not happening."

She padded down to the spartan kitchen at the back of the house. Bella sat by the sink, looking hopeful.

"Room service is late tonight, old girl. Coming up." Nadeen retrieved Bella's food bowl from the sink's drainer, tossed in a good handful of dog chow and set it on the floor. To the sound of gutsy crunching, she filled the kettle and clicked it on to boil. Light-headed from hunger, she peered in the fridge. "Looks like it's pumpkin soup and toast again. I need to get groceries. Soon." From a large saucepan, she ladled out congealed soup into a '70s stoneware bowl and eased it into the microwave. A couple of slices of frozen bread made it into the toaster, flew out again some minutes later, well-browned, hit the plate, were slathered with butter, and laid on the rickety kitchen table next to the steaming soup.

Nadeen slumped in the creaking pine chair with her head in her hands, inhaled the heady soup aroma, nearly too tired to bother. The phone messages flew into her head and she swatted them away. Food was the first priority.

"Vegemite." She hauled herself upright and rummaged in an overhead cupboard, found the jar, smeared a blob of sticky blackness on the toast, and took a huge bite. "Ah! Food of the gods. Butter and Vegemite make everything better."

Stomach placated, she retired to the sitting room's lumpy couch with a mug of tea, resting her protesting feet on the vinyl ottoman that had seen better days. Beside her, Bella curled up and buried her greying muzzle into Nadeen's left hip. Sipping the welcome tea, she idly stroked the Cavalier's super-soft and silky black coat, playing with the long tan strands falling from inside the dog's ear leathers. Bella snuffled contentedly and nestled more deeply.

The air-con was making slow work of cooling the stuffy room, but a pedestal fan set up opposite the couch made a decent difference. With high ceilings and quaint picture rails, the room had a solitary sash window that looked out to the street and a tiny yet dominating postwar fireplace with a too-large mantelpiece. Everything smelt a bit musty. Too bad she had no time for renovations. For now, there was more than enough to do in setting up the shop. Even if the house was absurdly rustic compared to the Melbourne apartment she'd shared with Greer, it was liveable. And tranquil, which she needed more than anything.

When widowed Uncle Garry died last summer, her father had inherited his estate. He rented the house out over winter and into spring until a few months ago. For want of a sale, Felix had moth-balled his brother's old pharmacy in the arcade off Toodyay's main street. The business had been heading for extinction anyway, a new pharmacy farther up the street having consumed the last of his meagre trade.

For Nadeen, it was perfect timing. When her nine-year relationship with Greer had ended four months ago, she decided to pack up everything, including her eclectic gift shop, The Prophet, to move it three thousand kilometres to Toodyay, her childhood home in Western Australia. About as far away from Melbourne—and Greer—as she could get and still be in the same country.

Tonight's phone message was yet another among so many received in the last three weeks that she'd lost count. She had no intention of returning Greer's calls. Not ever. More annoying was how Greer had got hold of her number. Nadeen hadn't given it to her and she most definitely didn't want to be found.

Being dumped for some brainless, Jockey-wearing bimbo likely half her forty-two years, coupled with Greer's obsession with said bimbo and utter disregard for her maimed heart, was more than enough reason to pack up and get the hell out of town.

Enough already. Whatever Greer was after, she could go take a flying leap through a rolling donut. Preferably all by herself.

Nadeen's throat ached—she blinked rapidly until moist eyes dried out. Firmly convinced it was best to make a clean break from the remains of their relationship, she was handling the grief well enough. And the last thing she needed was her ex popping up, just as she was getting over it and establishing herself anew.

Her gift shop had been doing very well in suburban Melbourne. At the breakup, her father had tried to convince her to move back to Sydney and find a vacant shop in an outer suburb. A retired Egyptologist and part-time teaching professor at Sydney University, Felix Quin was a minor international celebrity in his field, and not short of funds. In fact, it was less than six months ago that he'd bought a luxury high-rise apartment in Bondi Beach where he lived with Jodie, his latest young thing.

Truth be known, she didn't want to live that close to him because his attitude to her "choice of lifestyle" was fundamentally hostile. When she first phoned and told him she and Greer were splitting up, he made no attempt to hide his delight. Yet he was downright dubious about her setting up shop across country in sleepy Toodyay. His suggestion of a sprawling metropolitan city like Sydney was perfectly sensible.

Still, her childhood home had drawn her with a persistent urgency, even though the businesswoman in her knew that moving here was a sizeable risk. She was resolved, and had told him as much, without knowing how or when she might be able to make it happen. Ten days after that phone call, he rang and offered her Uncle Garry's house and shop, unconditionally. With little demand for rentals in Toodyay, it made sense to have her occupy the house and thereby look after it. Still, such unusual largesse gave her pause. But she took him up on it, no questions asked.

Something about his latest message left her uneasy. Notorious for a hidden agenda, what was his "great news"? What was her unpredictable, rather contrary Dad up to this time?

Such shenanigans were giving her a headache. As it was, she regularly questioned her own decision to uproot herself and take off across the country as if Toodyay were Neverland. Her father had grown up in Toodyay. When his wife fell pregnant while they were working in Egypt, he brought them home. But career advancement called and they moved to Sydney when she was only eight years old. She had few memories of the town, but they were precious and sweet. Now, was she being wildly idealistic, if not completely delusional?

What would tiny Toodyay make of her shop's richly diverse offerings? Probably not much locally, but the surrounding area was growing strongly as a tourist destination, particularly for weekend jaunts by more sophisticated, moneyed-up Perth residents looking for that special "something different." That, The Prophet would definitely offer. She was counting on it.


Nadeen arose, nudged the reluctant pooch off the couch and lead the way down the hall to the back door where she flicked on the outside light. She let Bella out to toilet on the scrappy lawn under the clothesline. Uncle Garry's greenhouses loomed next to the garage. They were surrounded by innumerable pots of stunted gerberas that had toughed out the summer so far, despite inevitable casualties. A substantial garden shed backed onto cultivated beds full of similar plants in various states of health. Since she moved in, she'd been hand-watering heavily to bring back from the brink those that she could.

Uncle Garry and Aunt Peggy had been keen gerbera fanciers, both quite besotted with the colourful, sturdy South African daisy that thrived in Perth's severe dry summers and cool wet winters. They had been stalwart Gerbera Society members, a hobby that saved Garry's sanity after Peggy died. As a small child, Nadeen had helped them pot up pups—young gerbera plants—which had left her with an enduring fondness for their sturdy foliage and cheerful durable blooms. When she had more time, she would see what she could salvage. A phone call to the Gerbera Society for advice was on her "to do" list. With any luck, someone would be prepared to make the hour-long drive from Perth city to have a look for her.

It was another hot night that wouldn't make for easy sleeping. She leant against the doorjamb and studied the stars, brilliant without a large city's light pollution. Bella snuffled about under the clothesline, then looked up sharply. A shadowy boobook owl perched on a wire, eyeing off the dog below. Without a whisper of sound, the owl launched off and disappeared into the trees, its hunting for mice or similar tasty morsels curtailed for now. The boobook's mournful call that imitated its name was as much a sound of her childhood as a magpie's warbling. This place was home.

What about that young girl…Mel something? Telling her to drop in on Sunday had been an impulse she couldn't resist because she needed allies in Toodyay. And a well-trained willing sidekick could make life so much easier. She hadn't dared to hope for such help, but when opportunity knocked, courage took the chance. Assuming Mel was suitable, of course. She seemed promising, but that could be mere wishful thinking. Only one way to find out.

# CHAPTER TWO

"Hi, Mum. How's it going?"

Lorna Chidlow glanced up from the paperwork laid out in neat piles across the desk. "Getting there, my girl."

In the office's doorway, her daughter shrugged on a backpack. Mel had recently taken to tying back her ash-blond hair—a move that immediately made the teenager look remarkably like Lorna. For years, Lorna had only seen Cormack's features and gold-specked hazel eyes gazing back at her. When had gangly Mel become such a memorable young woman?

"Where are you off to?"

Mel adjusted the shoulder straps. "I told you Friday, remember? I might get work experience in that new gifty-thingummy shop in town. I'm to meet the owner at nine."

Lorna nodded, then frowned. "How are you getting there?"

"Kelly's giving me a lift on her way to guitar lessons. But I don't know how long I'll be. Could you pick me up?"

"Surely can. Just give me a bell."

Mel headed for the front door.

"Good luck," said Lorna. Louder, "Proud of you!" She peered through the ranchsliders, spotted Kelly's battered utility motoring up the gravel driveway. Still getting the hang of the recently purchased vehicle, the teenager did a rough three-point turn outside the largest glasshouse next to the packing shed and stalled the engine. Mel climbed in and slammed the door. The ute restarted, took off and disappeared beyond a cloud of dust that obscured the open front gates of Morwood.

What gift shop? Lorna couldn't think where it might be. Historic Toodyay town was really a village in search of a town—one main drag, and that was about it. Yet it was a growing residential and tourist destination for those seeking a tree change, either permanently or for a holiday. Its main claim to fame was a rich history of convicts and pioneering landowners centred around the Avon River that ran close by. Notoriously, the original town site had started as a convict settlement in the 1850s and developed more diverse reasons for being since then. The whole Avon Valley had become prime orchard and farmland dotted with properties of various shapes and sizes, of which Morwood was one.

Lorna closed her eyes and breathed deeply. Four summers had passed since Cory's quad bike had slid in driving rain and rolled into a gully. A broken neck had killed him instantly. For Lorna, the memory of his loss could be rekindled by the oddest things, like a certain expression, or her daughter's eyes.

A shiver coursed down her spine and she exhaled in short puffs, forced herself to focus on the itemised consignment sheet that needed a final check. Tomorrow, she would drive the van's precious cargo to the Papsom Medical plantation at first light to avoid the day's heat.

The van was fitted out with purpose-built shelving to hold the multiple trays of five-centimetre-high plants. It was Lorna's task to germinate the tiny seeds. Contracted to the Federal Government, Papsom then grew them to full size in their carefully concealed facility located nearly fifty kilometres inland from Morwood. They would let them flower freely, ensure they were pollinated, and then collect the sap from the seed heads of *papaver somniferum.*

Opium poppies. Grown for the sole purpose of providing opiates for medicinal use within Australia.

Lorna's closely guarded technique that ensured an extremely high rate of germination was the lifeblood of the farm's business these days. While the apple orchard, cider production, and donkey stud paid modestly, they provided a front for Lorna's real passion of bringing the frail poppy seeds to life. She *loved* poppies: their tiny precious seeds, curling exotic leaves and glamorous flowers. Especially the brilliant red ones.

Generating a highly desirable and very expensive natural product, opium poppy cultivation was strictly controlled across the country, which made her propagating business necessarily secret. Rumours of her growing marijuana bounced around Toodyay—they came and went. Few knew what really came out of Morwood. Lorna intended to keep it that way.

Now fifty-six years old, she'd had their daughter after she and Cory had stopped trying, with his premature death depositing all parenting duties on her steady, lone shoulders. She intended to provide amply for her only child for as long as she was able.

At her side was Rocco, whom she employed to manage the apple orchard, oversee cider production, and supervise care for the donkeys. He'd been Cory's choice—Lorna wasn't too keen on him. And it had become obvious soon after Cory's passing that Rocco was a bit too keen on her. His surreptitious stares were disconcerting. Not that he'd done or said anything, but his manner wasn't helped by a lazy right eye that left her wondering exactly where he was looking. For now, she put up with him because he knew his stuff, did the work, helped out if needed, and left them alone nights. He was bearable and harmless.

With the final sheet prepped for checking, she'd have all the paperwork done in plenty of time before lunch.

An ominous rumbling gave her pause, and a pale-blue Falcon station wagon pulled up outside. She'd clean forgotten Murray had rung three days ago and said he'd drop in this morning. He was one of Papsom's production people who came to see her about once a month and had most recently visited only a fortnight ago.

Smiling brightly, she held the front door open. "Nice to see you, Murray. What's the occasion?"

"Morning, Lorna." Just taller than her and whippet-thin, he doffed his Akubra, deep-blue eyes flashing appreciatively. "You're looking fine, as usual. Any chance of a coffee?"

"The percolator must still be on. Come into the kitchen."

While she filled a sturdy mug, he dropped his hat on the kitchen table and settled into a chair. He stroked his jeans-clad inner thighs, watching intently when she slid the coffee in front of him. Nestled into a chair across from him, arms folded, smile on, she said, "So. What's up?"

He blinked, pausing to push a sandy fringe out of his eyes. "News from on high. We've received an injection of federal funding, with the proviso that we rapidly increase production. This new government wants the country to be self-sufficient in supply, as much as possible. Much of what is imported legally is compromised by illegal imports. In terms of biosecurity, it's better for the country, and also for greater ease in policing…catching the criminal element."

Lorna leaned forward. "What's that got to do with me?"

Clearing his throat, he said, "We'd like you to increase what you give us by forty percent. As soon as possible."

"What the—?" Lorna pinched her eyebrows. "Murray, that's simply not possible. No way. I'm at max in the greenhouses already. There simply isn't the space."

"I know. But if you're agreeable, Papsom will subsidise a new greenhouse and see it built on your land within the next six weeks."

Looking askance, she said, "Are you for real?"

"You're the best in Western Australia, Lorna, if not the whole country. This is a long-term investment in a niche market. We're under the pump and, as long as you can supply seedlings, Papsom will buy them. Government guaranteed."

Lorna sat back and studied the freckles that had filled in the white line where her wedding band had once lived—she'd finally taken it off at the beginning of summer. "May I think about it overnight?"

"Of course. But if you don't come to the party, we'll have to source supply from South Australia, probably the Adelaide Hills Nursery as it would have capacity. And Papsom management would rather deal with you as a local, reliable nursery without the freight costs and time lag. Which is why they're willing to put their money where their mouth is. A brand-new, state-of-the-art greenhouse on your land. Your choice. But it has to happen fast."

Lorna worried a hangnail. "No pressure, eh? I'll let you know."

At the door, he put a tender hand on her shoulder in farewell, and she stiffened.

She said, "Speaking of the criminal element, we had another break-in at the growing-on glasshouse last Sunday morning. That's where the more developed seedlings are stored."

"Anything stolen? Damage?"

"As usual, just a broken sheet of glass, some of the seedling trays shifted around. Nothing taken."

"You wonder why they bother." Murray scratched a thinning scalp and replaced the hat, its brim skimming his eyebrows.

"Oh, that's easy. They think we're growing marijuana. Once they've had a good look inside, even the dumbest dopehead knows what the plant looks like. Hm…not like ours. It's just a nuisance. We've had five break-ins since that first one twelve months ago. This is the first this year. No point in calling the cops for broken glass. The thing is, if we put in a swanky new glasshouse, that's going to attract even more attention. I reckon I'm already keeping the local glazier in regular beer money."

"What about some fencing?" said Murray.

"That would *really* gain unwanted attention because they'll think there's something definitely worth stealing. We know there isn't. Besides, fencing is a very expensive deterrent. There's no point as serious thieves will always find a way in and these idiots aren't serious. It's just a nuisance."

"Tsk. I worry about you, Lorna." He moved closer and lowered his voice. "You need a man around the place to look after you."

She backed up and laughed lightly. "I've handled Morwood perfectly well for the last four years. And I'm sure I'll manage just as well for the foreseeable future. Besides, Rocco is always somewhere around. Do try not to worry."

"You know I will anyway. See you later." Murray strode away to fire up the Falcon, its throaty V8 engine fading into the distance. Idly, she wondered why forty-something men like Murray and Rocco paid any attention to her at her age. And Murray with a young wife and kids.

But she had more important things to think about now. Choices—always choices. Most inconsequential, then some with massive ramifications that weren't always obvious. and fraught with traps for the unwary. It was times like these that she really missed Cory's input. Increasingly, she talked to her daughter who often had a surprisingly insightful take on things, and sometimes a left-field, curly thought process that contained startling wisdom. But this business situation was very adult—she'd have to carefully consider her options.

# CHAPTER THREE

While Nadeen unpacked books, Mel called her mother for a ride home. Since they'd gone through an hour of explanations and a sit-down cup of tea with a bickie, Nadeen was confident and frankly relieved that Mel seemed like a good match for The Prophet. However, only a decent tryout would justify that judgement.

Mel had hung up. "She'll be here in ten minutes, no worries."

"That's handy. Now, have you any questions?"

"I love everything! The books and posters and crystals. The range of statues and jewellery." Mel cast her gaze around the shop. "The different oracles are just amazing. The toys and games for kids. All of it," she said with a wide grin. "But I was wondering—"

"What? Go on, surprise me."

"What about some Aboriginal art? Or posters?"

Nadeen folded her arms and examined the enthusiastic youngster. "Do you think it would sell? I'm afraid I have to be a businesswoman to stay in business."

Mel shrugged. "I get that. But there are some local artists who do really cool stuff. We could try."

Smiling widely at the proprietary use of the word "we," Nadeen said, "I'll give it some thought. As a matter of fact, I am interested in local handicrafts that would appeal to tourists and Perth shoppers. And by that, I mean woodwork and jewellery. Maybe some leather."

"Oh, yes!" Mel clapped her hands. "My mum plaits leather belts. And bracelets and wristbands. Usually just for family and friends. I'll ask her, if you like."

Nadeen pictured Mel's mother as a well-rounded, craft-obsessed and merrily busy farmer's wife. "Sure, you can mention it and let me know." Nadeen started for the door, mindful of the numerous people who had peered in the windows while they were talking and walking around the shop. "For now, I need you to help me get the shop set up for opening by the end of this week, if not sooner. Just to take advantage of the school holidays' passing trade. Would you be able to start tomorrow morning? Be here by a quarter to nine, let's say. Does that work for you?"

"Yeah, that'd be rad," said Mel, peering beyond Nadeen. "There's Mum."

A woman knocked and stepped back aways, fingertips tucked into the pockets of a pair of well-worn jeans held up by a plaited belt. She wore a plain white T-shirt under a blue-checked shirt. Mel opened the door and went out. The woman's deep-grey eyes scanned Nadeen's physique, came to rest as a direct, unreadable stare that Nadeen couldn't help but return, drawn in by the woman's self-assured demeanour.

Nadeen straightened her collar and opened her mouth to say something—anything. But the woman briefly doffed her stockman's hat over tousled ash-blond hair, turned on a heel and sauntered away. With a shy smile, Mel gave a quick wave and bolted to catch up with her mother.

Nadeen stood in the doorway, fingers spread wide across her chest, as townsfolk waylaid Mel and her mother to chat, while others stepped back, smiling and nodding. The woman radiated an unmistakeable energy that people responded to, consciously or not. Was she aware of it herself? In less than a minute, the pair turned a corner and they were gone.

"Would you look at that? All falling over themselves," Nadeen murmured. "I bet you're a local celebrity. The town's shining light. And once upon a time, the Toodyay Festival queen, no doubt. Probably broken the heart of every bloke within a fifty-kilometre radius."

Soberly, she locked the door and leaned back on it for a few moments, musing to the empty room. "Oh-kay…She really is something else. For the love of Isis, what gives?"

Yet Mel's mother hadn't a conventionally pretty face. Those strong eyebrows, a thin nose, and maybe a mouth too wide? But she emanated something compelling, yet elusive, that would make anyone with a pulse look twice.

Nadeen speared soothing fingers through her dark waves and exhaled noisily, turned and strode back to unpacking that couldn't wait. Delving into the remaining contents of a carton of books, she weighed an illustrated guide to the tarot and a glossy astrology manual in her hands, looked up at a large poster of Isis and said to the Egyptian goddess, "Who would have guessed? A rogue stunner lurking in little old Toodyay." At the back of her mind, a seed sprung up into the unlikely thought that she had seen Mel's mother before. But where?

# CHAPTER FOUR

It was only when Mel was stacking the dishwasher after dinner that Lorna dared a tone of casual disinterest to ask, "Is Nadeen married?"

"Um, I don't know. Don't think so." Mel started the machine.

"No wedding ring?"

"Didn't notice. Does it matter? I mean, I like her. So far. And the shop is so cool."

Lorna nodded. "Just as long as she's good to you."

Mel rolled her eyes and flounced off toward the TV room. Lorna took a deep breath and exhaled through pursed lips. While she could usually keep a straight face, her daughter knew her too well, but she may have got away with it, this time. A fluttering pulse reported that she was considerably calmer than she had been a few hours ago. Calmer, yet far from calm.

She closed her eyes, which was a mistake. A sultry smile belonging to a face from ten years ago leapt into view, made her heart clamour. Nadeen's resemblance to that face was remarkable. Even more alarming was the feeling that they'd met before, and she couldn't think where. Or how. Or when. The familiarity was unnerving.

"Don't worry about it, easily fixed. Don't have *anything* to do with her. End of story." She leaned forward and rubbed her forehead briskly. "Get a grip, Lorna!"

"You all right, Mum?"

She looked up at her daughter. "Nothing coffee wouldn't fix. Put the kettle on, darling girl. It's all good."

At the witching hour and sweating freely, Lorna woke to a tension in the groin that she hadn't felt for years, alarmed to realise her fingers were dealing with the source. And Marissa De Leo's heady perfume seemed to hang in the air.

She flung off the bedclothes, swung her legs over the edge of the bed and turned on the bedside light. Breathing deeply to slow her thudding heart, she examined her shaking hands as if they belonged to someone else.

Marissa. All those years ago, the locum tax accountant had worked for just three months to help out the local firm of accountants that was swamped by end-of-financial-year tax matters. The Toodyay Valley growers had had a particularly good year, and Morwood was no exception. Cormack was frantically busy with cider production, while Lorna tackled the tax side of things for the first time, way out of her depth. Cory told her to get help, however she could. Well, Marissa had helped. And then some.

At first meeting, Lorna had been much taken with Marissa's warm, easy smile and dancing dark eyes—a light-hearted laugh never far away. And she knew her tax stuff, too—knew exactly what she was doing, to Lorna's relief. The paperwork got sorted over three meetings, heads together, deciding what should and could not be included in the return. Job done, Marissa dragged a protesting Lorna off to line-dancing classes in the town hall every fortnight, with a chat over a drink afterward—well worth a giggle. In fact, a lot of giggling. With a wicked sense of humour that secretly shocked her, Lorna couldn't remember when she last had so much fun. She was unexpectedly gutted when Marissa announced she was leaving town to work for a firm in Subiaco, near the centre of Perth city. But for her last night in Toodyay, Marissa invited Lorna out to dinner at a local restaurant. She jumped at the chance. They savoured yabbies with tagliatelle, washed down with too much unwooded chardonnay. Lorna was having a good time, yet aware she was about to lose someone surprisingly special.

Apologetically, she confessed that she'd drunk too much. In her BMW Z3 roadster, Marissa drove Lorna home too fast, pulled over just short of Morwood's gates and killed the lights. Without a word, Marissa leaned over and kissed her and the bottom fell out of Lorna's known world. Marissa's hands did what Lorna hadn't realised she wanted until it happened. She would never forget the look of fierce desire and animal knowing in Marissa's eyes. No one had looked at her like that, before or since. As it was, a surge of unspeakable passion and its urgent release left her gasping, blood ringing in her ears. Mute and close to panic, she had scrambled out of the convertible and bolted to the front door.

Lorna never saw Marissa again. Never told anyone—not even Natasha, her best friend. But she couldn't lie to herself. She'd never felt so alive as she had in the hands of a bold and fearless woman who knew exactly what she was doing. That it might happen again made her blood run like fire through her veins. And she didn't have to look far for the reason.

# CHAPTER FIVE

With its mellow weather, March was the perfect time of year to divide and propagate gerberas. Nadeen was out the back in the greenhouse, potting up pups into a soil mix that should make a good growing medium. Not knowing precisely what suited gerbera cultivation and which ingredients constituted a perfect growing medium, she had contacted the Gerbera Society for advice. They said someone would come out and have a look.

Uncle Garry had taught her to take an old plant out of its large pot, shake the soil off and tease the pups away from the main plant without doing them too much damage. The roots had to be washed free of soil, dunked in a watered-down bleach mix to kill nasties, and rinsed again before being planted in a small pot of fresh soil mix. It was messy but satisfying.

Nadeen daydreamed while she worked. Mel's mother's unblinking stare popped into her skull, as it had at random moments since they saw each other that day. What was it about that woman? And why the hell did she look so intensely at Nadeen? Unforgettable eyes—positively unnerving. Whatever passed between them in those ten seconds kept replaying in glorious technicolour that seemed to grow more vivid each time. Sure, she was attractive—so what? But there was something else. Mel's mother hadn't said a word at the time, but she didn't have to. It was like a physical zap—a connection that felt oddly like some kind of a reconnection. Nadeen shook her head vigorously. It was all too weird.

She tapped a filled pot on the bench to settle the soil around the young plant. It had taken long evenings of turfing out the sad casualties of neglect, scrubbing out and sanitising plastic pots, and trying to work out what plan, if any, Gazza—as his mates used to call Uncle Garry—had for organising the plants in garden beds and pots. Without the flowers, she had no idea what was what—just guessing, totally. This was going to take months, if not years to sort out. In the meantime, the best she could do was to propagate with a numbering system that tagged each pot and its offspring. Only flowering would reveal all.

Any minute now, she was expecting Irma Ledwith from the Gerbera Society to arrive. She had sounded very excited when Nadeen described Uncle Garry's substantial collection and explained that there could be some absolutely astonishing beauties in amongst the mayhem.

"Coo-ee!" A woman popped her head over the tall wooden garden gate.

Nadeen took quick strides and lifted the latch. "You must be Irma. Thanks for coming all this way." The neat and trim grey-haired woman wore a comfortable blouse, trousers, and loafers that were distinctly classy, if not quite designer. Definitely not gardening gear.

"No trouble. I'm intrigued to find what's here. Your uncle was well-known and respected within the Society."

"Wonderful. Let me show you around."

They did a slow and thorough circuit of the garden, with Irma frequently stopping to put on her spectacles and examine the plants. "You seem to have a good mix of standard and new vogue gerberas, likely singles, doubles, and triplexes. With nothing blooming, it's the wrong time of year to assess them properly. Sorry about that."

"That's all right. I'll just have to wait and see."

Irma tapped her nose with the folded glasses. "Are there any written records that might help with identifying them. Anything at all?"

"Nothing I know of. My father had the house emptied and thoroughly cleaned when my uncle died. Then it was rented out most of last year. Before I came, that is. And you know what tenants are like. They don't water gardens."

"What a shame," said Irma. "Tell you what. I can get one of those rubbish removal services to clear out the whole backyard so you don't have to deal with the problem. Someone in the Society might take them on."

Nadeen smiled. "Truly, I feel duty-bound to do my best by my uncle. He taught me a bit about gerberas…said I had a green thumb, which is debatable. Is there any information about planting, potting, fertilisers and so-on that you might be able to show me?"

Irma rummaged in her handbag and drew out a small booklet. "The Society gives this out to its members. I'm sure you'll find it useful."

"Why, thank you, Irma. That's very thoughtful of you. Can I offer you a drink?"

"Good of you, but no thanks. I drove over with a friend and she's waiting for me at that cosy café on the main street. We're doing lunch in Toodyay for a change. I promised her I wouldn't be long."

"I know the one. Be warned, it has the most irresistible Black Forest cake. As a matter of fact, I was thinking you didn't look dressed for messing about in soil."

"Ah, no…hardly," said Irma, putting out her hand. "It was nice to meet you, Nadeen. And if you ever want to become a Society member, you're welcome to join us."

Nadeen escorted her back to the gate, waved when she drove off in a navy Mercedes two-seater. She grinned to herself. Thar be gold in them thar hills—otherwise known as prize-winning and quite probably unique varieties of magnificent gerberas.

"Good thing I'm not as green as I'm cabbage-looking," Nadeen told a row of unassuming pots. "Or you lot would have been spirited away, never to be seen again by us Quins. Lucky for you, I'm willing to take a punt on Uncle Garry's knowledge and skill as a gerbera fancier, eh?"

Nadeen potted up another pup, enjoying the process of nestling a tender young plant in the soil mix. It had a good chance of growing strongly and turning into a living thing of beauty. She might set up a stand inside the shop and sell a few pots when they came into flower, just for the satisfaction.

More urgently, Easter's four-day holiday would start tomorrow with Good Friday. All the shops were shut, reopening on Saturday which promised a serious influx of visitors to the town as potential customers. The passing trade could be considerable, and after months of settling in and stocking up, she was ready.

It had been six weeks since Mel first started Saturday hours at The Prophet. She had blended in well and now needed minimal supervision. Mel would assist this Easter Saturday, with her bestie, Jared, on call if needed.

When she first met Jared, Nadeen was struck by his dazzling smile and thick black lashes that batted at her above dancing eyes as dark as a new moon. A barrel-chested teen in a colourful tie-dyed T-shirt and tight jeans, he'd hovered silently while Mel explained he was a budding Aboriginal artist who would like to one day sell his work but was eager for retail experience.

Nadeen had shown him around, explained how to work the till and what she expected from him when dealing with customers—all of which he had absorbed with effortless speed. Over a few Saturday afternoons, she'd warmed to his shy humour and willingness to step in and have a go at whatever she asked of him. She could rely on him to turn up at short notice—a rare treasure in retail. Between the three of them, Nadeen figured they could handle any challenges the coming Saturday's hectic trading might pose.

# CHAPTER SIX

By three thirty p.m. the store was all but empty of people. Jared had gone home, which left Nadeen and Mel sorting and counting banknotes tucked away under the tray in the till. Most people paid in cash, with only a few needing a card transaction. Nadeen was impressed by the number of tumbled semiprecious stones younger women and girls had bought. Costing very little each, they'd been very popular—she would have to order more. And source a stand to display gerberas.

"I've potted up more gerbera pups, Mel. They're going to be a hit in about a month's time. Just diversifying because I can."

Mel said, "Do green thumbs run in your family or something? They seem to in mine."

"Apart from Uncle Gazza, not that I know of. Don't all humans have farming ancestors in their DNA, somewhere in their distant past?"

They both turned when someone strolled into the shop. Only Nadeen stared at the moustachioed, olive-skinned older man in a jazzy yellow polo shirt. He held his hands wide and grinned at her, fingers thick with gold rings.

"Dad? Good grief, what are you doing here?" She touched his shoulders, and he pecked her on both cheeks. "Tired of Sydney? Is Jodie with you?"

He looked askance. "Daughter of mine, I've come to see you, of course." With a cursory glance around, he said, "And you're about to shut up shop. May I take you to the pub for a drink? And a catch up?"

"Oh, okay. I'll need another twenty minutes, or so. Will I meet you there?"

"Please. There's lots to tell you." He backed up, grinning wickedly, then strode out the door.

Mel said, "Were you expecting him?"

Nadeen barely shook her head. She had tried to phone him back, any number of times after that last message on her phone, but no one had picked up. She had assumed they were away on holiday somewhere. And then, the last time she called an automated message told her the number had been disconnected. He was up to something.

Nadeen weaved her way into the main bar of the Victoria Hotel that was doing a roaring Saturday trade. The place reeked of beer and cigarettes, which wouldn't suit her father. More likely, he'd be in the outdoor garden behind the main building. And there he was, talking animatedly to a lipless bloke with short blond hair who looked vaguely familiar.

"Nadeen! Come and say hello to Derek. You remember him, don't you?"

With a smile that was more a grimace, she tried not to stare at the man who she went out with for five minutes in her late teens. What on earth?

"Of course. Hi, Derek." She shook his too-enthusiastic damp hand. "Fancy seeing you here."

"Fancy. Gee, you look great. Haven't changed a bit."

Nadeen caught her father's glance and raised an eyebrow. In reply, he rubbed his hands together like a used-car salesman. "Well, Derek, I'll be in touch."

Derek grinned at them both, then offered Nadeen a wink and a scoutmaster's salute, and turned on his heel.

Nadeen glared at Felix. "Derek The Dork. Pompous arse. What the hell, Dad?"

"Don't know what you mean. He's a good bloke. Well, maybe not the sharpest crayon in the playroom, but a handy real estate agent. Now, sit down and listen up. I've got great news." He paused for effect. "I've bought an apartment in Cottesloe. Derek handled our purchase to our best advantage. Jodie and I have moved in already. It's the perfect spot, with plenty of rooms and stunning views across the Indian Ocean. You're going to love it. A thousand sunsets await you."

"Is this a permanent move, or what?"

"Certainly is. I've retired from my position at Sydney Uni. To be honest, your move here inspired me. We're hoping to see a whole lot more of you now that you're single." He leaned in and peered at her. "Not that I expect you'll have to put up with that sorry state of affairs for long, my girl. There's plenty of worthy talent out there, and it's time you took your future seriously instead of mucking about with the other team. I know you've got it in you to call time on all that nonsense. You're an adult, now."

Nadeen didn't know whether to laugh or cry. With one hand over her mouth, she just looked at him and nodded for a few moments. "Well, it's been interesting. I know I'm wasting my breath, but I really wish you wouldn't meddle in my private life. As luck would have it, I've work to do." She backed away from his tetchy, disconcerted expression. "Enjoy the new place. Have to go." She didn't look back when he called her name. Disappeared into the crowd.

On any Saturday night she was glad to be home with her cuddly old dog. She'd gone through the store's books, checked what they'd sold and their takings, and couldn't be anything but pleased. A surprise was how well the Egyptian-style blank greeting cards were selling—simple, plain white cards with prints of Isis, Osiris, Anubis, and Bast, plus a few meaningful hieroglyphs in a variety of colours. People could use them for any occasion.

Nadeen had designed them, made the linocuts and printed them herself. She would have to do more tomorrow—Easter Sunday. While the town was closed down, she could do whatever she liked. She was looking forward to mucking about with inks.

The spare room had become a default stock room with various cartons stacked neatly at one end. She'd found a folding trestle table in the garage, brushed off the redback spiders and managed to wrestle it inside where it had become her printing table, amongst other things. She rummaged through the printing inks. Supplies of metallic blue were low—it seemed to be a favourite colour.

At that moment, she let herself think about her father's words. Getting upset or offended was pointless. And protesting was even worse when he professed his parental love and concern for her happiness. Fully convinced that his way was the only way, experience told her there was no point arguing or trying to educate to the contrary—a lost cause, as much as he thought she very nearly was. But he just couldn't help himself. A no-win situation for them both. It didn't have to be that way. If only.

Someone was knocking on the front door—not something that had happened of an evening since she'd moved in. On the way, she flicked on the outside light.

"Oh, it's you. You'd better come in."

Felix shut the door. "I didn't get a chance to ask how you're settling into the house, or how everything's going for you. Are you okay?"

"Of course. Do you want a cuppa?"

He drew a paper bag from behind his back. "How about a red?"

"I'll find some glasses."

In the kitchen, he opened the bottle and poured. "A pinot shiraz. Cheers." They both pulled out a chair and sat at the table. "Do you like the house?"

"I do. It's homely and surprisingly comfortable. I've cleaned up most of the backyard and had fun potting up Uncle's gerberas. I don't know what most of them are yet. When they flower, I'll have a better idea. But it's very peaceful. In fact, I found it difficult to sleep for a while. It's so dark and deathly quiet after Melbourne."

"Is everything sorted with Greer?"

"Yep. She paid out my share of the apartment months ago, no problem."

"Good." He swirled the wine in its glass. "Are you involved with anyone new?"

"What? No. And I've no inclination to be otherwise, thanks. Why are you even asking?"

"Because if I don't ask, you don't tell me a blind bloody thing. I just wondered. You were so reactive about Derek." He took a swig and rested the glass on the mottled timber, crossed his arms. "You know, you should really consider your options, now that you're free. Stands to reason."

"Reactive? Options?" Nadeen examined the ceiling that badly needed a lick of fresh paint. "Would you please get it through your skull that being lesbian isn't optional for me. Making my life more difficult than most was not my first choice. It's just how it is."

"You see?" He waved a finger at her. "That's your problem. Right there. That 'no can do' attitude. Where did that come from? Not your mother and me. We brought you up to adapt, survive and make the best of it. Just change your mind. How hard can it be?"

Nadeen laughed—a loud, hooting laugh. "Oh, give me a break! I've heard this all before. I heard this nine years ago when I moved in with Greer and you called me a lemon." She pushed back the chair and paced the kitchen. "I heard this when we invited you to every occasion and you refused to come. And when you invited me to yours, as long as Greer didn't come with me—"

"That was your mother, worried about losing friends."

"Like you were any less twitched? You know that's why we moved to Melbourne and stayed well away. To save us all from these stupid, toxic arguments!"

He glared at her. "Listen, you ungrateful…I helped you get away from her, to get out of Melbourne, let you have this house while you set up shop. Wake up and work it out!"

She ground to a halt. "Is that what this is about. All your so-called help has a price? News flash—who and how I love isn't something I can change. It may be for some, but not for me."

"Yeah? How's that been working for you?"

Nadeen sagged. "I know it's hard for you to understand but being gay isn't difficult in itself. In fact, it comes naturally. What makes it difficult is wrangling the dramas created by panic-stricken straight people. You all need counselling."

He snorted and blustered. "Comes naturally, my arse. You're the abnormal ones. Go get some counselling yourself."

"Not abnormal. Uncommon, as in less of us. Just a bit different. And who, by the way, is a hundred percent normal? Never met such a beast. But I can see I'm wasting my breath, yet again." She tidied chairs back under the tabletop. "If you want me out of here, I'll find somewhere else. How long have I got?"

He drained the glass and stood. "Don't be like that. I didn't mean it that way. I just want—"

"What *do* you want? I can't be someone else. They're all taken."

With a reluctant smile, he said, "All I want is for you to find happiness. When you come to your senses, you'll have every chance to do just that. That's what I want."

"How very caring." Nadeen swallowed hard. "But I'm sick of listening to the same old crapola. Would you please leave me alone, now? I'm tired. Seriously."

Pulling a face, he rose stiffly and put an arm across her shoulders as they made their way to the front door. She shrugged it off and said, "We would get along so much better if we didn't talk for a while. I'd appreciate you respecting that."

On the step, he opened his mouth as if to say something, closed it. And slipped into the encroaching darkness.

# CHAPTER SEVEN

The new glasshouse financed by Papsom had been erected five metres away from the older glasshouses. It hadn't had its glass installed but was due any day now. The empty frame and metal benches inside were shiny and new. Pristine. Untouched.

The intruders had broken into the nearby shed and older greenhouses sometime during the early hours of Sunday morning. Or at least that was Lorna's best guess. They'd used glass cutters on the first two greenhouses that housed yet-to-germinate seed trays, then must have got frustrated by the time they got to the third, most distant glasshouse and had ripped off the glass door. In the first two greenhouses, they'd up-ended seed trays all over the floor. In the last greenhouse, the tiny poppy plants had been emptied out to create one large mound of potting mix dotted with their first leaves. The door had been flung on top, the glass smashed and stomped into the soil by someone with heavy boots who must have been in a foul temper. Sheer bloody-mindedness.

Lorna had found the mess at six thirty a.m. By the time she got to the last glasshouse, she was weeping freely. Weeks, if not months, of work destroyed. At the mound of soil, she fell to her knees and tried to scoop up the wilted poppy juveniles to put back in their trays—cried out when hidden glass sliced through flesh. No one heard her.

She hurried back to the house, trying not to drip a bloody trail. When she whispered softly at Mel's bedside, the young woman roused, eyes stretching at the sight of Lorna's hands slippery with gore.

Down at the local medical centre, the on-call doctor cleaned up Lorna's hands, put five stitches in the ball of her right thumb, a few more in her first and second fingers, then two in her left ring finger and thumb. Hurting significantly by now, he gave her a prescription for antibiotics and a heavy-duty painkiller. And a tetanus shot as a matter of course.

Drugs in hand, learner-permit Mel drove them home again.

* * *


On Sunday afternoon, Nadeen was in the middle of guillotining sheets of white card stock into the exact size for printing. The phone rang.

"Hi, it's me. Sorry, I can't work at the shop tomorrow. Mum has had an accident."

"Oh, no. Is she okay?"

Mel's voice was high-pitched and wavering. "She cut her hands on broken glass. Very deep cuts. Had stitches this morning."

"Whoa, that sounds serious. Look, don't worry. I'll call Jared, see if he's available. Otherwise, I'll manage somehow. No worries."

"Thanks. Have to go."

"Hey, Mel? Let me know if there's anything I can do to help, okay? I mean it. Anything."

"Yeah, right. Thanks."

Nadeen put down the phone, picked it up again and left a message on the machine at Jared's share house. Would he get it? She could only hope, but if not, she would manage.

* * *

Lorna sat on the edge of the bed and let bitter tears fall. Even if her hands weren't injured, the damage done by the intruders had severely compromised her ability to supply seedlings to Papsom on schedule. But with her hands worse than useless as well, it was nothing short of catastrophic. Papsom had just invested thousands in the new glasshouse to increase production, while the damage had achieved the reverse. A setback in supply, precisely when they wanted more, would not go down well.

For any task not associated with seedling production, there were any number of locals who would offer their time. Some years, the apple harvest could be bounteous, and people willingly turned up to help with the picking. But for poppy seedlings, the necessary secrecy excluded all of them except her best friend, Tash, who was away up north, indefinitely. Lorna needed help right now. And a very specialised kind of help, at that. In fact, she needed a band of angels.

With her right arm in a loose sling, Lorna chased peas around her plate with a spoon in the other hand. "How about some tomato sauce to glue these tearaways together? Doesn't exactly go with mushroom omelette, but I'd be grateful." Silently, Mel got up and poured some sauce on her mother's plate. "Thank you, my girl. Ow…ouch." Her fingers weren't working well. "Nice omelette."

Mel said, "I'll try making apricot chicken tomorrow."

"Sounds great. With Tash up in Geraldton, I was thinking we need a miracle."

With a slight shrug, Mel stood up and stacked their empty plates and cutlery. "What would a miracle look like?"

"How about my hands healed perfectly overnight?" Lorna sat back and examined her mangled mitts plastered with assorted dressings.

"Why is Tash in Geraldton, again?"

"Her elderly mother has had a fall and her brother up there is useless. He couldn't organise a bonk in a brothel, let alone a care-home placement for the poor old chook. Tash flew up there two days ago to get it sorted. Anyway. Now what? Let's find a mob of expert botanists with nothing better to do. Ha! Just dreaming, here. Maybe a mega-efficient nurseryman on speed."

Mel paused, plates in hand, and looked down at her mother. "That last one." She put the dishes in the sink and ran the tap. "Just minus the speed."

"What? You've someone in mind?"

"Well, yeah. My boss at the shop. You've met her, remember?"

*How could she forget?* "Oh. Really, Mel, that's a stretch. And what would she know about seeding poppies?"

"I dunno for sure, but I reckon she's got green thumbs. And she's fast. Everything she does happens in no time. She told me she divides flowering thingies and pots them up into more flowering thingies. Whatchamacallits. Yeah, gerberas. That's them. She's going to sell them from the shop, she said. She's offered to help."

"I don't think so." Lorna was mumbling. "Don't know if anyone, let alone a complete stranger can be trusted with my seeding protocol, which I would have to spell out. Wouldn't want to risk it. Or impose."

"Well, Mum." Mel turned off the tap and leaned back against the bench. "As you've said before, if you don't ask, you don't get. You asked, and my boss happened to offer. I can help with the simple things like refilling trays with mix, and other stuff like that. And Jared would too, for some pocket money. It's worth running it past her. Just saying." She stooped and began loading the dishwasher.

It was a rare moment when Lorna Chidlow felt a bit silly—a bit churlish in front of her daughter. A bit told-off. But her seventeen-year-old was somewhere between child and woman—a difficult time of transition during which the dumbest thing might be said, and then the most sensible.

"Melanie."

She straightened sharply and met Lorna's gaze.

"I need you to be very clear about that woman. In a nutshell, our future depends on it. Do you understand?" Mel came back to the table and sat down. "What is she like in the shop? With you and Jared."

"She teaches us exactly what to do." Mel pursed her lips. "A bit strict. If we make a mistake, she tells us how to fix it and we have to do it. She's always nice about it, but she wants it done right or not at all, she says. Taking payment has to be smooth and accounted for in the till. Helpful and polite and not too much chat with customers."

"Do you think she's honest? Trustworthy?"

Mel blinked and examined her fingernails. "She makes *me* feel trusted. That's what I really like about her. She makes us responsible without being patronising or pushy. I feel like we're a team because of it. Respected. Yeah, I reckon she's trustworthy."

Lorna said, "Good enough. Because, short of telling Papsom we can't supply what they want, we are short of options. As it is, for the next ten days or so while my hands heal, I'll have to buy us some time to catch up on the damage, which won't go down well. The glass will go in the new greenhouse any day now, and then we'll be expected to increase production." She couldn't help but drop her forehead into a wounded hand.

"Come on, Mum. It'll be all right." She reached out to rub across Lorna's shoulders. "I reckon my boss would calmly row a dinghy through a tropical cyclone, no worries."

Lorna had to smile. "Well, *that* won't be necessary. We'll find out, eh?"


Mel was watching *Buffy the Vampire Slayer* on the goggle-box. In the office, Lorna swung gently back and forth in the chair, composing a possible conversation with Nadeen in which she asked her to help in her free time, if she was either willing or able. Next to the desk, there was a small, decrepit safe bolted to concrete blocks under the wooden floor. Lorna put her feet up on it to help her think.

Other than Tash, her in-case-of-emergency helper, there were at least two local Country Women's Association members who she knew well and would help, if asked, but they weren't gardening types. And security was an issue. The less attention their nursery attracted, the better. Truth be known, even the sweetest of Toodyay souls loved to gossip. Nadeen didn't seem to be like them. Beyond being an outwardly polite and nice-enough business owner, she kept herself to herself, according to Mel.

Lorna shut her eyes and pictured Nadeen's even features, dark wavy hair in an unruly shoulder-skimming cut and lovely warm eyes. An attractive woman who didn't advertise herself as such with makeup and too-snug clothing. Marissa's face popped up and she wondered if they were alike in personality. From what Mel had said, Nadeen seemed a more earthy, in-control-of-herself character than Marissa—that firecracker in search of a willing match. There couldn't be another quite like her, surely? Lorna was reassured and resolved. She could do this.

Yet she hesitated. So far, she'd carefully avoided having anything to do with Nadeen. They'd never actually spoken in the many weeks since Mel started Saturday hours at the shop. Lorna's right hand couldn't grip—she couldn't drive. And casually dropping into the shop with Mel wasn't ideal because it required a very adult, face-to-face conversation. That left phoning Nadeen at home and inviting her to Morwood.

Asking for specific help from someone she'd never technically met was off-putting. Not to mention that Nadeen pushed some disturbingly primitive and private buttons. She couldn't afford to think about that—it was totally inappropriate to react so strongly to a perfectly innocent stranger. Nadeen must never know. Too embarrassing for words.

She would just have to woman up and do it. Tomorrow evening, maybe? Easter Monday. She could do this.

# CHAPTER EIGHT

Nadeen stirred a tall saucepan of "mince surprise," so named because it tasted surprisingly good for mince. Simply, browned beef with generous quantities of herby passata, seasonal onions, garlic, root vegetables, and greens simmered gently for ninety minutes—should be edible, if ordinary-sounding. But she never told anyone about the grated beetroot and teaspoon of Vegemite that transformed it beyond ordinary into remarkably moreish. Most of it would be packed into convenient portions for the freezer—her version of fast food for reheating after long days in the shop.

The phone rang. She slid the glass lid on the saucepan and loped down the hall.

"Lorna Chidlow here. Mel's mother. How are you?" Her throaty, lilting tone was a surprise.

"Coasting along, thanks. She told me you were injured."

"That's right—"

"Is there anything I can do? I mean, I'm often tight on time, but whatever. Mel's such a find for the shop. A real credit to you."

"Well, thank you. As a matter of fact, I was wondering if you might come to Morwood for a chat over a cuppa. I can't drive. At least, not yet."

"Hmm." Nadeen looked at the phone. "As it happens, I can. How's tomorrow looking? It's my day off. I've a few things to do first thing, but midmorning works for me."

"That would be perfect. Say ten thirty?"

"Fine. Can I bring anything?"

"Just your charming self. You know where we live. See you then."

Nadeen put down the phone, frowning as she walked back to the kitchen. Charming self? Lorna Chidlow—the town's poster girl—she of the unblinking stare. Maybe she was just being friendly, Toodyay style? The place had changed dramatically since she was a child in this sleepy Australian country town infamous as a place of redemption for reformed convicts. It was only because Lorna was a single parent and Mel such a bonus that she was offering to lend a hand. Not that she knew exactly how she might fit into the Chidlow scheme of things. She was a tad stunned to have the offer taken up at all.

Her recent move to Toodyay had its challenges. Still, leaving behind metropolitan Melbourne, and by association Greer, had been a refreshing shot in the arm of creative freedom. She was enjoying her new life way more than she had anticipated.

She sampled the braised mince for seasoning and licked satisfied lips. And admitted that it wasn't entirely that Lorna was a single parent in need that motivated her. Lorna had a certain indefinable something that was interesting, if not outright compelling. Could they be friends? That would be great—she could do with a few friends in town. More entertainingly, Nadeen had heard rumours about marijuana cultivation—heady stuff in such a small community. However, whatever facts she might become privy to, she was quite capable of keeping to herself, no problem. Growing up lesbian in a less-than-impressed world, she was well practised at keeping her mouth shut.

On this Easter Monday in 1996, things were definitely better than in the '70s, yet far from a cakewalk. Mouth shut.

* * *

When tyres crunched on the gravel out front, Lorna had just switched on the percolator. Having one-handedly wrestled the machine into submission well enough to produce coffee, if she'd had any doubts about how useless her right hand really was, they had been swiftly quashed.

With a self-conscious check of her attire in the hall mirror, she opened the front door and clocked Nadeen getting out of a mustard transit van. Striding over in Reeboks, a pale-blue cheesecloth Nehru shirt and well-worn boot-leg jeans, Nadeen seemed impossibly young and vibrantly alive. In that moment, Lorna felt old enough to be her mother, which was reassuring. And likely technically true. She exhaled easily and relaxed. Too easy.

"Hi. Come on in. Coffee's on."

Smiling warmly, Nadeen looked her up and down. "Thanks for the invite. I'd shake hands, but I can see that's not an option."

"Right first time." Lorna returned the smile and led the way down the cool, shadowed hall to the kitchen. "Thanks for coming. I can manage some things well enough with my left hand. Melanie is doing the lion's share of the domestics. For now, I can't even peel a potato. Do sit down."

Nadeen nestled in a padded chair and crossed her ankles. "Have you any idea when your hand might be usable again?"

Lorna slid a mug of black coffee in front of Nadeen and fetched her own. "There's milk and sugar on the table." She took a seat as Nadeen poured a good splash. "The doctor said ten days, depending on how well I heal. I really don't want to push my luck because some of the tendons were nicked and won't heal quickly."

"That's not so good." Nadeen blew across the top of the mug, her gaze searching intently. "So, Mrs Chidlow. How can I help in the interim?"

"Aah…" Lorna lost herself in Nadeen's melting dark eyes— lost her train of thought—scrambled for it. "It's complicated. I'm sure you've heard rumours about the nursery? Sure. It's not what people think, and I'd like to keep it that way. For good reasons, one of which is security, another is that what we do is officially sanctioned by the Federal Government. May I have your assurance that what I divulge goes no further?"

"The feds, you say? As long as everything is legal and above board, I'm agreeable. Totally."

Lorna said, "Perhaps you're aware of a growing demand for medical-grade opiates both nationally and on world markets? Well, we germinate *papaver somniferum* seeds, otherwise known as opium poppy, for a large federal government nursery located inland from here where they grow them on to flower and develop seed heads. It's from those heads that they extract the raw liquid opiate."

"Now I get the need for secrecy." Nadeen twirled her mug in her hands.

"Exactly. The germination process is something I've perfected so that the poppy seeds, which are prone to fungal contamination and subsequent failure, have a very high germination and thrive rate. The seeds are tiny and difficult to handle, but we have a process that simplifies all that. And, as you can imagine, the seed-raising mix has a tightly controlled proportion of ingredients and fertiliser. It's all fiddly and time-consuming, and needs a safe, fast and meticulous pair of hands. Something I don't have right now. And I'm hoping you do."

"Uh-huh. One question. Why doesn't the government do the germinating themselves?"

"Attrition. Failure to thrive. An awful lot of seed can be spoiled and wasted which interrupts the continuity of production. Which is money down the drain. It's all about saving government money, and they can't be bothered messing about with unreliable seed-raising. They prefer to pay me to supply seedlings sufficiently sturdy for safe transport and highly likely to survive transplanting. From then on, they are easily grown, robust plants that love a warm and fertile growing medium in low humidity. Their facility does all that. Not my problem, thankfully."

"All right. I'm getting the picture. May I see your setup?"

Lorna paused. "It's a mess at the moment. Last Saturday night we had a fool or two smash their way into the glasshouses and run amok. That's how I wrecked my hands, trying to rescue seedlings. Rocco, my manager, is sweeping up debris right now." She stood up. "But if you still want to have a look?"

"Yes, please." Nadeen trailed Lorna down the hall to the back door.

They toured the three glasshouses, Lorna outlining processes as they went. In the last one, she introduced Nadeen to Rocco who was shovelling the last of the contaminated soil into a wheelbarrow destined for a sturdy box trailer and a trip to a landfill site.

On the way back to the house, Nadeen asked, "Have you worked out a minimum target of seeds planted and seedlings ready for consignment?"

"There's a target. And then there's what is actually possible. Realistically, the two are far apart." Lorna shouldered the back door open, stepped inside and let Nadeen close it. In silence, they walked back to the front door.

Lorna said, "Come and sit down outside." Nadeen followed Lorna out to the deep front veranda and to a generous wooden swing suspended by heavy chains secured in the rafters. Well-padded and strewn with assorted cushions, it was comfortable.

"So, Nadeen, what do you think?"

"Bluntly? That you need as many hours of concentrated effort as possible within a short time. Seeds have to be sown *en masse* before anything else can happen. We're starting from scratch."

"That's the priority. But at the same time, new beds of mix can be made up, ready and waiting. The seeding is the most critical and technical process. I can get you up to speed on that, quick time. Thereafter, results depend on speed and efficiency. And how much time you are willing and able to commit to it."

Nadeen nodded without comment. Wafting around them, an intense scent of roses filled the warm morning air. At one end of the veranda, an impressively large and gnarly old rose bush reached out with vigorous branches laden with deep-pink flowers. Nadeen glanced at it and leaned forward, elbows on her knees, and rested her chin on her knuckles. A sturdy silver chain swung free of her open shirt. On it hung a silver pendant in the shape of a silhouetted eyebrow above an eye filled with a vivid turquoise gemstone.

Lorna got up and paced, then stood awkwardly over her guest. "Look, I know it's a big ask." The vibrant pendant against the backdrop of Nadeen's warm olive-skinned cleavage was distracting. She wet her lips. "And if there were anyone else to ask, I would, believe me. I mean, why would you do this?"

With a soft snort, Nadeen looked up at her. "Because I offered. And made a rod for my own back, by the looks of it. But I confess that I have an ulterior motive. I plan to be in Toodyay for the foreseeable future and, having left friends behind in Melbourne, I need a network here. My memory of growing up in Toodyay is that people look out for each other, and I want to be part of that. And you know I'm very impressed with Melanie who's willingly done so much for the shop. Well, I figure that, by association, her mother might prove to be an equally decent human being."

"I like to think so. Does that mean you'll have a go?" Flushed, Lorna returned her gaze.

"I'll do better than that. The week after Easter is always quiet, barely worth opening for the occasional walk-in. To give it a fair shot, I'll shut up shop until next Tuesday. Let's start this afternoon, eh?" She rose abruptly.

"You mean right now?" Lorna stood up and steadied the swing.

"No, I'll be back after lunch, about one p.m. as I've a few things to do at home first. Does that work for you?"

"Yes, definitely."

"Good, let's do it." Nadeen started down the steps to where her van was parked. "I'll bring my Cavalier back with me. She'll be no trouble. Oh, and one other thing."

Lorna's eyes crinkled in the sharp sunlight, and she shaded them with her good hand. "What's that?"

"Have we met before?"

*In my dreams.* "No. I'm sure we haven't. Not that I recall."

Unsmiling, Nadeen looked hard at her, then turned and strode off to the van.

Back on the swing, Lorna sat for a while enjoying the heady rose scent—the last flush of blooms before winter. That Nadeen had readily agreed to help out was a relief, as was her own excitement at such a promising solution to what had seemed hopeless. In amongst that reasoning was a disquiet attributable to nothing more than Nadeen's sheer presence. On one level, Nadeen's help was nothing but welcome. On another level, her proximity was intrinsically alarming.

Yet, she'd handled the situation well and achieved the desired result. Why, then, did it feel like she was merely in the calm eye of a cyclone created by the break-in, and about to cop the full force of its return? An image popped into her mind's eye of Nadeen rowing that dinghy through a tropical cyclone. A storm was approaching, but from which direction? What was she getting herself into, and might she be sunk by its consequences?

There was a lot riding on Mel's assessment of her boss, coupled with Lorna's gut instinct that Nadeen was both trustworthy and capable. Yet, right now, her gut was churning for some mysterious reason. Was it excitement or anxiety? What did she *really* know about Nadeen Quin, outside of Mel's workplace experience? Diddly-squat.

For one panicky moment, she again wished her bestie, Tash, wasn't out of town. Now, like it or not, she had to risk letting this enigmatic, disturbingly attractive stranger into their home and business. Was it wise? She was about to find out.

# CHAPTER NINE

During the drive home, Nadeen pondered the wisdom of her offer to help Lorna. It wasn't as if she had oodles of spare time, what with the shop and its upkeep, not to mention mucking about with gerberas. So she needed new friends, but did she need to be quite so keen? Sometimes she confounded herself with less than logical reasoning. Sure, she was very comfortable with Melanie, but her mother? Her mother was something else. Whereas most of the Toodyay folk she had met so far were about as deep as a summer mud puddle, Lorna was like a still pool in a hidden clearing surrounded by massive mother trees guarding its depths. Its secrets.

As she swung the van into Ellery Street, she replayed looking up at Lorna, deciphered the longing in Lorna's eyes and where she had tried not to look. And failed. Blinking rapidly, she couldn't quite believe it. Surely, it was only the turquoise Eye of Horus that had drawn Lorna's gaze? In a wave of shock and surprise, her gut flagged it was way more fundamental than that.

A lopsided grin beginning, she whispered, "Well, Mrs Chidlow, I'm flattered. It's been quite a while since I caught that kind of attention. A momentary aberration, perhaps?" She lifted the pendant to her lips, then let it drop. "Thank you for your protection, Horus. You always sort the women from the girls. The truth will out."

She pulled into the driveway. She had company. Felix. Again.

He sat on the front step stabbing agitated fingers through his dark teddy-boy curls that were greying at the temples, looking anywhere but at her.

"Dad. What brings you here again? So soon."

"Jodie threw me out."

She stepped past him and unlocked the door. "Oh, come on! Drama queen. You'd better come in. I'll put the kettle on."

Down in the kitchen, he hovered like a dog with a tasty bone and nowhere to bury it.

"Tea? What do you mean, she threw you out? I'm making a cheese toasty. Do you want one?"

"Wouldn't say no. She did…well, sort of. We had a big fight. And it's your fault." He tugged out a chair and sat, one knee bouncing madly.

Nadeen said, "Even though we've never met, I'm warming to her. How old is she, your fitness-trainer bimbo?"

"Hey, that's not necessary." He drummed fingers on the table and fixed her with a beady glare. "She has a science degree. Plays tennis like the best. Has washboard abs." He stopped drumming. "She's two years younger than you."

Nadeen laughed out loud and sloshed boiling water into a dented stainless-steel teapot, clanging its lid on with glee. "And this fight was my fault because—?"

"I told her all about you and your problem. She had the nerve to call me old and out of touch. *Me?*" He slapped his chest with both hands. "She called me a dinosaur. How dare she? I'm cool with it. It's just that's it's a dumb choice that you can un-choose. I told her that."

Nadeen was buttering toast. "And she agreed, just like my mother would?"

He coughed and spluttered. "Hardly. In fact, she stood there and lectured me about all the alternative people she knows who have every right to shack up with their object of desire and be left to wallow in peace."

"Amazing. Smoked cheese or gruyere?"

"Gruyere. Then she asked me what I thought gay people wanted. Which was awkward. I said they…you…want to turn everyone that way. She looked at me and called me a moron. *Me*…a moron? I'm a professor of Egyptology—"

"I wish I'd been a fly on the wall. Mustard or chutney?"

"Chutney. Are you listening to me? I'm your father, remember?" He took the mug of tea handed to him. "She said I sounded like an old man. I mean, she's gorgeous and I love her, but that was *really* low. Jeez, I'm only sixty-five. Yeah, I got ropeable and walked out."

She slid a plate of neatly cut triangles of toasty in front of him. "I see. So, you threw yourself out?"

"Not quite." With a grudging smile, he said, "She told me to come and ask you what you *really* want. That gave me a moment. I've never done that. So, I'm here. Asking." He took a man-sized bite of toasty, rubbed his fingers crumb-free and looked intently at her. "Talk to me."

Nadeen was tempted to do an eye roll, but bit into her toasty instead. "Eat. Before it gets cold. And I've a busy afternoon ahead with things to do that just won't wait."

They ate in silence, punctuated only by Bella drinking, her name tag rhythmically pinging against the metal water bowl with each lap, long ears dripping artistically across the linoleum on the way back to her well-worn bed.

Nadeen shook her head and cracked her neck, took another gulp of tea. "After all the arguments and the crapola you and Mum dished out, I'm finding it very hard to believe you'll listen."

Between chews, he said, "Jodie called me old. That hurt. And she may be right, but this old dog is willing to learn new tricks. I promised to listen. And while I may be far from perfect, you know I keep my promises."

"That's true. Yet I'm not sure you really want to know what I want…what I think. If I asked you what most straight people want, what would you say?"

"Most people?" Felix's brown eyes relaxed their focus to out beyond the kitchen window. "The usual. Career, money, partner, family. What of it?"

She smiled thinly. "That's pretty much what not-so-straight people want, too. People like me. Very ordinary, really."

He frowned, blinking rapidly. "There has to be more to it."

"Why? Not enough 'gay agenda' for you?" Abruptly, she gathered up crockery, let it clatter into the sink, and stood frowning at him. "Do you really think I want to 'turn everyone that way'? Now, there's one hell of a fright-night conspiracy theory, and equally batshit crazy. And why do we all have to be one way or another, anyway? What's wrong with variety? Answer this—how is it any skin off anyone's nose if two men or women happily share each other's lives and beds? I just bet you listened to our former Prime Minister saying two blokes and a cocker spaniel don't make a family."

Felix grunted. "He had a point."

"And a valid one from an ignorant, smug straight guy's point of view. But I call bullswool on his sorry opinion. There's the family we're born into, and then there's the family we create with others we care about. I know quite a few same-sex couples who have built a successful life together, in spite of the naysayers. Frankly, I think it's none of anybody's business, including the government's, what consenting adults do in private."

Nodding rhythmically, he said, "If it's consenting adults, I guess. I know what you mean about family, though. I'll think about it."

Nadeen took empty cups to the sink. "Yeah, sure. At least you heard me out. Now you'd better go because I really do have to get on. I'm helping out a friend this arvo."

"You've made a friend? Who? How?"

"Not really a friend. Just networking. My casual's mother. On the other side of town on a property called Morwood."

"Morwood? That's the Chidlow place. You must mean… whatshername…Cormack's wife."

"I don't know about any Cormack bloke. Her name is Lorna. She's injured her hands and needs a stand-in. I volunteered."

Felix grinned. "Oh, hey. She was once a Northam girl and became Toodyay royalty. If you're after friends in this town, she's a great start. I went to school with him."

"You know her?"

"Never met her, but someone who went to their wedding showed me photos, years ago. She was a real cracker and much younger than him. Cory copped a heap of flak on both counts. And I heard she's tight with the local oldies. There are some tough nuts out here. You can be sure that's quite a feat."

"She's certainly charismatic. In an artless way, I might add. Despite townsfolk falling over themselves to get her attention. Being unaffectedly luminous can be a liability." He was studying her, tight-lipped. "What? You think I don't notice a good-looking woman when I see one? Oh, for the love of—"

Silence hung between them like swamp fug. She said, "You mentioned my mother earlier. Do you know where she is?"

He scratched his moustache and shivered. "Last I heard, Carla's still swanning up and down the Nile, tomb hunting. Thebes is the red-hot spot of the moment. Friends are putting her up when she's in Cairo proper. I guess she's somewhere between digs and cocktails, who knows? I certainly don't care, do you?"

Nadeen shrugged. "Just keeping tabs. So, you'll report back to Jodie?"

He muttered, "If I don't want to sleep alone tonight."

"Do give her my regards. We must meet one day."


With the rest of the house in darkness, the bedside light threw deep shadows in her bedroom. Nadeen took off the turquoise pendant and draped it over a protective amethyst cluster on the bedside table that it shared with two silver rings. Her father had given the pendant to her for her eighteenth birthday, and she'd fallen in love with it instantly. In fact, she wore it most of the time.

She shimmied between the sheets and turned off the light, lying back with her hands above her head on the pillow.

Had she *really* mistaken Lorna's wandering eyes? For sure, they were remarkable eyes under a strong brow, with deep laugh lines at the corners—not a frown line in sight, as if she'd never had a problem, which couldn't be true. More the reflection of a positive attitude—an optimism that found solace in faith and hope, rather than dwelling on life's miseries. Lorna's easy presence lulled her into being so relaxed and comfortable around her that she forgot herself. Too good to be true. In fact, there had to be something wrong with her.

Oh, yes. That's right—not like you.

Just when she'd spotted the kind of woman she was inclined to get utterly nuts about. Nadeen punched the pillow into shape and turned onto her side.

Go to sleep, you silly bugger. Yeah, dream on!

# CHAPTER TEN

In the first greenhouse, Nadeen cut butcher's paper to fit the metre-by-metre germination trays that were already prepared with soil to a depth of five centimetres, having been screed and tamped, and screed again. She laid the sheets into three of the trays set out on the long benches. "What happens next?"

Lorna said, "This particular paper has a very open weave and minimum of sizing in it. In other words, it falls apart fast. Now we spray the paper with the sterilising mix, just to make it slightly damp to the touch."

Nadeen aimed a pump pack at the trays, nose wrinkling. "That smells peculiar, like a spice. What's in it, and should I be wearing a mask?"

"Not necessary. It's not toxic to humans. Anything but. Cinnamon is one of the ingredients, but I'd rather not say if you don't mind. That should be enough. Now the seed spreader."

By its handles, Nadeen picked up a square board with raised edges that was drilled with tiny holes. Notches on the side had to align. She lined them up and gently laid the board on the paper in a tray. "Is that about right?"

"Good enough." Lorna held out a small stainless-steel jug. "Now the seed. This is premeasured to hold three point seven grams. Pour it out in the shape of an infinity symbol. Then you need only brush it in, first horizontally, then vertically. Trust me, there's method in this madness."

Eyebrows knitting, Nadeen followed instructions, pouring out the tiny grey seeds into a neat pattern, then wielding a wide brush until all the seed had disappeared. "Fascinating. Now what?'

"Take out the seed spreader and lay another sheet of paper on top. Very gently. Then you can spray that, too." Lorna danced around Nadeen as she worked. "Okay, now we need about five millimetres of vermiculite like a light blanket covering the paper. If it's patchy, don't worry. Once in place on the benches under lights, we'll mist the trays regularly from above."

Nadeen scattered the ultra-lightweight vermiculite evenly and Lorna examined the result. "You're a natural at this. Let's do a couple more trays, eh? Then I reckon you've done enough for one day. What do you think?"

Nadeen fetched another tray. "Your call. I can be here seven thirty a.m. tomorrow and work until we've all had enough."

"Would you like to stay for dinner? Mel's attempting apricot chicken."

With a wry grin, Nadeen said, "I've food at home, but thanks anyway. And Bella needs special chow, now that she's a senior. Have to look after my one faithful companion."

"As you wish."

At the front door, Lorna waved at Nadeen's disappearing van and took a moment to ponder the poignancy in Nadeen's voice. "Her one faithful companion? There's a story there," Lorna muttered to herself. "We all have our secrets. Just some more than others. None of my business."

In spite of that resolve, her heart reached out with instinctive tendrils that easily detected the walking wounded. Nadeen was one of them, of that she was certain. And she couldn't help but feel for her.

"Cut it out. It's not healthy for you to be caring and sharing with all and sundry. Leave well alone."

* * *

Early-morning light entered the glasshouse at a sharp angle, warming the room from its overnight chill. Nadeen blurted, "What *is* this stuff? It smells really odd." She worked the sprayer above yet another tray of paper-covered seeds, one of the many laid out and waiting on the bench. She turned when Lorna manoeuvred another tray across an adjacent bench. "Excuse me, but you really shouldn't be doing that."

"I have to do something with myself. Better than nothing," said Lorna.

"If you stretch healing wounds, no, it's not. Please stop. Sit down and talk to me while I work. Seriously. What's in this stuff?"

Lorna lowered herself onto a dilapidated plywood chair and straightened her sling. "Does it matter? You don't have to know."

Risking a sideways glance, Nadeen said, "A business secret. Got it. I'm just curious because I'm going to try breeding from my Uncle Garry's gerberas. They came with the house. For now, I'm propagating from pups, but once I've identified and catalogued what's there, I aim to cross pollinate by hand and see what I can develop. And improving germination with something like this stuff? I'd like to have such an advantage."

Softly rubbing the back of her right hand, Lorna took her time answering. "Are you planning some kind of mass production, much like what we're doing here?"

"Certainly not. It's a hobby. At the same time, the market for gerbera plants and cut flowers is sizeable because they are so long-lasting. Cut gerberas can last for weeks. Floristry is big business when it comes to blooms that survive international transportation. And gerberas fit the bill."

"I see. As a matter of interest, I love peonies so much I cultivate them in a gully east of the house. It's rewarding with such beautiful blooms. So, why gerberas?"

"Nostalgia, perhaps. I associate them with my childhood. Those times I spent mucking about with my aunt and uncle in their garden. Carefree, easy and peaceful times. Really, gerberas are just a daisy. Except they are remarkably resilient and can be hybridised to create stunning flowers. My interest is in new colours and styles for showing within the gerbera fanciers' realm. Nothing beyond that." Nadeen caught Lorna's glance, paused and leaned against the bench.

"In that case. The main ingredient is, unsurprisingly, worm juice as a soil conditioner and fertiliser. Two home gardeners in Toodyay have worm farms and supply the liquid to me, which is measurably diluted. The other ingredients are cinnamon and myrrh."

"Myrrh? Wow, that's pretty exotic for Australia. Why on earth—?"

Lorna said, "Because the ancient Egyptians used it, together with cinnamon, as a powerful antibacterial and antifungal treatment. They used it on just about everything. Plants, animals and humans. That combination resolved all kinds of infections, whether from wounds or bites…whatever. Saved many lives, or so my research tells me. Those two and the humble poppy, of course, which was their only reliable pain killer. It was vastly revered in their culture. The poppy was more precious than gold. Seeds were soaked in a solution much like what's in that spray bottle."

Nadeen held up the bottle and resumed spraying. "Interesting stuff. Now, would you please go away while I work? I'd prefer to get as much done as quickly as possible. I know what I'm doing now. You resting up and healing is about as helpful as you can be."

Behind her, Lorna pushed open the glasshouse door. "Would you stay for dinner Friday evening? However far you are by then, a thank-you celebration is in order."

"If you insist."

The door had already closed.

Nadeen put down the sprayer and sank onto the plywood chair. Her enthusiasm dampened, she rubbed her cheeks and stared sightlessly at the door, as if it held answers. Had she simply imagined the look in Lorna's eyes only two days ago? Since then,

Lorna had been all business, which was understandable given the stress level.

She chewed a lip. Bottom line, all she wanted was a decent friendship. Maybe she gave off a gay vibe that Lorna had picked up on and felt threatened by? It wouldn't be the first time that had happened with a straight friend. That kind of minefield she did not want to tiptoe through.

Sure, Mrs Chidlow was both easy on the eye and blessed with a haunting presence. That lively, generous mouth would attract attention from anybody and everybody. And Nadeen had a pulse. Of course, she found her attractive. Who wouldn't?

Head in hands, a visceral yearning threatened to overwhelm her. "Great idea, folks. Let's get my heart trashed twice in one year." She slapped her cheeks. "Don't you *dare* fall for her. Do *not* make a fool of yourself. Forget it."

Spray bottle in hand, she got back to work. It should have been the perfect exclamation mark for her grim resolve, were it not for a nagging sense that she knew Lorna from somewhere. As a powerful presence. In a dim dark past? She always did have a vivid imagination.

# CHAPTER ELEVEN

The roast lamb was about forty minutes away from coming out of the oven to rest when Nadeen appeared at the kitchen door. Lorna left the string beans and beamed at her weary volunteer. "How are you feeling?"

"Like going home for a shower and a beer, but whatever you're cooking smells too delicious. I wouldn't want to miss out."

Lorna took a step. "There's a shower in the mud room, just to the left of the toilet. I'll get you a towel."

"I don't want to trouble you. I'll be fine."

Lorna had walked straight past Nadeen and was halfway down the hall. "It's no trouble." She stopped at a hall cupboard, grabbed a fluffy blue towel and kept walking. "Come on, it's in here. There are brushes, moisturiser and deodorant in the medicine cabinet in here. It's all for communal use." She opened a less-than-obvious door, breathed in and let Nadeen squeeze past. "Take your time."

She did a few skips back to the kitchen, quite disconcerted by the lingering exotic scent of spicy, earthy, perspiring woman. Is that what she herself smelt like when doing that task?

She paused at a sturdy waist-height bookshelf. It was dominated by a full set of Encyclopedia Britannica—a long-out-of-date relic of Mel's early school years when they were useful for homework. The volume with "P" on its spine scored a fond pat, in passing. Few knew that its inside had been partially hollowed out with a box-cutter to accommodate a thick wad of recipes for soil and fertiliser, plus years of annual production records for the poppy seedlings—precious information. Farther along the shelf the "V" volume, similarly hollowed out, contained valuables— some jewellery items and a few thousand dollars in hard cash, kept handy for emergencies.

The beans needed her to finish the top-and-tailing before steaming. They'd already taken longer than she would have liked. Admittedly, Nadeen was distracting. Great body. She had a "picky type" vibe, likely only a chosen few had seen her naked. Beans. Get on with it.

Mel took the large tray of roasting cut potatoes and pumpkin out of the oven and shook it. "These need another half hour, Mum. They're cooked but could be crisper. Should I let Nadeen know when it's tea time?"

"She's in the mud room shower now. I've nearly finished these beans. Would you fetch a couple of beers from the garage fridge? Just in case she doesn't fancy our cider." Lorna took to the remaining beans, chopping fast with one hand, still getting the hang of being a wounded leftie. Mel had put the steamer on a hot plate awaiting Lorna's contribution. She made several trips with small amounts of beans, finally nestling a lid on top.

The dining table had been set for the three of them. In pride of place in the middle stood a polished brass Victorian oil lamp with a white, bowl-shaped shade decorated with perfectly painted pink rosebuds. It was only lit on special occasions, and this was one of them. It had been a while since they had a dinner guest. Lorna checked everything was as it should be, added the salt and pepper mills, and extra napkins.

Footsteps of the four-legged variety had her look down at a black-and-tan dog wagging her tail furiously. "Hello, Bella. Where's your mother?"

"Right here. She tried to join me in the shower. Funny girl."

*I can relate.* "I'm sure you're feeling better for it."

Mel bounded in and waved a bottle at Nadeen. "Would you like a beer?"

"Yes, please! You're a life saver. May I borrow a bowl for Bella's chow?"

"Of course," said Lorna, tugging open a low cupboard door that revealed assorted crockery. "Pick one. Bring your beer into the den. Dinner isn't far away."

Nadeen decanted a baggie into a bowl and stood near the hungry dog.

Lorna held out a bottle opener. "There's a chilled beer glass for you in the fridge, if you want."

"How civilised. It always tastes better in a glass." Nadeen took the bottle and opener, found the glass and followed Lorna into the next room. "Oh, this is cosy. Very comfortable."

"That's why we call it the den. We spend most of our down time in here, rather than the lounge room, which is a bit formal. Do sit down."

Nadeen sank into a very long and low L-shaped suite covered with an autumnal chintz. In the middle of the room was a large square of polished marri timber that had been made into a striking coffee table. It was scattered with cork place mats and coasters. On the opposite wall was a Victorian-style fireplace and mantel piece with various *objets d'art* festooned across its considerable length. The firebox was full of kindling, paper and skinny logs, just waiting for a match.

From a beer poured with a deep snowy head, Nadeen took a good few gulps and asked, "Do you use the fire?"

"This time of year, yes. It's not so cold, but one thing Morwood never lacks is firewood. Mel will light it when we have dessert. It gets lovely and warm in here. We enjoy it."

Mel poked her head in. "Mum, when do you want the beans on?"

Lorna said, "I'd better go supervise. Just take it easy and rest up. You've earnt it."

* * *

Nadeen wandered around the room with her glass which she emptied in a matter of minutes—that beer had barely touched the sides. But it refreshed and enlivened her, even more than the shower. The room had all sorts of odd things like a rusty horseshoe here, a scruffy teddy bear there, a forgotten Rubik's Cube, and old-fashioned porcelain ornaments. A side table held reels of coloured leather thong, brass and steel rings, and a half-made plaited belt in two-toned leather. Some completed in a variety of colours were curled up in a box. Must be hand-made by Lorna—her hobby?

She had lovely hands, did Lorna, despite the current wounds. Elegant, strong fingers, accustomed to handling all manner of things with a casual dexterity. Nice to touch and be touched by—to be held and to hold. With a crooked smile, Nadeen raised an eyebrow at herself. Don't go there.

When did she and Greer last hold each other that way? Definitely not this year, but when? She couldn't remember, which said it all.

In a dark corner was a collection of framed photos of people, some obviously quite old. A rogues' gallery of ancestors, perhaps? And a deep, glass-fronted wooden frame that stored a few items: a small child's shoe, a pack of ancient playing cards and something wrapped in fabric—all very random.

A disembodied voice called, "Nadeen, would you carve for us, please? I can't and Mel's not confident."

"No worries." Nadeen took the glass with her to the kitchen.

# CHAPTER TWELVE

Mel shouted, "Bye, Mum!" The front door slammed.

One-handedly carrying a tray with two glasses, Lorna hesitated at the door to the den, raised her eyebrows and smiled. Nadeen reached out and took a glass. "Thanks. Is she staying over at Jared's?"

"It's a teenage party, his parents supervising. I don't expect she'll be back before late morning." Lorna slid the tray onto the coffee table and made herself comfortable on the other couch. Bella had taken up residence in the corner between the two of them. "Would you like anything else? Coffee, chocolate mints?"

"I'm very full, thanks. That passionfruit flummery was delicious. Mel's handiwork?"

Lorna said, "She did most of everything. But I stood over her with the flummery. It takes a lot of beating to get it right. She did well."

Nadeen sipped the night's second glass of cider. "This brew is excellent. Not too sweet, not too alcoholic. How long have you been making it?"

"The farm has for at least a hundred and thirty years. The hotel has been selling it just as long. Morwood…home to farmhouse cider since 1865, give or take. Or so the story goes. The hotel remains our only retailer."

"Surely not?" Nadeen held her glass up to the chandelier's light. "You could sell this anywhere."

"Ah, but commercialising would take the fun out of it. This life needs all the fun it can muster."

The fire crackled and spat cinders onto the hearth, filling a silence. A flame rose higher for a few moments, then settled to a steady licking of its prey.

"Speaking of fun, I'm not too sure about Jared. He smiles a lot and makes Mel laugh. That makes me nervous for my daughter." Staring into the flames, Lorna took a gulp of cider. "Sorry, I don't mean to put you on the spot. It's just that you've had him working for you."

Tempted to smile, Nadeen said, "I think you can be confident that Jared is only interested in Mel as a friend." She caught Lorna's narrow glance and shrugged. "What I mean is, even though I'm gay, my gaydar is not so good. But I'm pretty sure Mel is as safe as houses with Jared. He's a lovely young man and has a big future ahead of him. Mel could do far worse than to have him as a friend."

Lorna's eyes had widened, jaw clenched.

"Don't worry, Mum. She'll be right, eh?"

"Eh," said Lorna. "Not something I notice. It's a new world."

Nadeen sculled the last of her cider and sat forward, hands on knees. "Not so much. I believe Whoopi Goldberg said, 'homosexuality has been around since air.' We've always been here. Just more visible, these days. Anyway, I should go." She stood up. Bella stirred, yawned and rattled her ID tags.

"What? No, please don't. Give me a moment to digest all that, will you?" Lorna leapt up and took a quick step toward Nadeen. "Besides, I'd like your opinion on a family photo." She tucked bandaged fingers into Nadeen's elbow and steered her to the den's darkest corner. "See that one in the black metal frame? Lift it down and we'll have a look at it together. Humour me."

Nadeen lifted the postcard-sized photo off its hook, took it back to the coffee table and found her still-warm place on the couch. Bella had hunkered down again.

"I fancy a shot of apple schnapps. Won't you join me? It's very good and rarely offered to anyone who isn't a Chidlow. Consider yourself honoured."

Nadeen glanced up at Lorna who seemed to be in search of the Eye of Horus again. Only when she wasn't looking intently into Nadeen's eyes.

"I do, believe me. Whatever you're offering."

Lorna turned and left the room. Nadeen swallowed hard and took a few quick, deep breaths. "Not fair. You're like moonlight. Can't grasp it, can't fight it."

The photo's metal frame had been punched outward into small playing card symbols—hearts, diamonds, spades and clubs. Repoussé work? One corner had been damaged, like it had been dropped. The glass was thick and possibly original, as was the backing board—a black painted card that was missing a hinged stand for putting on a shelf. The photo itself looked ancient.

Two shot glasses hit the table. Lorna took a stubby brown bottle from under an arm and sat beside Nadeen, thigh against thigh. "Sorry. Getting between you and your dog isn't easy. Would you pour?"

Nadeen eased out the squeaky cork, sent a viscous gold liquid into each glass. "That looks like it means business."

"Yep, forty proof. Just sip it. Slowly."

Nadeen had a taste, took a cautious sip. "Right. Sweetish with a complex fruitiness. As becomes an ageing apple. Delicious. Potent. Addictive."

"Like many things that are not so young, don't you agree?" Mere inches away, Lorna's twinkling grey eyes dared her.

All too conscious of their bonded thighs, Nadeen said, "Oh, absolutely."

Lorna laughed out loud and shouldered Nadeen who returned the gesture. Amused looks passed back and forth until Nadeen took another sip. "Could you use it as a mixer?"

"You mean like, in a cocktail? The problem with mixing a strong ingredient like schnapps into some innocent tasting substance like soda water is you could imbibe a whole lot more alcohol than you meant to. And the drinker could get herself in a heap of trouble before she knew it."

"I take your point. That could apply to many things."

"Far too many. You may know they once added powdered opium to alcohol to make a tincture, called it laudanum and flogged it as a cure-all. Nineteenth-century women who were trying to manage menstrual pain got addicted, their lives ruined. The takeaway is there's a fine line between a potent elixir and a deadly potion."

"Which comes down to how it's combined?"

"You could say that." Lorna caught Nadeen's look. "You could also say it's wise to know the true nature of the individuals... ingredients you're putting in the mix."

"Uh-huh." Nadeen picked up the photo and held it between them. "Who are these ladies?"

"This is my husband's great-great-grandmother, Violet Wood." Lorna pointed to the smaller of the two grey-haired women seated side-by-side on a bench, likely a prop in a photographer's studio. Behind them was a large screen enhanced with stylised leafy trees. Both wore high-necked, floor-length dark dresses and buttoned boots. The taller woman rested her right hand atop a walking stick. Violet cradled the other hand.

"Are they sisters?"

"Not even remotely. But it's bit of a tale, so forgive me. You must be tired after all your work."

"I'm okay for now. In the morning might be another story. But do go on."

Lorna took the photo and leaned back. Nadeen joined her.

"You see the frame? Probably made around 1900. Cory reckoned it's solid silver that's gone black with age. We didn't dare clean it in case it crumbled away. The other woman is Alice Moreton. Both were British convict women sent to prison here in Australia. In Toodyay, in the late 1850s."

"What for...what did they do?"

"We don't know. In those days, stealing a loaf of bread could get you transported. Any minor transgression would do. Their government wanted people to colonise the country. So-called criminals were grabbed off the streets and sent here to be virtual slaves. It was brutal."

"But they must have gained their freedom eventually."

"In time. Those who worked off their sentence were called emancipists. And if they were lucky, they could get a land title and make a life here. Which Alice and Violet did. They put their surnames together and built Morwood. It was only a two-room thing initially. Must have been a cold hole. Subsequent generations extended the house at intervals. When we did yet more renovating, right around the time Melanie was born, we knocked down a few old walls and found a stash of stuff above a doorway—a small child's leather shoe, a pack of playing cards and two claddagh rings wrapped in fabric—one silver, one rose gold. When they were put there, we don't know. But if you look closely at Violet's left hand, you can see the claddagh shape."

Nadeen peered at the photo. "That needs a magnifying glass but could be. Does it matter who the rings belonged to?"

"Not really, but they're matching, you see. And too small to be men's rings, although men used to wear that style, long ago. Very Celtic."

Sipping schnapps, Nadeen examined the photo. "The thing of it is, for Violet to be your husband's ancestor, she must have given birth to a child. Where was the father in all this?"

"All we know is she had a son in 1866, Alvin Morwood. In those days, unwilling fathers-to-be absconded, ran off to another town, changed their names, remarried and nobody was any the wiser. Ex-convicts weren't the most law-abiding citizens, unsurprisingly. Even the law itself was far from law-abiding. We're living in Australia's version of the Wild West. That Violet and Alice survived to whatever ages they are in this photo is impressive. In fact, they did quite well, thanks to cider. That's what made them a living."

"And here we are, drinking Morwood cider and schnapps. Here's to Violet and Alice. Cheers." They clinked glasses and drank. "So, what did you want my opinion on?"

"Ah." Lorna crossed arms and legs. "Cory reckoned the name Alvin is a near-enough combination of Al and Vi...Alice and Violet. He reckoned they were a couple."

Nadeen leaned forward and looked back over her shoulder at Lorna. "I can see why. Still, it looks to be an unlikely coupling for those times. On the other hand, some things were just not spoken about, let alone given technical names. What looks obvious to us would not have been to most back then."

"You think they could have gone unnoticed?"

"There's a good chance." Nadeen massaged her eyebrows— she'd been seeding poppies since seven thirty a.m. "That said, the consequences to being pegged by the authorities as anything other than church-going ageing spinsters would have been dire. Towns revolved around the church and the local pub. People were more religious then—more righteous about severe punishment. As I'm sure you are aware, there is no hatred quite like Christian love."

"Let me get this straight. In spite of the fear of being found out, you reckon they were hiding in plain sight."

"Possibly? They must have been very careful to appear above any hint of impropriety. Who knows what story they told anyone who had the temerity to ask? And the problem with living a lie is having to lie constantly and consistently. It's tiresome." Nadeen sat up straight, hands on knees. "Anyway, as I said earlier, we've always been here. Just not as visible as we are these days. So, yes, I think your husband was probably right. But, if you don't mind, I think it's time Bella and I hit the road."

Lorna roused herself off the couch. "Of course. Let me walk you out."

At the front steps. Lorna said, "I can't thank you enough for all your hard work."

"You already have. That's the best dinner I've had this year. No bull. But I have a special request. Regarding Jared, please don't share what I said because I don't know for sure, and I've been wrong in the past. It can be devastating for young ones when a rumour goes around, accurate or otherwise."

"I understand. I'll keep it to myself." Lorna reached out as if to touch Nadeen's shoulder, but Nadeen stepped away.

"Appreciated. Come on, Bell-bell. Home time!"

She legged it to the van, lifted Bella inside, and gave a brief wave as she drove off down the driveway. In the rear-vision mirror, Lorna's rigid silhouette vanished only when Nadeen steered onto the main road into town.

With her help no longer needed, she had no clue when they might see each other again. It was purely for Jared's sake that she outed herself to Lorna, which was always a risk with straights. A lady might freeze, or panic, or feel obliged to flirt. Lorna had done some of the latter, which was entertaining and flattering. She couldn't help but grin—they'd had some fun. But quite obviously not to be taken seriously—pointless to hanker after the impossible. She'd had that experience.

"Tsk. Traps for young players. Not this little black duck."

Still, the story of Morwood's origin was a good yarn, and the faces of the two colonial women in that photo memorable with their bold assurance frozen in time. They must have been tough, single-minded and deeply committed to negotiate the perils of colonial life together.

# CHAPTER THIRTEEN

*May 1866*

"Get a wriggle on, Biscuit!" Alice Moreton let the reins down with a soft slap on his back. The dun donkey tossed his stiff mane and sped up only a little. Winding along the bank of the Avon River, the rutted track was muddy and narrow, a light drizzle making the threat of bogging more likely. But she didn't want to push him too hard with the heavy dray lumbering behind him, six empty wooden cider barrels strapped on board.

A hardy Australian donkey, five-year-old Biscuit was unusually lofty at fourteen hands high. He weighed as much as six men and was reputedly as strong as a mallee bull. She'd bought him last Christmas from old man Mackenzie who'd been bitten and kicked once too often, giving further weight to a story told by a previous owner that the donkey—then named Stomper—loathed and abhorred the male of the species. If she hadn't offered a decent fifty shillings, he was destined for a warning shot between the eyes. When she led the beast away, Mackenzie couldn't resist sneering, "Bloody good luck to you, missus. You're going to need it. Mad bastard."

Alice renamed him Biscuit at once, kept him dry and well-fed, brushed him down in the drafty barn whilst whispering sweet nothings in his long ears, praised him relentlessly, stroked his furry grey cheeks often, and never raised a whip to his solid flanks. Initially suspicious and taciturn, he had steadily transformed into a loyal, biddable help over the last five months. She wasn't in the habit of violence—of pushing either person or beast past their tipping point.

The river had widened, running deeper and faster than she'd seen it run so far this year. Alice wrinkled her nostrils at the persistent reek of rotting, sodden undergrowth and gum leaves. Across her square shoulders, a woollen shawl had become swiftly saturated, and atop her head, a drooping faded bonnet was worse than useless at protecting her pinned-up hair from this early-winter rain. Still, Morwood was less than a mile away—she'd just have to put up with it. Violet would have the cooker stoked and rabbit stew on the hob. Despite being very pregnant, nothing could keep that particular woman down. Violet's merry eyes popped into her mind and Alice swallowed, smiled a crooked smile and shook her head. She was dead nuts on Violet and had been for at least three years. The feeling was mutual.

Both ex-convicts, they had managed to get title to an allotment of land together, the granting of titles to two men or two women being less common, but not unusual as the local authorities were keen to have productive farms in the valley. Alice and Violet had built a simple stone homestead and planted an orchard of Cox's Orange Pippin cider apples that were just starting to crop. Over the last few years, Alice had bought other farmers' excess apples for not much and made cider for the local hotel. Originally from county Kent, she'd learnt the craft when very young. The English loved their cider that was always a safer bet to drink than anything out of the local waterways. As did Australians—beer and cider—always sought after. With good soil and the Avon close by, their enterprise had prospects.

Biscuit he-hawed deep down low and slowed. Up ahead stood a uniformed figure on horseback, complete with rifle resting across the pommel. Through clenched teeth, Alice said, "What rotten luck. It's Fuck-knuckle. Woe betides me."

* * *

Police Constable Ozias Digby spat tobacco, keeping one eye on the approaching dray. He had an itch that badly needed scratching, but was he this desperate? His groin said "yes." Violet was his usual relief, but she was so swollen with child she'd protested, and he couldn't get near her. This fair cow would have to do. He whispered, "Nothing like my pretty Vi, this one. As rough as a sack of spanners." And spat the last gob of tobacco. "Not even a tide would take her out."

Then he barked, "Stop! Get down here. Make it quick."

When Alice swung herself onto the muddy track and approached, he holstered the rifle and eased out of the saddle, ambled toward the woman waiting with her arms crossed. The donkey shied away.

"What's on your mind, Digby?" Her voice was dark and strong. He hesitated.

"Violet is indisposed…her condition. And I've a mind for relief where I can find it. Lift your skirt and be quick about it." Swift fingers unbuttoned his trousers, exposed his problem.

Alice gaped at him. "What's this? Is having her week after week for a year not enough for you? Getting her up the duff against her will? And now you want to stick that in me, too? You perverted maggot. Nincompoop! Get away with you!" She turned aside.

Digby grabbed an arm and wrenched her back. Grimacing, she twisted and squirmed in his grip. He said, "We can do this civilly or we can do this any old who. Hold still, you stupid cow!" Alice dragged a hand loose and lashed fingernails across Digby's left cheek, drawing blood. He punched her in the temple and she fell to her knees, face in the mud. With a gleeful grin, he stooped to lift her skirt.

Someone grabbed him by the back of his neck, lifted him high, shook him like a pair of wet long johns, and flung him to the ground. He screamed when blows crushed the air out of his lungs, splintered his spine. When his skull caved, there was silence. Except for the triumphant braying.

*  *  *

Alice coughed, muddy muck drooling. Back arching, she lifted her throbbing head, fingered her temple and winced. Only then did she spot the body. And nary a soul in sight—just her and Biscuit. Frowning, she got to her feet and stared at the hoof marks on the copper's jacket, clasped a hand to her mouth and turned to look hard into Biscuit's bold brown eyes. He batted long black lashes and snickered. She began to tremble, mind racing.

She could be up for murder, a hanging certain.

They'd shoot Biscuit.

Violet would be alone. With a babe. How would she survive?

Evidence—had to get rid of the evidence.

Breathing hard, Alice tugged and pulled and rolled Digby's glassy-eyed body down the river bank and into the rising water where it drifted, sinking fast.

She washed mud off her face and hands, drying her lips on a damp hankie. With as much calm as she could muster, she approached the copper's horse, loosened the saddle's girth strap and tossed the reins back over the pommel. The rifle irked her. Throw it in the river? No, that would be a dead giveaway that he hadn't just fallen off for some innocent reason. She patted the horse's shoulder and gently shooed it down the track where it broke into a trot and disappeared.

Back at the dray, she scrambled up and drew breath. Then, and only then, bile rose in her throat and she began to shake, ducked her head between her knees and dry retched over the buckboard between her boots. Clammy, she rested her head in her hands and rocked for a while, slowly calming down enough to think clearly.

When they'd moved into the homestead, local Constable Digby had twigged to the fact they were sweethearts. He'd called them a pair of filthy tribadists, threatened to have them locked up again and their house razed to the ground. But, for certain favours from Violet, he'd do none of that, he said. Did they have a choice then?

Now they did. With him floating down the Avon, it was all over, bar the brouhaha as Digby's superiors sort to figure out what happened to him. Within the fast-moving river, a body could travel a fair distance in no time at all. And with a bit of luck, it might never be found.

Might.

Should she tell Violet? What her beloved didn't know, she couldn't tell. But, maybe. Maybe one day. Long after it mattered. Certainly not now while Violet needed all the wherewithal for her about-to-be newborn.

Maybe never.

She straightened her bonnet and reached for the reins. A dozen yards away on the opposite river bank, an Aboriginal man balanced on one leg, motionless. Beside him stood a woman with a naked toddler at her hip. How long had they been there? No love was lost between black fellas and police. Alice nodded with a grimace that passed for a smile. A return flash of teeth settled her nerves.

"Walk on, Biscuit. Good donkey!"

# CHAPTER FOURTEEN

Down by the Avon at dawn, kookaburras cackled their heads off and Lorna stirred. It was the morning after the night before when things had got complicated.

Nadeen. What on earth was she thinking, cosying up on the couch with Nadeen, who seemed to take it with good humour? She was a lot younger than her—what would she think of her? Actually, how much younger—sixteen, maybe eighteen years? Could she blame the alcohol? Except she wasn't drunk. Not like that time with Marissa.

Lorna squirmed and tossed back the doona. Dressing gown and sheepskin slippers on, she paused by the wardrobe's floor-length mirror. "I never thought I'd say this, but there's no fool like an old fool."

Apple jam with peanut butter on thickly sliced toast—very moreish with a mug of belting-hot Assam tea. She flicked through the morning's paper, but no news was either good enough or bad enough to distract her. Patently, it was all Nadeen's fault. She shouldn't have told her she was gay. None of this would have happened. She would have kept her distance and her dignity intact. The current penchant for self-disclosure was annoying— too much information.

She shoved the paper across the kitchen table. At least she was out of the sling, only three days away from having stitches out. Mug in hand, she strode into the den where Alice and Violet stared back at her, unmoved. "What do you know that I don't, eh?"

The front door opened and closed. "Where are you, Mum?"

"In the den, darling."

Mel looked her up and down. "Why aren't you dressed?"

"It's Sunday morning. Who cares? I didn't hear a car."

"Jared was in a hurry. He dropped me off at the main road. Are you all right?"

Lorna turned to meet Mel's gaze. "I'm fine. Why wouldn't I be?"

"The garage door is doing its thing again, going up and down."

"Oh?" Lorna took a deep breath and bit her lip. "Oh. I'll get dressed."

"Are you stressing about the poppies?"

"Ah...no. They're all right. Everything is under control. I'll go for a walk down to the peonies, check how they're doing. Don't you worry, I'll be fine. Please go and switch off the door's motor and unplug it. You know it'll reset. Thanks."

The gully easily went unnoticed. Flanked on both sides by steep hills, a narrow creek trickled through dense trees and undergrowth—a trickle that never completely ceased, even in the hottest summer, and would deepen into a steady flow with winter rains. It was here that Cory had slipped and overturned the quad bike, got himself killed. She always sent him a silent blessing as she passed by the spot where he had been found pinned beneath the bike, wet through and lifeless.

Lorna picked her way down the track beside the creek to where it flattened out into a wide area of alluvial soil that had accumulated over millennia. Deep, rich and fertile, it had a microclimate that was perfect for growing peonies—neither too hot nor too cold.

Now in autumn, they were beginning to die down for winter. In spring, they would emerge to flower prolifically in November and December.

Fallen logs made for passable seating. Lorna perched and stretched her legs out, inhaling the fusty lush air. The peonies needed mulching. She would bring a bag of lucerne next time.

Mel's report of the gyrating garage door had unnerved her. It had been years since it last happened. Twice when Cory died, in fact. Before that, it was Marissa. That's when it started and continued for ten days. In the end, Cory had the motor replaced. It did it again and he threw up his hands—cursed the thing. But then it grew still and only stirred itself again for his passing.

Lorna never knew if it was her doing something inexplicable, or the spirits of Alice and Violet. Maybe they reacted to what happened to her? Or maybe it was just her. Either way, she couldn't fathom it. When Cory died, Melanie was barely thirteen and, on the matter of the garage door, she was silent. She would have been too young to recall the first occurrence. Well, hopefully. But Mel knew it had something to do with her mother. This morning was proof perfect.

In the cold light of day, she pondered her behaviour with Nadeen the previous night. She liked her, and…? Her heart said it was a whole lot more than "like." She'd liked Cory as a friend. They'd been buddies—good mates. She would have been happy with that, but he wanted her—wanted marriage. In 1970, that's what you did. With kindness, mutual respect and similar values, they'd made a good team. And she grew very fond of him. Built a life with him. Eight years later, Melanie's arrival had been a glorious bonus, one for which she would be eternally grateful. Her adorable darling girl.

And Marissa? Like? Love? More like lust. Shocking. Compulsive.

But Nadeen seemed much more. Every heartbeat near her was boosted by a sense of anticipation that promised more—a soaring joy. Inexplicable and undeniable, though she'd tried to skip around it. If not for Marissa, she would have succeeded. Marissa had been a volcanic eruption that Lorna had swiftly plugged. But the magma remained below. All it needed was a larger volcano named Nadeen to explode to the surface, unleashing a lava flow of desire that made it perfectly clear who she really was. This was her, being fully herself. Both exciting and frightening, what might such a liaison cost her?

People could be awful, while the silent majority were not. Cormack had copped flak for being ten years older than her. What might they make of her and young Nadeen, and was she willing to go there and find out? If nothing else, she felt more alive today than she had since forever ago. More alarmingly, very much alive from the waist down. Postmenopausal, she was supposed to be past such urges, wasn't she? So much for that myth. The less she thought about it the better—way too distracting.

"So," Lorna said to the wilting peonies. "I'm a middle-aged woman having an identity crisis by falling for another woman. Great idea. Not."

The peonies nodded in the breeze.

"The only positive is she's gay. That's one less hurdle." But what did that make her? "Damned labels. It is what it is. But there's no getting around the age difference. I really must be old enough to be her mother. And in my birthday suit, a sure bet to win a show prize for 'Best Dried Arrangement.' Heck, I don't even know if she likes me. All this is purely theoretical. I have to be worrying about nothing."

What was so attractive about Nadeen, anyway? Realistically, the resemblance to Marissa was by the by. Yet, back then, she must have flirted with Marissa, completely oblivious to the fact. But she couldn't plead innocence about last night. And Nadeen had taken it—played along, good-naturedly. Humoured her, which was charming. What a lovely soul—gentle and generous. Yet underneath that unassuming amiability lurked something intensely passionate. Just behind those dark, enigmatic eyes. And it drew her…insisted she pay attention. Whatever you do, don't walk away.

Restlessly, Lorna rubbed her breastbone. She wanted to grab hold of and immerse herself in life, every day for as long as she was able. With Nadeen, perhaps she could. And would, if only she dared go after it. Like tapping into some primeval power—a mother lode of lifeforce that she'd be foolish to turn her back on. Wouldn't she? At what price? No, it was pointless even thinking about it.

She stood up, stretched her back and bent to caress the largest peony's withering leaves. "Thanks for listening. You're right, this is such a dumb idea. My dumbest, ever."

Winding her way up through the dense bush, Lorna had the inkling of a way forward that would sorely test her nerve. By the time she got to the top, all became clear. She stopped when she reached open ground and spoke to Cory.

"This may not be what you had in mind for me, old fella, but it's what I want. This woman feels right. She might be the future…*my* future. It scares me witless, but I feel so vitally alive! So help me, Cory, please let it be so."

This was no time for prevarication—not any more. Just in case, the garage door would remain unplugged, because needlessly freaking out her child was not an option.

# CHAPTER FIFTEEN

She couldn't get out. Nadeen screamed soundlessly, beat at the stone above, choked. Ran out of breath.

Lurching upright in the dark, she sucked in the night air, hands strung out over her thudding heart. She rubbed her upper arms until her breathing slowed, the bedroom cloaked in an eerie gloom lit only by a full moon forcing its rays between the curtains, cleaving the bed like a white-hot blade.

Eyes half-shut, she caught snippets of the dream. In a confined space, much like a shallow stone box. A simple dress. Flashes of a tropical place, a river flowing nearby. Underground. She was shut in. Alive.

Nadeen clicked on the bedside lamp, clambered out of bed, fumbled her way to the kitchen and put on a light. She slid a water-filled mug with a teabag into the microwave, pushed buttons and blinked at the timer counting down. It beeped, and the clock read 3:47 a.m. A few hours before dawn.

Back in bed, she switched on the clock radio for a hint of normalcy, stacked up pillows and sat sipping the comforting tea.

Joan Armatrading sang of love and affection which only made her tear up. She turned it off, put the half-drunk tea to one side and switched off the light.

More sleep was unlikely. She shut her eyes to the gloom, welcoming any kind of rest that would be better than nothing and sunk into a fitful doze. In the stone box, she hadn't been alone. It couldn't be, but it felt like her. It *was* her.

Lorna.

With daylight, Nadeen bolstered her back with pillows and unpacked the Egyptian oracle cards. To get the right answer required asking the right question. What was the dream trying to tell her? She smoothed out the doona, shuffled the cards and meditated for long enough to calmly hand over the question to a knowing beyond her earthbound self. With the cards fanned out, she gave her left hand to that knowing to choose as it saw fit.

Bast, Tehuti, and Selket, with the final word from Sesheta.

The cards seemed to tell a story. Nadeen stared down at the first three. Bast spoke of love from long, long ago. Tehuti of past-life marriage vows. Selket of great danger averted by powerful protection. In that box—sarcophagus, or whatever it was—she'd been anything but protected. And here, Sesheta heralded a star soulmate as a potential friend and lover for life.

She winced at "soulmate," fully aware that everyone of consequence in her life was a soulmate of one kind or another who shared the same soul group. From incarnation to incarnation, they acted out roles for each other like parent and child, grandparent, sibling, friend, lover, mentor, tormentor, abuser…assassin. The course of such relationships was one of life's mysteries. Some might last a mere moment. Or a year. Or a lifetime.

Her relationship with Greer had cycled through friend, lover, and partner until they became estranged. She didn't know what they were to each other in a previous life. Or would be in the next. Regardless, they would always be soulmates.

The demise of their relationship still hurt, but its end had shipped her home to Toodyay. And, despite the initial grief and anguish, she was grateful for that. Now, the onus was on her to not let the past determine her future. To carve out a new life, which was exactly what she was focussed on doing. And enjoying, mostly.

What if Melanie's mother was someone she knew aeons ago? Her familiarity was a powerful indication that they too were soulmates. So what? Oracle cards were only guidance. The gods inclined—they did not compel.

Yet, she had to pay attention. The dream had been powerful enough to wake her, its vivid details readily recalled. Pointedly, she had been made aware of the possibility of an impossibility becoming possible, which would require making the right choices at the right time. "Right" being the critical word. And the only part of her that could do that—the only part she trusted—was her heart. For now, it was busy feeling its way through the vagaries of life in sleepy Toodyay. Beyond that?

There was Lorna Chidlow. The "possibility." A self-assured, mature country woman with a hands-on, can-do attitude who was a community favourite and at ease with the townsfolk of all shapes and sizes—quick with a smile and a kind word. That generous mouth gave her away. So familiar. Just not in this life.

Without doubt, she was a fine figure of a woman who rocked a pair of snug-fitting Levi 501s with both grace and style. Lorna seemed to know she was attractive, but she didn't cash in on it. Why not? In more come-hither clothes, the blokes would hang around like flies. And when first widowed, she would have scored a second husband in a heartbeat. Maybe she didn't want that particular kind of attention?

Nadeen rubbed a tight brow. Guilty of dressing innocuously herself, even modestly, to avoid the male gaze, maybe Mrs Chidlow was much the same? More to the point, she had made it clear she found Nadeen attractive. Which could have been just a straight woman's game. Or the alcohol.

"I don't think so," murmured Nadeen. "You wouldn't be waking me for that. She's delightful, and I know her. Already, I know her."

Nadeen gathered the cards, shuffled and repacked them in their box stored with other such treasures. The day had taken on a brighter hue, lit up by the hint of a tantalising path that she hadn't dared contemplate. A path that could only materialise with both the boldness to succeed and the willingness to fail—to be hurt—in equal measure. Life was a love game, the future a mystery that dared the willing to step off the edge into the unknown. Did she dare? If a sign flagged the path, maybe. Then the choice was hers. She was ready.

Amongst the letterbox's junk mail was the usual windowed business envelopes and an unexpected letter from Melbourne, its writing all too familiar. Nadeen was tempted to bin it unopened but tossed it on the kitchen table while she made a pot of tea. She was looking forward to dinner—leftover coleslaw and a piece of salmon thawing in the fridge.

Mug in hand, she pulled out a chair and steadied herself in front of the letter, dreading it. What now, Greer? She'd ignored every phone message, and they'd dwindled, then ceased. What now?

Two pages explained how sorry she was. That she'd made a mistake. Deeply regretted losing her best friend, the love of her life. All those years taken for granted. Not anymore, no. She wanted her one true love back. Love never dies—it just transmutes, don't you know? They could rebuild everything lost. Where there's a will, there's a way. Another chance was fair. Trust is knowing nothing will be abused. Love conquers all. Worth another chance, they were. No time for regrets. The future awaits.

She read it three times, scrunched it up and threw it at the bin, where it bounced and landed in the dog's water bowl, floating aimlessly. In the humble kitchen with its dodgy cupboards, rickety table and a snoring Cavalier passed out in her doggy bed, Nadeen was very much at home. Exactly where she wanted to be. In little old Toodyay.

To a shout of "Bella!" the dog opened one eye. "What do you think of this, eh? A grandiose missive, dripping with gag-worthy cliches. Too little, too late."

Yet the letter didn't sound like anything Greer would say out loud. The trite sentiments could have been dictated by a well-meaning somebody, trying to help out. Did Greer really think it would move her? If so, she didn't know Nadeen at all. After nine years, did they know each other well? If not, whose fault was that? Both of them, probably. Nine years of familiarity breeding contempt. All too common and no less lamentable for it.

It was only much later when she slid between the sheets that she found herself counting the number of times Greer had let her down. When she ran out of fingers, she stopped and had to chuckle. Given how little she knew about what was really going on behind her back, if she'd genuinely been Greer's best friend, she would have hated to have been merely a vague acquaintance. Because that's how she was treated.

Early in their relationship, she'd wondered why Greer had so few friends. It took a while to work out that, in fact, she didn't have any real friends—just people she could use. Good-hearted people who would do a favour when asked. Those who knew her passingly well said she was notable for just one thing: Greer was more arse than class.

Come Sunday evening, the phone rang. Nadeen eyed it off, waited for the call to go to the answering machine, heard a familiar voice and picked up.

"Hi, Lorna, how are things?"

"Glad I caught you. Can you spare me a couple of hours tomorrow? The glaziers have been, so the new glasshouse is ready for set up. Trouble is, Rocco is flat out with the apple harvest, supervising pickers as we've got a bumper crop. If you could just give me a hand to position fittings, that would be great."

"How are your hands?"

"The left is pretty good, but the right one thinks I'm joking when I ask it to grip anything. If you can't make it, I'll think of something."

"No, that's all right. But I have to drive down to Fremantle first thing."

"Oh. That's a bit of a hike. Do you have to?"

"The Customs people want to eyeball me and have a chat. I import clay statuettes from India, and they're always wary of concealed contraband. Turning up in person usually allays their suspicions and saves them damaging any stock. I used to get the same treatment in Melbourne. Can't say I blame them. But I can get to you around midday or just before. Does that work for you?"

"Perfect. Do bring Bella…she's such a sweetie."

"Will do."

A bubble of excitement surfaced in Nadeen's chest and she quelled it with a muffled chuckle. Just quietly, she'd been waiting for such a call. And it was highly likely she'd be smiling all the way to Freo and back. But she'd have to tone it down or Customs would wonder what mischief she'd been getting into.

# CHAPTER SIXTEEN

"Show me your hands."

Lorna stuck them out for Nadeen to hold. "You have very warm hands."

Nadeen smoothed her fingertips around Lorna's livid scars and murmured, "Warm hands, cold heart."

"Ha! Whatever you're selling with that line, I'm not buying it."

Nadeen didn't look up. "You need extra padding on that palm. An inner soft glove within your work glove would help."

"Somewhere, I have a pair of ancient kid-leather gloves that might do. Let me find them. Won't be a moment." Lorna left Nadeen in the kitchen and went to rummage in a bedroom drawer. She paused and shut her eyes, still absorbing Nadeen's searing touch, Nadeen's tumbling hair and long lashes only a breath away. How close had they been? Within kissing distance. Tempting—very tempting. A deep and steady, calming breath later she found the gloves, and slid the drawer slowly shut.

At the kitchen door, she waved them to Nadeen who nodded as she pulled them on, the heavy work gloves next. "Good to go."

They walked out to the new glasshouse, all fresh and shiny. Inside, stainless-steel benches were jumbled up one end, ready to be positioned.

Nadeen said, "What's the plan?"

Lorna yanked a folded paper from a back pocket and laid it flat on a tabletop. "This is the layout, in theory. If we set everything in place, then have another look at it. It's only in use that we can judge what works best."

Nadeen lifted the table's edge. "Not too heavy. When you're ready."

They manoeuvred all the tables, had to reposition them twice, which had Lorna gritting her teeth, determined not to let Nadeen see her struggling in pain. But they managed it in less than an hour.

Lorna ambled back to the door and stood with her hands pinned under her armpits, surveying the result. "That will do. Come in and I'll make you a strong cup of something."

In the kitchen, Lorna washed her hands under soothing cold running water.

Nadeen said, "Show me."

"I'll be fine." Lorna patted her hands dry with a towel.

"Yeah, right. Show me." Nadeen took a good look. "Do you have any wound cream with anaesthetic in it?"

"In the top drawer by the sink."

Tube in hand, Nadeen pulled out two chairs and sat waiting. Lorna joined her, closed her eyes when the cool cream hit the still-healing, fiery cuts. "I can do that myself."

"But you weren't going to, were you? Being strong doesn't mean being tough with yourself. Strong is smart, tough is less than. That said, you really should do daily stretches so the scars don't heal too tightly."

Lorna wasn't really listening, too busy relishing being cared for so tenderly, which hadn't happened for far too long. Nadeen spread the cream in gentle swirls as the anaesthetic was rapidly absorbed. "Thank you. That really helped. You're right, I wouldn't have bothered." Nadeen looked into her eyes and she forgot to breathe, and could have sworn there was the barest hint of a smile in Nadeen's expression.

Nadeen stood and put the tube away. "Shall I put the kettle on?"

"Yes, please." Lorna sucked in a breath and roused herself. "Actually, I was wondering if you might help me make Dorset apple cake. My knife skills are still very ordinary, and I could do with a hand peeling, coring, and slicing. Can you spare the time?"

Nadeen had filled the kettle and switched it on. "Sure, I've never heard of that recipe. Something you make regularly?"

"Always. The harvest is particularly large this year. I bake and freeze and use the apples any and every which way known to man." Lorna put two mugs on the countertop and popped in teabags. "The recipe is very old. I particularly like it because it's more apple than cake. Basically, layers of sliced apple held together by a light batter with cinnamon and a few sultanas chucked in for good measure. Tastes good too. Mind you, that's only because the Cox's Orange Pippin is famously delicious." She opened a tall pantry door and tugged at something. "Sorry, I need an extra pair of hands. Would you?"

Nadeen stepped in and lugged out a basket of yellow-and-red-mottled apples that she put on the kitchen table.

With a paring knife, Lorna cut a thin wedge from one and offered it to Nadeen. "Try this."

"Whoa." Nadeen kept chewing. "It's sweet and tart, all in one bite."

"Isn't it amazing? Good for eating, baking and brewing. They don't come any better." She poured boiling water into the mugs. "Now, I've got the flour mix prepped, just need to rub in the butter. I'll park you at the table with apples and implements, if that works for you?"

"How about a chopping board and a bowl to put the slices in." Nadeen started peeling an apple. "What do you do with the waste?"

"The donkeys love the peelings. If you could keep the cores separate because the seeds aren't too good for them in any quantity.

The chooks will eat them." Lorna put a board and a bowl in front of Nadeen. "How are you at rubbing in cold butter?"

With a shake of her head, Nadeen said, "Warm hands, remember?"

*How could I forget?* "Of course. I'll manage." Lorna took the mixing bowl with flour to the table and stood over it, cutting in pieces of butter, then massaging it in with her fingertips. They worked in silence broken only by the sounds of peeling, slicing, and scraping.

"What do you do with your excess apples?" asked Nadeen.

"If they're not suitable for cider, I make cakes and a mountain of apple jam that gets sold through the CWA opportunity shops."

"Is that worthwhile commercially?"

"The CWA keeps the proceeds, but they provide the jars. I've been a member for aeons. My mother signed me up when I was a teenager. She was passionate about the CWA, and was their president for a few years, back in the day."

"Pardon my ignorance, but I would have thought they're fast becoming irrelevant."

Lorna protested, "Goodness, no. Not at all. The CWA may have been around since the 1920s, but things haven't changed that much for country women. For those in rural areas, sometimes hundreds of kilometres away from neighbours, it's a lifesaver. It's not all about the best scone recipe—more like a trusted community in which people will help each other out. Sometimes with physical labour, sharing resources or equipment that saves money. Sometimes it's just about being supported, no matter what. Even here in Toodyay, people owe life-long friendships to the CWA. At the moment, I'm acting vice president for my friend Tash who's up in Geraldton dealing with a family crisis. All a bit fraught."

Lorna stole a glance at Nadeen. "I've been meaning to tell you that the poppy germination rate is excellent. All your work is proving itself. I really can't thank you enough."

"Oh, I don't know. How about a chunk of Dorset apple cake?"

Grinning, Lorna said, "If you hang around long enough. It bakes in about forty minutes. I can show you around the place while it's in the oven. Speaking of which—" She stepped to the stove and switched the oven on to preheat. Sugar, sultanas, and cinnamon went into the flour mix. A couple of eggs and a slosh of milk were beaten together. She had a quick look in Nadeen's bowl of prepared slices. "When you've finished that one, it should be just enough for this cake." The bowl's contents were emptied into the flour mix and folded in. "Nearly there. Now, where did I put the cake tin? Ah, found it."

Nadeen said, "If you don't mind me asking, how did you get into the poppy germination enterprise?"

Lorna greased the tin with a knob of butter. "I'm not too sure. I grew up in Northam and remember seeing the flowers many years ago and being amazed by them. The gold rush in the last decade of the nineteenth century would have attracted Chinese folk carrying seeds to grow their own opium. They're so beautiful. I was oblivious to their medicinal properties, of course. But when I found out about that, I found them even more fascinating. A few local farms had poppies growing wild, with most people unaware of what they were. But I collected seeds and grew them in my parents' garden where they self-seeded and went rampant. Which was so wonderful. I loved it! Such an outrageous, captivating, huge red bloom harbouring a powerful medicine. A plant with both charisma and real power is unusual, wouldn't you say?"

"I guess the same could apply to just about any living thing." Nadeen brought over the bowl with the last of the sliced apple. "In fact, I can think of the occasional exceptional woman who would fit that description. Charismatic. A commanding presence. She can be intimidating."

Lorna risked a glance at Nadeen, stilled her hands, then wiped them and took the bowl. "Are you intimidated?" She emptied it into the mix, poured in the beaten egg mixture, and lightly folded the contents together.

"To some extent. All living things have a unique energy…an instinct to survive and, given the chance, to thrive. What comes along to help us thrive can take us by surprise. You see, I'm guessing what it might be that you want…"

Lorna emptied the batter into the tin, smoothed it flattish, and sprinkled the top with demerara sugar. "Would you put it in the oven for me? Middle of the middle rack. Thanks." At the sink, she rinsed and dried her hands. She set a timer for forty minutes.

There were only a few steps between her and Nadeen. Her heart beating way too fast, she approached slowly, placed one hand on Nadeen's breastbone. "I'm flesh and blood, with all its associated needs and desires. Nothing unusual."

Nadeen covered the hand with her own. "We both know it's way more complicated than that. And right now, I feel it's wise to be cautious."

"Some people would say you're talking in riddles."

Nadeen dropped her hand. "You're not 'some people.' Energetically speaking, you're far more aware of nuance than the average mortal. You know that."

Lorna's fingertips moved up to the galloping pulse point at Nadine's throat, rested there. "I've never met someone with a near-perfect poker face. Why do you wear it so well?"

"Because I'm not straight. And it's preferable, most of the time, for others not to know what I'm thinking or feeling. It's my armour. At the moment, it's falling apart. You have that effect on me. Satisfied?"

"Nowhere near it. But I'd like to be. Satisfied. With you." Lorna licked her teeth and slipped both hands around Nadeen's neck.

Nadeen's mouth on hers was both a relief and a release. A hand in the small of her back arched her against Nadeen's hips. Another hand in her hair, holding her, was unwilling to let go. Lorna's body surged with want, with wanting to be wanted. She came up for air, ecstatic, delighted, looked deep into Nadeen's dark, dancing eyes and kissed her again. "I want you. Something bad."

"Lead the way."

Lorna grabbed the timer in one hand, Nadeen in the other. "Mustn't burn the cake."

# CHAPTER SEVENTEEN

On a sunny afternoon in rural Toodyay, with the blinds down and curtains closed, Lorna's bedroom could have been mistaken for a secluded scene of tranquillity, except for two women in a hurry. Lorna had flung back the bedclothes, but otherwise, their undressing was random and happened only where it mattered—where hands needed access.

Nadeen said, "No time for niceties, my lovely."

Lorna let it happen, rode a wave of desire that reached a crescendo way beyond her control, left her clinging to Nadeen until she subsided onto the sheets, heart still thudding.

Nadeen scooped her into her arms, held her in silence until her breathing slowed. "Are you all right?" Lorna simply turned her face into Nadeen's throat. "Sorry, but that had to be a quickie."

Lorna murmured, "How could you tell?"

"Hm. Your pupils were so dilated, I thought you might launch into the stratosphere and never come down. And that would be a crying shame because I'd like to see you again."

Lorna managed a giggle, reached up and stroked Nadeen's cheek. "Ha, ha, you're very funny. And talented, with it. What have I got myself into?"

"As a rule, I'm very mature and sensible. Just not today," said Nadeen, licking her lips. "Rules are for breaking, especially personal ones." She slipped off the bed and very casually undressed with a tiny smile, ignoring a mesmerised audience.

She sat on the edge of the bed, unbuttoned Lorna's blouse and caressed bare skin. Lorna sat up and took off her remaining clothing, pulled Nadeen in for a kiss that deepened into something savage. Hands on hot skin over undulating muscle, flexing against hips in sync with taut backs and bellies.

The timer went off.

Muttering, Lorna flew out of bed, dragged on her dressing gown, raced down to the kitchen, turned the oven off, grabbed the oven mitts, pulled out the cake tin and plonked it on the stove top. Equally fast, she ran back to the bedroom, wriggled out of the dressing gown and jumped on Nadeen who burst out laughing, turned her over and licked and kissed her way down the back of Lorna's neck to the base of her spine. Then she crawled back up and lay beside Lorna, whispered sensual drivel in her ear, ignoring the protesting giggles.

Tentatively, Lorna ran hands over Nadeen's form, touching the intriguing soft places, the curve of belly, breast and inner thigh, a wrist where a pulse thumped visibly. All of it, a miracle for her to marvel at, even if she was unsure quite where to start. But Nadeen's dark pools for eyes drew her, serene yet alert.

Lorna said, "What's on your mind?"

"May I ask if you've been with women before?"

"Not exactly."

Nadeen's eyebrows shot up.

Lorna cleared her throat. "Once upon a time, I let a woman have her way with me, as it were. And didn't return the favour. It never happened again. To be blunt, it shocked the pants off me, scared me silly. This? This, I was more prepared for. Older and wiser and all that. But honestly, still a bit scared. With good reason, I suspect."

Nadeen started to say something, but Lorna bolted upright and looked at the bedside clock. "Oh, shit! Mel will be on her way home, about now!"

They found their clothing, dressed at breakneck speed, and hurried down to the kitchen.

On the way, Lorna said, "Sorry to do this to you, but it's not a conversation I want to have with my child right now."

"Me neither."

"Please take some of this with you." Lorna lifted the cake out of its springform pan and slid it onto a plate. A large wedge cut, she wrapped it in clingfilm.

Nadeen took it gingerly. "About us. Nobody has to know."

"This is Toodyay. It's only a matter of time, if we were to carry on. Sorry but, maybe it was a very bad idea. Shouldn't have happened at all."

Nadeen froze and whispered, "Please don't say that. Please?"

"Oh, God, Nadeen. I'm sorry. I didn't mean it that way. It's just that—"

"Look, I get it. See you later." And she turned away.

Midstep, Lorna grabbed her, and pulled her into a tight hug, kissing her hard. "I *really* like you. No matter what happens, don't you dare think otherwise it. I want you and nobody else but you. Now, make yourself scarce. Skedaddle!"

# CHAPTER EIGHTEEN

The autumn days were still light late enough for Nadeen to potter about in the back garden after shutting up shop. She'd discovered a whole row of gerbera pots behind the garage that she hadn't realised were lurking there, barely alive for lack of water. They could be ordinary, or they could be treasures. There was no way to know without seeing them in flower, which meant refurbishing the plants and potting them up for a new lease of life. Up to her elbows in soil, she stirred together a fresh mix of ingredients, tailor-made to suit the waiting plants.

Three days had passed since she'd seen or heard from Lorna. When she'd started toward home that day, she'd driven past Mel on foot just before the main road junction. They'd smiled and waved at each other, leaving Nadeen slightly queasy, as if she'd betrayed her loyal sidekick. It didn't feel good, that's for sure. And she'd been trying to make sense of their interlude ever since. Was it a one-off—just a moment's afternoon delight? In fact, she was tired of thinking about it: what they did, what was said. What wasn't.

It was the indecent haste of her exit that troubled her. As if they'd done something shameful. And she'd had a gutful of guilt and shame to last her entire adult life. Did she need more of the same now? On balance, it was a whole lot easier being single. Apart from the odd misguided straight bloke like Derek, people left her alone. No pain involved. Singleness had its pluses.

Except that meant living her life within the status quo, with zero hope of the many joys of a loving relationship. Presuming love had something to do with her and Lorna. With her hands in a tub of soil enhanced with animal droppings, she may have merely dug a lusty hole for herself—one extra heavy on the manure.

Speaking of which, she'd never heard Lorna swear before. It was startling at the time. She smiled wryly to herself and muttered, "Beware of putting anyone on a pedestal. She may have feet of clay."

The phone rang. She would check the machine when she went indoors. And the letterbox probably needed clearing, unopened since last week.

There were two letters. She opened the earlier postmarked envelope first and gingerly extracted the card. The cover was a sea of gold-edged pink and red hearts, the handwritten contents a vehement protestation of undying love. Nadeen blinked at it, put it to one side and opened the second one. Its cover featured a rosy-cheeked winking cupid with a quiver full of heart-tipped arrows. Inside, Greer must have mined a thesaurus for every romance-related word in the English language. Nadeen gulped and clasped her cheeks.

"Oh, for the love of…have you lost your mind? Am I the next 'shiny thing'?" Greer had tended to flit from one passing obsession, to another temporary hobby, to crushing on a celeb, to the next latest have-to-have thing. Initially amusing, it had grown tedious with time and exposure. Behaviour Nadeen knew only too well. Now that Greer couldn't have her, she wanted her. To quote Lorna, "Oh, shit!"

But with no response or gratification, in time Greer would run out of enthusiasm and find some other poor, unsuspecting soul to dazzle and conquer. All smoke and mirrors. Or, in Toodyay parlance, all piss and wind.

"Not my problem. And I'm not going to let you make it mine." The cards went in the bin.

She pushed the "play" button on the answering machine. Lorna asked her to call back when she had a spare moment. In the cool of the dark hall, she folded her arms and shut her eyes, breathing in the simple serenity of the humble cottage—its peace and solitude. This was what she stood to lose. In the town, she was a newcomer with primarily tourists for customers, therefore already an outsider. It wasn't like she sold rainbow pride flags and wasn't about to start.

In Lorna's world, as Toodyay royalty, she stood to lose much more.

Already, she was far too fond of Lorna. Just her voice made her heart hum a sweet ditty, now tuned in to Lorna's by their lovemaking. That couldn't be undone. But was it enough to get them through what may come? And may continue to come in the ensuing fray? Queer people spent their whole lives repeatedly coming out. Tiresome. How would Lorna handle all that? Presumptuous to consider, but she had to take some responsibility for wrecking Lorna's life, didn't she? Maybe, maybe not. It was Lorna's decision—her choice. And not for Nadeen to determine what Lorna could or could not handle.

Bottom line, what did she really want? Her heart sang out, loud and clear. She picked up the phone.

* * *

Nadeen said, "It's getting dark out here. I hope you've brought a torch."

Lorna muttered, "City slicker. Of course I have." Ahead of Nadeen, she picked her way down the track toward the peony gully. "Are you all right, back there?"

"Sure. Enjoying the view."

Laughing, Lorna stumbled. "Ouch! Nearly cracked my ankle. Behave yourself. At least until we get to level ground."

"Are you really showing me peonies, or is this just to get me alone?"

"A bit of both. Ah, here we are. Come and sit on a log. It's a challenge for your bum's padding." Lorna took Nadeen's hand and led her to a fallen gum tree trunk. "Isn't this lovely? No mozzies at this time of year, fortunately. Or we'd get eaten alive."

"Any wildlife out here?"

"The usual bandicoots and possums. Maybe a lizard or a fox looking for a drink. But they're more scared of us than we are of them. Otherwise, you're safe. From the wildlife, at least."

"Not from you?"

"Afraid not. First, we need to talk."

They sat in silence, exchanging glances. Lorna sheltered Nadeen's hand in her lap.

Nadeen said, "Tell me what you've got planned for this secret peony garden."

"Well, I plan to propagate and grow maybe sixty to eighty plants of different shapes, sizes, and colours. I haven't worked out how many years it will take before I can offer a product to the cut-flower wholesalers, but it's likely the first three to five years will establish that. It is results driven, of course."

"Why peonies, why now, and what about the poppies?"

"Good questions," said Lorna. "I'm aware that industrial chemists keep finding ways to create synthetic versions of all sorts of drugs. I figure that, one day, they'll come up with a synthetic opium. And then, what I do will be superfluous. While manufacturers already make fake flowers, I figure they'll never make one that smells like the real thing. Peonies, like roses, are both beautiful and perfumed. It's likely there will always be a demand for the real thing. And people will pay a premium for the privilege."

"I see you've done your research."

"Thank you, my dear. There is one more reason. The poppies are difficult, technical, fiddly work, with a whole lot of lifting and carrying. I'm thinking about my future, you see."

Nadeen nodded. "Indeed. Your future. Makes sense."

"So, what do you think?"

"It has legs. If anyone can make it run, you can. But I suggest we need to make a move back to the house, or Mel will be wondering what on earth we hope to see out here with only a torch."

Lorna stood up, tugged Nadeen to her feet. In the fading light of day, they stole a few minutes to touch, look into each other's eyes and kiss. Breathless, light-headed…oblivious. In a crushing hug, hearts thumping in time, they swayed, ever so slightly. Lorna said, "I love being with you. Just the feel of you, your arms, your warmth. So, so good. Can we make a date for more?"

Smiling, Nadeen stepped back. "Let's go, eh?"

Lorna switched on the torch and they weaved their way up the path, concentrating on not taking a misstep.

Near the top, Nadeen said, "I've been thinking. Correct me if I'm wrong, but it would be only fair for you to return the favour. You know…you could come to my place and give me advice about gerberas. Sundays and Mondays are my days off. You might pop in and stay for a cuppa. And whatever came up."

Out in the open again, Lorna flashed her teeth. "Well, Sunday first thing is looking perfect for me. Suit you?"

"Absolutely."

# CHAPTER NINETEEN

With one hand, Lorna clung to the carved wooden bedhead. "What are you doing?" Her other hand gripped Nadeen's wrist.

"Exploring your most responsive bits. The arch of your foot. Such pretty feet and ankles. The backs of your knees are so, so soft. Shapely calves…strong, yet elegant. The inside of your thighs and the crease at the base of your spine. Both too delightful. It's doing it for me. How about you?"

Lorna spluttered and managed a weak chuckle. "Somewhere between utter tease and torture. Have pity on this old lady, will you? Oh...oh…" She sucked in a sharp breath—sank into a white-hot oblivion—and allowed herself to be gathered into Nadeen's arms. Warm and soothing hands stroked the length of her back. Kisses fell on her forehead and temples.

Blinking, she focussed on the ceiling and sighed. "You should come with a health warning. Positively dangerous."

"I'll take that as a compliment." Nadeen's eyes glittered, and she leaned in. Lorna kissed her, caressing her lover with a tenderness that somehow shocked. This close wasn't close enough, but it would have to do. Short of climbing under Nadeen's skin.

Eyes closed, they lay in silence. Still.

Nadeen said, "Cuppa? Water?"

"Water, please."

"Back in a minute." She took up a silky robe on the way out.

Lorna slid off the low bed, gathered pillows and silver-threaded turquoise cushions and set them up to support their backs against the ornate bedhead. Nadeen reappeared with two glasses and a carafe.

"I've a spare robe somewhere. Sorry, not used to bedroom guests." She opened a sliding door and came back with a white robe stamped with blue stylised ankh symbols.

"Thank you. I'm getting that blue's your favourite colour."

Nadeen sat on the bed and poured water. "Especially turquoise. I love it with silver."

Lorna said, "I don't know what I was expecting but it wasn't this." She climbed on the bed and waved a hand in the air. "White bed linen, brown bedspread, dark timbers, cane chairs, turquoise accessories. Silver trinkets and ornaments. With the fabric hangings and Egyptian posters, it's certainly got a theme to it."

"Too over the top? When it comes to Egyptian décor, this is very tame. They love lots of black and gold, with red and deep-blue furnishings. Plus, wall-to-wall posters and hieroglyphics. I used to have a canopy over the bed, but it collected too much dust. It's only because I grew up with Egyptophile parents. We had so much stuff, it defied belief. This is my version…the toned-down one. These posters are of Isis and Sekhmet. No male gods staring at me while I sleep, thanks very much."

"What about those statuettes?" Lorna pointed at items on the cane-fronted dressing table.

"What, those? I sell them in the shop. Osiris or Isis, Anubis or Bast. A man or woman, a dog or cat. We Aussies love our dogs and cats, don't we? When people want something Egyptian, they buy one of them. Hand made in India." She cocked her head at Lorna. "I hasten to add that everything in here is chosen for its symbolism and energy. Nothing is random."

Lorna took a sip of water. "Some of that symbolism strikes me as morbid, as if Egyptians were obsessed with death."

"I can see why you'd think that, but for them it was all about an afterlife in the stars. They fervently believed that the pleasures of earthly life should continue to be enjoyed by the deceased in the afterlife. That's why they prepared their dead so reverently and equipped them for the journey. It was an act of love."

"That makes sense. This room feels peaceful. Safe. Protected."

"Do you prefer to live in an always safe and protected way?"

"That's a strange question. I mean, who would?"

"For security's sake, some do." Nadeen glanced over and dropped her shoulders. "I know there are things you want to talk about. But I feel I have to warn you how hard things could get if people find out about us. And you said yourself, it's inevitable in Toodyay. May I ask if you've ever been discriminated against?"

"That has to be rhetorical." Lorna exhaled heavily. "As a woman, certainly. Happens to every woman, doesn't it? And as I get older, I have to fight harder to be heard. Respected. Ageism, I suppose."

"Sure. Suffice to say, if you get labelled as 'one of those,' by that I mean lesbian, you could be ostracised by some people."

"Why are you telling me this now?"

Nadeen pursed her lips. "Because your life could become quite uncomfortable. Look, you have a better idea than me how Toodyay folk would treat a different version of you. And a better idea how you would handle their reactions. I know you're a strong woman of considerable integrity, but you're used to being accepted without question. This is all very new to you. You may want to consider your options. Before too many folks get wind of it. Before Mel finds out."

"I admit I haven't thought that far ahead." Lorna managed a wry smile. "How have you coped with this kind of stuff?"

"For the sake of my sanity, very pragmatically. I stopped caring what other people think a long time ago. And I've learnt to trust my instincts about people. It saves time and a whole lot of heartache. For the rest of it, I think of myself as a fox in the middle of a pack of hounds. That is, I look straight ahead and run with the pack. It's remarkable how the hounds don't notice me. And every now and then, I spot another fox in the pack, doing exactly the same thing. We nod at each other and just keep going."

"Ah-ha. I see, Foxy Lady. Come over here. This vixen needs a pashing."

Nadeen grabbed her. They rolled around on the bed, kissing and giggling.

"And here I was worrying about bringing up the difficult topic of the age gap," said Lorna. "It rather pales into insignificance."

"What? Please explain. What is its significance?"

"Considerable, I think. For the record, how old are you?"

"I'm forty-two."

"Not as bad as I thought. I'd pegged you at thirty-eight. Still, that's a fourteen-year difference. I could be your mother."

Nadeen coughed and laughed. "That's ridiculous. You would have been a child bride."

"In some cultures, not unusual. But seriously, it's an issue. How do you feel about it?"

Eyes narrowing, Nadeen said, "Frankly, I don't care. I might have ten years ago, but now? I'm no longer young and feel youth is somewhat overrated. What's important to me is how we are with each other. And bite me if I'm wrong, I think we're good together. It's early days, but I enjoy being with you. So much."

"What about in ten years' time?"

"What about it? We'll both be ten years older. And there are only two options for us mortals—get older or join the afterlife. Anyway, it's a bit early for this conversation."

Lorna frowned at her. "You've just been telling me we have to have this conversation now. Before every one of the three thousand-plus souls in Toodyay has their head explode with the news. While I can still get out while the going is good, yes? That's what you meant, isn't it?"

"In a nutshell." Nadeen rubbed her eyebrows. "You're quite right. My experience of straight society's disregard has gone on most of my adult life. Things are improving, albeit slowly. And your experience doesn't have to mirror mine. It's just that I would never forgive myself if I didn't warn you. Sorry." Tears sprang from nowhere and she covered her face with her hands.

"Oh no, my honey-babe. It's okay, it's okay. Shh…" Lorna held Nadeen's face to her bare chest. "My tough lady fox with a tender heart. And I love you for it. Listen to me." Nadeen rubbed away tears, sniffed and blinked at Lorna. "Maybe if there was a bloke on the planet just like you, I'd be interested in him. But there isn't. You're a one-off. Only one Nadeen Quin here, in this place, at this time. And I have to confess to myself and you, and others, if necessary, that I prefer that you're a woman. Are you hearing me?"

Nadeen gaped for a moment, then she swallowed and nodded.

"Good. Bear with me, because I'm still none too happy about the age gap. But I'd better get going. Mel will be wondering where I am. She won't believe how fascinating and time-consuming chatting about gerberas can be."

Grinning, Nadeen said, "Hang on. There's something else I wanted to ask you."

Lorna was dressing. "Talk fast."

"Right. I'm just curious. Do you experience inexplicable phenomena around you?"

"Like what? Where's my bra?"

"Here." Nadeen swung it over. "Objects moving that shouldn't. Electrical faults, or things turning on and off."

Lorna hooked herself up. "Electrical things, yes. When I'm worried, distressed, disturbed, out of sorts. It's rare, but it happens."

"I suspected as much because you radiate such a high-level energy, like a mini power station. It's just telekinesis. You leak energy under stress."

"And here I was, for years, silently accusing the ghosts of Alice and Violet for orchestrating mischievous shenanigans. Should I be worried?" Lorna pulled her hoodie over her head.

"It's pretty harmless, if sometimes disturbing. Look, this is going to sound whacko, but I dreamt we were together in a sarcophagus. In ancient Egypt."

Lorna frowned. "You mean thousands of years ago? Have you seen my watch?"

"Jeans back pocket. No, the other one. Yes, before the Christian era. Somewhere BCE."

"Assuming reincarnation, previous lives and suchlike. So, what if it were so? Which we'll never know."

Nadeen crawled over and dangled her legs over the edge of the bed. "Does it resonate with you?"

Through thoughtful eyes, Lorna examined Nadeen, stepped between her knees into waiting arms and looked down at her. "Honey-babe. I've never called anyone that in my life. Weird. Anyway, somewhere deep inside, it does resonate. And I wonder about the poppies. I've always been fascinated by them. Maybe too much. Anyway, on some level, you and I seem very in tune with each other."

"Yes, I feel it, too. Remember when we first met, I asked you if we'd met before? I figured we must have."

"And I thought the same. You reminded me so much of Marissa."

"Who's Marissa?"

"The tax accountant. You resemble her, except your hair is wavy whereas hers had a distinct curl. I thought I was seeing things."

"Well, maybe it was something else."

"Could be. Walk me out?"

"Just to the door. I'm not decent."

"Oh, but you are. You're just right, exactly as you are."

They hurried down the hall and, just before the front door was opened, Lorna said, "Can we do this again? I mean next Sunday morning. If I can wait that long. I know I'm a rank amateur, but is that okay?"

"Love to. Don't worry. Don't overthink it."

Lorna wrapped herself around Nadeen, buried her face in her throat and inhaled her scent for just a little while longer. Abruptly, she let go and grabbed the door handle. "You're holding me up, honey-babe. Gotta go!"

* * *

Nadeen shut the door, still smiling. In the sitting room, she stood motionless and tweaked the curtain open to catch a glimpse of Lorna's white van as it left the driveway. The fact that they both thought they'd met before left her inexplicably disturbed.

She nudged open the curtain a smidgin farther to reveal a dark sedan parked three doors down. Tinted windows hid its interior, with no apparent movement. Her neighbours on both sides were long-term, elderly residents who rarely had visitors. Staring, she untied her dressing gown, wrapped it more snugly and retied it.

Foreboding grew as the unknown hazards of a future with Lorna competed with the echo of an ancient familiarity for her attention. She shut the curtain.

# CHAPTER TWENTY

*Thebes, Egypt 1108 BCE—Peret (growing season)*

In the House of Life in the Temple of Horus, Nadiyya sat on the floor, as usual. The walls bore colourful paintings of people and their exploits, with hieroglyphs explaining their significance. All was framed by rows of stylised poppy seedheads that encircled the room.

One leg was under her, while the other's knee acted as a slanted table for the small slip of papyrus on which she was writing. Already, the reed was losing its point. She would have to stop, wash out the black tint, and chew the reed into a fluffy fibre to form a fine point again. She had just written "myrrh" and was about to write "cinnamon," the last ingredient of the healing recipe. Nearly there.

"Nadiyya!" Her father's voice made her start and smear the hieroglyph. She bit a lip and slumped, hand quivering.

"Have you finished?" Akil stood over her and she handed him a thin pile of papyrus. As befitted a *wabu*—a priest physician to royalty—he leafed through the slips and threw half of them on the floor beside her. "Not good enough. These are medical texts. They have to be perfect for the records. You understand?"

"Yes, Father, but I've done my best—"

"Your best is not good enough! You are my daughter and now fourteen years old. I have to decide your future. Do you want to be a medical scribe, or do you want to be married?"

"A scribe! I must be a scribe."

Akil glowered at her. "That you are my daughter is the only reason you have the chance to be a scribe. Do not have me shamed. You must be perfect to be a scribe. Do the recipes again. Practice makes perfect." And he strode out of the room.

Tears welling, she shifted to stretch an aching right hip and legs that had grown numb. On her writing hand's wrist, she wore a woven band with a crude ceramic scarab beetle as a protective amulet. She lightly rubbed tired eyes that were ringed with kohl every morning to protect them from dust and dirt. Only recently, her scalp had been reshaven to keep the lice away. And, no matter what she did, the pale linen dress that she constantly wore was dusty again. When she could, she would wash herself, the knee-length sheath, and her triangular loincloth in the Nile. Everything either went into or came out of the great river, including the fish they ate.

Probably, Laani was down by the river talking with her friends—those older, more noble girls who scorned Nadiyya. But sixteen-year-old royal daughter Laani always smiled at her, beckoned her over and hugged her like she deserved it. Which she didn't, of course. Certainly, she was Akil the wabu's child, therefore a step above a common street girl. But not by much.

She closed her eyes and found herself in Laani's arms, Laani's lively grey eyes smiling into hers. She adored Laani, would do anything for her, swim the length of the Nile and back for her. And Laani knew it. She would giggle and coo at Nadiyya, rub her ears and cuddle her like she was one of the royal pet monkeys. Nadiyya would snuggle up and finger the broad gold cuff bracelets Laani wore on each wrist, both enhanced by a raised Eye of Horus inset with an almond-shaped turquoise. Once, Laani kissed her on the mouth and Nadiyya nearly fainted. All the girls pointed, and two laughed so hard, they slipped and fell in a heap of helpless giggles.

But Nadiyya didn't care. She had seen a look in Laani's eyes that had ventured well beyond pure fun. Yet she would mean less than nothing to Laani who was Tyti's—the Great Wife of Rameses X—youngest daughter. Whereas Nadiyya was a nothing—a nobody going nowhere. Except to be married off. Or become a scribe if she were so fortunate. But she could and would dream. Dreams that always featured her beloved princess.

Nadiyya squeezed her eyes and squatted back into the writing position. She washed the reed in a nearby large jug of water and stuck it in her mouth, grinding the end with her back teeth to soften and feather the fibres.

"A scribe. I *will* be a scribe. Or nothing at all."

* * *

They ran behind the boat huts, giggling and exulting at having escaped the prying eyes of the other girls scattering along the river's edge. Old reed boats were piled up in disarray, some upside down on top of others. Laani squeezed into an opening between two tatty craft that served as a private cocoon. She dragged a willing Nadiyya in behind her, and they sat listening, clutching their knees to their chests, exchanging smirks.

Laani said, "What have you brought me?"

Pulling a small clay pot from under her dress, Nadiyya said, "Honey. I got it in the market yesterday, just for you."

Laani took the pot and tugged out the linen-wrapped reed stopper. She licked its tip and smiled at her young friend. "Delicious. Much better than what we have at the palace. How did you manage to steal it?"

Nadiyya gasped. "I'm not a thief! I'm the wabu's daughter. I would never do such a thing."

"Forgive me, my always honest honey-babe," Laani teased, measuring the girl's outrage. "I did not mean to offend, but how can you get it otherwise?"

"Same as everyone does. I barter."

"You barter." Laani stuck a pinkie into the pot, then into her mouth, savoured the sweet stickiness and licked her lips. "With what?"

"I'm training to be a scribe. My father is teaching me to write. And I—"

Laani blurted, 'You can't do that…you're a girl!"

"He says I can, but only if I'm better than all the boys. And I will be, with practice…I *will* be a scribe. He lets me have scraps of papyrus that are too small for anything else. I write people's names in a cartouche and barter them in the market. Most cannot read or write, but they love having the writing or a picture about them, or a loved one. I don't get much for them, but it adds up. That's how I got your honey."

"Well, I'm impressed. Thank you for the hard-earned gift." Gazing intently, Laani leaned in and pecked Nadiyya on the cheek. "Now I appreciate it that much more. And I see there is more to you than meets the eye. My budding businesswoman. But I've never heard of a female scribe. Aren't you supposed to marry?"

"One of my cousins. But not if I become a scribe. I will earn my keep, and my freedom."

"I envy you." Laani considered Nadiyya. "I am contracted to marry my cousin too. I have no choice, but it could have been my awful brother. He smells out of his mouth like donkey dung. Their second choice…my last choice!"

"But you live in a palace surrounded by servants. You can have every pleasure the world provides, can't you?"

With a hollow laugh, Laani stroked the girl's cheek. "My pleasures are limited to what my parents allow. This time alone with you, hiding in a boat? Something I treasure more than you might imagine. And I dream of further pleasures with you that they wouldn't begin to understand." She pulled Nadiyya into too-long-empty arms. "All of which will be beyond my reach very soon. I have to comply with the marriage contract and live with my cousin. When that happens, doing what I desire with you will not be allowed. Only because I'm a princess. You must know that."

"Could we not meet in secret?"

"They would find out. And that, my sweet-sweet girl, would be the end of me. And this moment with you, honey-babe? Gone forever. Kiss me."

Nadiyya didn't hesitate. "You taste of honey."

"Now you do too." Suddenly fierce, she guided Nadiyya's free hand under her dress. "Use your hand on me. Yes, there...right there. Don't stop for any reason. I command you!"

"Yes, princess."

It was hot and humid in the boat. Nadiyya licked sweat off Laani's throat and nibbled an ear lobe, her free hand roaming in outline beneath the linen shift, caressing the responsive skin over ribs, belly, and hips.

Laani gently bit Nadiyya's shoulder and said, "You're full of surprises."

"I've learned that being inconspicuous allows me to get where I want to go, quicker than if I were loud and demanding. People dismiss me...don't see me as competition...don't see me coming. And I beat them to it."

"Clever girl. Can you get me some happiness?"

Nadiyya leaned back and stared for a moment. Then she sat up and edged away. "You mean thebaine, don't you? Poppy juice. I've heard it called happiness before." Laani met her gaze and blinked. "It is closely guarded because we have a very precious and limited amount, harvested from our Thebian fields. And even my father has to account for its every use. It is a medicine that is always measured and recorded. I have no access."

"Not even a few drops?"

"None."

"Not even for me, honey-babe?"

Nadiyya slumped back, arms folded. "Please don't ask me." Silence widened a deepening chasm between them. "Are you in pain?"

"Not physically, no."

"Have you had it before?"

"Of course," said Laani. "For bites and stings. Stomach pain. And sore teeth."

"Why do you want it now?"

Laani sighed. "When I had it in the past, everything about my life suddenly became more pleasant, even bearable. Very soon, my life will be completely unbearable."

"But you are so privileged!"

"So you keep saying. The reality of being a royal daughter is far more confined than you could ever understand. Everything I do will be commanded, and obedience will be enforced. My only value to Pharaoh, my father, is to continue his royal line. My sister married Pharoah's brother and is heavy with her fourth. All her others have died. I will be expected to bear many children in the hope that at least one survives to be an heir. And if I do not, I may sadly…mysteriously…die. As I said before, once married, pleasures such as those we just shared will be forbidden. I can't bear it. Please. I felt you cared for me."

"That's not fair. I adore you. Would do anything for you."

"Except this." Laani stared her down, head shaking. With her dress straightened, she snatched up the honey pot and climbed out of the boat. "Think about it."

* * *

Nadiyya wept over another papyrus and ruined it. If she didn't stop soon, she would be in trouble with her fastidious father again. But at least she only did so when she was completely alone. She kept going over and over again what had happened, what Laani asked of her. It was heartbreaking. No amount of thebaine would be enough to ease Laani's pain in the years ahead. Nothing was permanent. The medicine's relief was potent, but it would leave the body and have to be taken repeatedly. Laani's suffering would be endless, and a dose of thebaine good for less than a day's relief.

She hadn't been entirely honest, though. Only recently, her father had taken her to see the poppy fields for herself—a sea of brilliant red flowers in the midday sun. And to attend several patients, primarily to note what he did when administering medicines, but also to explain what they were and why they would heal the patient. He was teaching her to be a physician, as if she were an apprentice. Not that he said as much. She kept her mouth shut and listened.

But she also got to be his trusty porter, lugging the pots in a cross-body linen and leather bag, and handing him the potions when he asked. She knew which one was the thebaine pot. And where it was carefully concealed in their house, in case a patient had an accident or a need during the night.

If she could have healed her beloved with a few doses, she might have been tempted. But "a few doses" was a drop in the Nile compared to what Laani needed. All the juice from all the poppies ever grown in Thebes's fertile soil would never be enough to take away her misery. There was no way out for her beloved Laani.

A stream of tears ruined yet another papyrus. Nadiyya hung her head and let them fall.

# CHAPTER TWENTY-ONE

The original linocut Nadeen had made years ago had split. Every time it went through the rollers as part of the printing process, it was under stress, and the lino had finally given way, rendered irreparable. It was of three hieroglyphs that, together, loosely meant "happiness." She had printed innumerable greeting cards from it as the image had been a consistent favourite with customers seeking a general feelgood card. Nadeen was cutting a copy as exact as her skill would allow, even though every linocut was unique, no matter how carefully the blade was wielded.

She sat back and examined her work-in-progress compared with the original. The border at the top and bottom was so obviously stylised poppy seed capsules. Why hadn't she noticed it before?

Under her breath, she said, "We see what we want to see."

The two main glyphs were discernibly real-life things. One was a heart with two tubelike "ears" representing where blood entered and exited, while the other resembled a bridge with planks that meant "wide." Thousands of years ago, the Egyptians were aware of the heart as the most important organ, both physically and spiritually. To them, the two glyphs together meant "wide heart"—a big, open, full heart. Full not just of blood, but of joy as well. The smaller, third glyph resembled a sun rising on the horizon—a symbol of increasing light and the hope of more. Together, the three glyphs were a representation of "happiness" that still made sense.

Someone was banging on the front door. On a Monday morning—her precious day off!

It took a few moments to recognise Greer without the trademark white stripe in her chestnut forelock—one that had emerged from a scar after a cycling accident in her twenties that had threatened to scalp her. Now, the once-stark stripe had almost disappeared into a sea of silver.

"Greer? What are you doing here?"

"Nice to see you too. How are you?" Greer loomed in the doorway, one black boot on the step. "Can I come in? I'm not disturbing you, am I?"

Nadeen stood her ground. "Actually, you are. I'm busy." She stepped back to shut the door.

With one hand, Greer slapped the door and held it ajar. She was taller than Nadeen, but barely as strong. "Christ, Nadeen! I've come three thousand kilometres to talk to you. You owe me. A conversation, at least."

"Let's be clear. I owe you absolutely nothing. You don't want a conversation. You want an audience." Her heart was racing so hard, she pushed back with shaking hands. "Go away and stop bothering me."

"You don't mean that."

Nadeen dropped her hands and laughed out loud. "Don't you get it? I don't want you here. I don't want to listen to your old crapola. Forget it. Bugger off!"

"Old crapola? Okay. How about some new crapola? I want to explain a few things. Ten minutes of your time. Just hear me out. Then I'll bugger off. Deal?"

Nadeen crossed her arms. "Be advised. If you're not gone in ten, I'm calling the cops."

"Uh-huh…as if. Can we take this inside? It's too public out here."

Nadeen scoped out the empty street, noted the parked black sedan and opened the door wide. "Whatever. Come on, then." Greer trailed her down the hall to the kitchen. "Have you been stalking me?" She topped up the kettle and turned it on.

"Hardly. Although I did have a stickybeak yesterday, just to see where you live." Surveying the room, Greer pulled out a wobbly chair, sat down and straightened her black bootleg jeans. "This is quaint."

"Skip the small talk, please. My private time is precious. Cuppa?" She spooned leaves into the teapot and took out two mugs.

"If you're having one. What did I interrupt?"

"Lino cutting. Printing. Come on, then. Tick-tock."

"You're looking well—"

"Oh, for the love of—" She poured boiling water into the pot. "I couldn't give a rat's arse how you think I look. Say your piece and leave. That's the deal. Don't make me regret it any more than I am already."

"Okay, okay!" Greer's voice climbed to a squeak. "Can we just sit down together, in peace for a while?" Bella climbed out of her bed and wandered over. "Oh, wow! Hi, Bella." She stroked the dog's head. "At least someone's pleased to see me."

Nadeen stirred the tea in its pot, put the lid back on and poured the brew through a strainer that had seen better days. She topped up the mugs with milk and plonked one in front of Greer. She sat down with hers, in silence.

Greer cleared her throat. "Lucy left me." She cast a look at Nadeen who was busy cradling her mug and sipping daintily. "You and your endless cups of tea."

"If you don't like it, you know what you can do. I'm just being polite."

"Aren't you going to say something?"

"Like what? Was it a surprise?"

"Of course it was. Can't you be civil?"

"I'm doing my damnedest." Nadeen stifled a chuckle. "So. Young Lucinda left you. Is that what this is all about?"

"No. Yes, well...no, it's not. I want to explain my behaviour. At least give me a chance and listen."

"All ears, as usual."

"My doctor explained it all to me. She said I've been going through early-onset menopause for years. Hormonal imbalance has caused me to be erratic and impulsive, and to make poor decisions, she said. I should have been on HRT from my early thirties. I had no clue about any of this."

Nadeen said, "Sorry to hear that, but I've known you a long time. It can't all be explained away by hormones."

"But it can, don't you see? I wasn't in my right mind when I got involved with Lucy. I only found out all this in March, and was going to tell you, but you'd gone. We went out to dinner to celebrate my fortieth and I told her what the doctor said. The next day, she moved out with virtually no explanation. It was like a kick in the guts. I was shocked."

"I bet," said Nadeen. "It was probably the words 'menopause' and 'fortieth' all in the one sentence that did it for her. As it would for most twenty-six-year-old, tighty whities-wearing sorts. Tell you what. I reckon you've had a lucky escape."

Greer gaped at her. "Don't you see what this means? I made a mistake, Nadeen. You and I...we're meant to be together. You *must* see that. I want you back where you belong. With me in Melbourne." She swept a glance out the kitchen window into the backyard. "Not in this one-horse town in the middle of nowhere. I mean, really. Perth is an isolated backwater. A forgettable stopover on the way to Scott Base in Antarctica where no one would live, even if the penguins are friendly. Come home with me. We can start again and build a life together. I know you still love me."

Now it was Nadeen's turn to gape. "I hate to break it to you, but no, I don't. Not anymore."

Greer waved her hands in the air. "I don't believe you! What we had in the beginning? That was something special. The kind of love that endures. You must admit it was wonderful."

"Sure." Sagging, Nadeen said, "It was, way back then. We were young. Things have changed since then. A lot."

"But surely it endures, in spite of it all?"

"Even the deepest affection can endure only so much contempt…so much disrespect. And you dished it out so casually. Remember?"

Greer shrugged. "I wasn't myself. I'm so sorry. I never meant to hurt you."

"One never does." Nadeen studied her greying, long-lost lover. "Tell me honestly. Were you happy with me?"

"Ah." Greer wrung her hands. "Not at the time. When I met Lucy, I mean. No, but I wasn't myself."

"I appreciate that. So, why would you want to do it again?"

"We can start anew." Leaning across the table, Greer said, "We know each other so well. We have history. And still care for each other. We can make it work. Where there's a will there's a way."

"Great idea in theory." Nadeen drained her mug. "I think I've changed too much—"

Greer pushed back the chair. "Look, I'll go now. Think about it and, before you answer, consider the possibilities and the many pluses that I won't try to convince you of right now. You'll work it out for yourself. When you think about it, it's what's best for us both. If we can talk again in a day or two, I'd be grateful. But if you want to find me, I'm staying at the Victoria."

Nadeen smirked. "That must be a novel experience for you. The Toodyay watering and carousing hole."

"It's clean and the bed's comfortable. They're polite and friendly enough. And happy to take my money. Can't complain."

At the front door, Greer fleetingly rested a hand on Nadeen's forearm and intoned, "Thanks for listening. I'm leaving Wednesday night. Let me know, eh?"

Nadeen hovered, only until the dark sedan pulled away from the curb.

"Seriously? There's my day off interrupted. Time waster."

# CHAPTER TWENTY-TWO

By late afternoon, she had twenty of the sky-blue prints hanging on one clotheshorse and eighteen of the cobalt hanging on the other, all in various stages of drying. For each print, she'd used a sponge dipped in red ink to colour the heart glyph, and a blackened brush to colour a small cartouche shape with her NQ initials nestled discreetly in one corner. When completely dry, they would all be folded, stamped on the back with The Prophet's details and paired with an envelope, ready for sale. A good day's work in the end.

She'd let her mind wander, lightly mulling over their conversation while she worked, considering Greer's words, analysing her own responses and feelings. Its meandering took her down some old, painful paths and even some dead ends. None of it was pleasant.

Once upon a time, she had loved Greer—very much so. But they'd stopped being friends, probably for the last three years. Pinpointing when that had happened eluded her, but it was critical. Greer had become more unpredictable and unreliable.

She would commit to something then change her mind—go off and organise, or do something that affected them both, without consulting Nadeen, then bluff and bluster when it was queried. True to the adage, she really was all over the place like a mad woman's knitting. After a while, it wore thin, and Nadeen grew tired of cleaning up after Greer's dubious decisions, tired of shouldering joint responsibilities all by herself.

When Lucy came along, Greer's eyes were out on stalks like in a cartoon, which Nadeen thought too funny to take seriously. Big mistake. And in a very short space of time, her feelings mattered less and less until they didn't seem to matter at all. How long the two of them were carrying on behind her back, she didn't want to know. What was perfectly clear was, when it came out in the open, they had no intention of stopping. For Nadeen, the betrayal was sickening. And final.

What had Greer been thinking, getting involved with someone so young? With a huge gap in maturity between a twenty-six-year-old and a forty-year-old, obviously she wasn't thinking at all! Hormones?

Nadeen carefully lifted the drying prints. Some were not completely dry, and she nestled them back in place.

Yet here she was at forty-two and Lorna fifty-six—exactly the same gap. She had to smile at herself. Even if she was in no position to criticise, it didn't seem anything like the same disparity. It helped that Lorna was healthy and fit from a lifetime of rolling up her sleeves and "getting on with it" on the farm—she was no slouch.

Hormones. Was that an adequate explanation or a mere excuse for her ex? In all the time it took Greer to explain why it wasn't her fault, Nadeen couldn't shake the feeling that, if Lucy hadn't walked out, Greer would never have come looking for her in Toodyay. She was Greer's Plan B. If things didn't work out with Lucy, there was always good old Nadeen to look up and fall back on. Mark Twain said it best with, "Never allow someone to be your priority while allowing yourself to be their option."

Her better judgement would struggle to trust Greer ever again. Not fully, and that was imperative for a durable relationship. At least in her view. Greer would likely view it very differently, as was her prerogative.

Would she say as much to Greer? There was one very obvious "elephant in the room"—a dealbreaker that Greer wouldn't be able to come at—that rendered everything else that might be said unnecessary. It was a less hurtful way of resolving things and would save a whole lot of acrimonious discussion.

* * *

They sat on a park bench looking out over the Avon River. Nadeen had suggested a walk and a chat in the fresh air. Greer seemed eager to oblige.

Nadeen said, "What happened to your hair?"

"This?" Greer fluffed up one side and tucked strands behind an ear. "I started the HRT, which helped. I'm sleeping better, which is always a plus. And seem to be able to focus and concentrate for longer. It's a relief. But I went grey very fast. Like it happened in a matter of a few weeks. My doctor was flummoxed. Crazy. But it's still as thick as ever." She glanced across with a smile. "Not as thick as your lustrous raven stuff. Although I see you have a few white strays, these days."

"Old age creeping up on me. For the record, I have thought carefully about what you said, and there's a couple of considerations you need to factor into your decisions, too. One of them is sex."

Greer blinked. "I didn't see that coming!"

"Well, you should have, because I don't think we're particularly compatible in that area, if we ever were. Please accept that I'm not criticising. Just pointing out telling differences. Because of your interest in loosely…er, Lucy—"

"Hey! Now you're milking it."

Nadeen pulled a face. "Couldn't resist. And she deserves it. She knew you weren't single. Anyway, I think you enjoy more novelty than I do. For me, it's all about an emotional bond, connection, skin-to-skin contact. Intimacy, you might say. Whoever does what with whom is by the by."

"What, you don't like to mix it up a little?"

"Sure, we did all that, years ago. And I did lots of that in my twenties. You know…strawberries and cream in all the right places, etcetera, etcetera. Harmless fun."

"And who was that, then? Wasn't me!"

"I won't kiss and tell. Anyway, it's all long ago. The point is, I don't need endless variety and I think you do, which is awkward. Everyone is different. I suspect you'd be more fulfilled with someone other than me. For instance, pornography has always been a mystery. What is even vaguely arousing about two mute actors being paid to have sex on camera? Nothing natural about it. The appeal is beyond me."

"It can be amusing, if not titillating," said Greer.

"Hey, if you want amusing, you're in the right place. I hadn't been here long when, early one morning, I was driving along the road leaving Toodyay and came to the roundabout. Two horses were mating in the long grass, right in the middle of the island, with cars, trucks and utes whizzing round. I saw a lot of wide grins, but otherwise, no one blinked an eye. I thought, 'welcome to Toodyay!' where Mother Nature is proudly on display."

"How on earth did they get there?"

"No idea, but someone would have been missing their roan stallion, likely worth thousands at stud. And if he wasn't supposed to be covering that particular mare, there would have been hell to pay. Anyway, not a common issue in suburban Melbourne. Which brings me to my second point."

Greer sat back with wary eyes.

"I don't want to live in Melbourne again. Do you want to live in Toodyay?"

Greer coughed. "You must be joking! I'd shrivel up and die if I had to live here. My worst nightmare. Come on, Nadeen. You can't be serious?"

"Afraid so. I love it here. And, while my teeny house may be rustic, I'll do it up one day. In the meantime, I'm enjoying the peace and quiet, the countryside, the village atmosphere, the lovely people who walk by and smile, or start a conversation out of thin air. Very unlike Melbourne. And you're a Melbournite, through and through. We both know that."

"Lovely people," muttered Greer. "I saw a particularly lovely lady leaving your place on Sunday morning. She looked very pleased with herself. I was going to knock on the door after she drove off, but I guessed it unlikely you two were playing Uno." Nadeen matched Greer's quizzical look. "Ah. In which case, I would have been wasting my time. Is she part of the attraction?"

"Possibly. It's early days. It may go somewhere. And just as easily not."

"Oh. She's not straight, is she? Oh, Nadeen!" Greer was laughing. "You should know better. Tsk, tsk. Not a good idea."

"Yes, I figured that." She waved a forefinger. "For the record, it was *she* who cracked on to *me*, not the other way around."

"And you fought her off valiantly, eh?"

"Why should I?" Nadeen frowned, raised her voice. "I'm single…free as a bird. Unlike when you and I were a couple. That didn't slow you down when you hooked up with Lucy, did it? You forfeited any right to my person when you laid Lucy. Honestly. Get a grip!"

Greer dropped her chin and examined her boots. They sat in silence as waterfowl floated past, intent on a mission upstream.

"Besides." Nadeen nudged Greer. "Is there anything more exhilarating…intoxicating than a fine-looking woman making it perfectly clear she's dying to jump your bones?"

Greer hooted and grinned. "Oh, yeah. Nothing better for the morale. And wow, doesn't it make you feel so very glad to be alive? And hellishly hard to resist."

"Ditto. So here we are. You can tell I'm enjoying the moment. How long it will last is anybody's guess."

With one arm draped along the bench's backrest, Greer said, "If you don't mind me asking, are you emotionally invested in this thing…whatever it is?"

"I am, but not fully. Just protecting myself. The tricky part is, I'm a newcomer, an outlier, a ring-in who doesn't easily fit into this town. My plan was to build a modest business and live a quiet life with a few locals for friends. I didn't imagine for a moment that I'd stumble over someone like her. Even so, she is an established figure in Toodyay with a certain reputation that makes me think that, in no time at all, she's going to decide I'm more trouble than I'm worth." She cast a glance at Greer. "And you know how that feels, eh?"

"Doesn't every woman-loving woman?"

"The point is, regardless of her, I'm happy here. Don't look at me like that. I truly am happy by myself. With Bella, of course."

Greer put her silvered head in her hands and groaned. "Toodyay and a likely other woman. I've got Buckley's, haven't I?"

"Pretty much."

"Too bad for me, dammit. Look, you can say what you want, but I know we still can make a red-hot go of it. If this thing goes pear-shaped…if you change your mind, you know where to find me. Deal?"

A wood duck made a less than elegant landing onto the murky river. Nadeen shook her head. "Deal."

With Greer having left town, Nadeen got back to hand-watering recently potted up gerbera pups. The hose's handpiece fell apart in her hands, made brittle by long-term exposure to the fierce Australian sun. Under pressure, the hose thrashed about until she managed to grab it. Moleskins lashed with water, she turned off the tap and went back into the house, adding the purchase of a new handpiece to her mental list of "to-dos." In the bedroom, she shrugged off the soggy pants and sat on the edge of the bed in front of the tall dressing mirror. Staring back at her was a conflicted being.

Truth was, she was far more emotionally involved with Lorna than she made out to Greer. This "thing" with Lorna was a passion so insistent, it was doing her head in. Did her heart muscle need another workout, so soon after the last relationship? It was a big ask.

One thing was certain: regardless of how things worked out with Lorna, she and Greer would be unlikely to ever meet again. Which suited the part of her that enjoyed being a free spirit for a change. Yet another part was drawn to Lorna and a relationship that held the potential to be the most rewarding experience of her life. But would it work out?

"You're completely nuts if you think this is going to end any way other than belly-up. Protect yourself. Just stop, before you're in over your head. Crazy."

The intensity in her own eyes said such wise advice was way too late, and she smiled wanly. "Some wise person said, if it isn't a little bit crazy, it isn't love. Like it or not, you're going to have to ride this one out. Buckle up, sunshine."

# CHAPTER TWENTY-THREE

"Do we know when Beth's getting back from Yorkshire?" Lorna searched the faces of her CWA subcommittee co-members for news of their president. She was the youngest in the room, with octogenarian Cynthia waving the flag for an older generation. Martha, Robyn, and Cynthia looked at her blankly. "No? Last I heard, she should return this Friday. But Tash won't be far behind, which makes this the last meeting that I'll be acting chair for her. Before we close, any more business? All done? Excellent, and thank you." She shuffled papers into a pile and pushed back her kitchen chair. Noone moved.

A busty woman with a short grey haircut, Robyn, said, "If you don't mind, Lorna, we'd like a word." The ladies exchanged wide-eyed glances. "Off the record."

"Sure, what's up?" Lorna stood and circled the table, collecting teacups and cake plates. "Just briefly, or do we need another tea?"

Dentures whistling, Cynthia quavered, "We just want to let you know there's gossip going around. We thought you ought to know. What's being said."

Lorna placed crockery next to the sink less delicately than she would have liked. Then she turned sharply, stepped back to the table, sat down and crossed her arms. With a tight smile, she declared too brightly, "Ooh, that sounds exciting. What am I supposed to have done now? More of me growing whacky-baccy? Or is it an affair with Rocco, again? Maybe Murray, this time. The Morwood widowed temptress mired in yet more moral turpitude. What's the latest salacious gossip? Do tell." She looked at the three faces around the table. None met her gaze.

"Nothing quite so tame," said Robyn. "Far worse, I'm afraid. An association with a woman friend of yours is rumoured to be questionable." She exchanged a glance with Cynthia who pursed her lips. "We think it's a case of someone putting two and two together and making five. The story goes that your friend had an interstate visitor who was, shall we say, indiscreet about her previous relationship with your friend. The visitor stayed at the Victoria and had one too many scotches while chatting with a female customer at the bar. Apparently, she got a bit loud and her statements were overheard by other customers."

Lorna held the knuckles of one hand to her mouth, eyes darting.

"To add fuel to the fire, some have noticed you often visit your friend at her home." Robyn exhaled heavily and waved her hands in the air. "It's probably just a storm in a teacup, but these more sordid stories spread like wildfire. We're concerned not only for your reputation, Lorna, but for the reputation of the CWA by association. It's an ugly rumour that we could all do without."

"I see." Lorna stood up and slowly pushed in her chair. "This is news to me. Thanks for the heads-up. Now, if you don't mind, ladies, I need to get on with a few pressing things."

Hastily, the three women rose and headed for the front door. Cynthia and Martha made their escape as soon as was polite, but Robyn slowed to a dawdle at the threshold. Through clenched teeth, she said, "I'm sorry, Lorna."

"So you should be. We've known each other too long to play silly games. What was that all about?"

"Beth." Robyn shrugged. "You know what she's like."

"Our committed God botherer? She might have a meltdown when she gets back and hears all about it."

"Correction. She *will* have a meltdown. I had to make a pompous arse of myself just now for Cynthia and Martha's benefit, because they'll report back to her what I said. They'll be very pleased with that performance. Me telling you off for possibly being a *very* naughty girl."

Lorna muttered, "It was bound to happen, I suppose."

"See, I've known women like your friend. We've had a very few in the CWA, over the years. They didn't last long, once found out."

"It's ridiculous. This is 1996, not 1956. Attitudes have changed…are changing."

"Not so much in country towns. I'd extricate myself from that friendship, if I were you. It would be prudent."

Lorna turned and met Robyn's gaze. "As it happens, my friendship with Nadeen Quin means a good deal to me. I won't be extricating myself any time soon."

Eyebrows raised, Robyn said, "Be careful, because it could cost you. I've heard Beth wants either you or Tash to take over as CWA president when she retires at year's end."

Lorna looked askance. "Tash is welcome to it. That role is largely ceremonial. An awful lot of speechmaking and poncing about looking important. It's not my thing. And they wouldn't dare chuck me out. I've been a member since Jesus wore short pants."

Robyn nodded, then shook her head. "I hope you're right. Is it for want of available men?"

Whooping with laughter, Lorna twinkled at Robyn until her erstwhile colleague cracked a wry grin. Lorna said, "Believe me, there's no shortage of suitors, which never ceases to amaze me, were I so inclined. I guess it's the 'lonely widow' thing. They'd like to help me out, if you know what I mean."

"What is it with her, then?"

"Ah…no. I couldn't begin to explain. But it's no passing fancy. No small thing. She means a lot to me. At least as much as Cormack. Are you getting my drift?"

"Surprisingly, I am. Does Melanie know?"

"Not yet unfortunately. This is forcing my hand a whole lot sooner than anticipated. Which isn't fair on either Mel or me. But life isn't fair, is it?"

"No, it's not. And even less fair on those outside what's considered normal. However, there are some just getting on with their lives, regardless. Have you heard about the new bookshop in Northam?"

"Uh-huh. Big and glamorous, or so I'm told. Something… Jones?"

"Tatchell Jones. It's extremely popular and they're making a mint. By 'they' I mean the two fellas who own and run it together. They keep it quiet that they're a couple, but everybody knows. Style and finesse outclassing bigotry. You'd be surprised how many people are more open-minded these days, because they know someone who knows someone who knows someone in their family. Be that as it may, bigotry persists. Now I have to head off, but I sincerely value our friendship, Lorna. Regardless. You take care."

"Thanks, Robyn. You too."

# CHAPTER TWENTY-FOUR

Lorna slid the last tray of seedlings into the tall multishelved trolley and tugged off heavy gloves. "I'll put them in the van in the morning, but they should be safe here overnight."

"Do you want me to sweep up?" said Mel. "It's just that we have to get the spare bed into my room for Sarah."

"Let's both sweep. Won't take long."

Mel grabbed the wider broom and took off, brooming madly between the work benches. Lorna grinned and took to methodically sweeping patches of potting mix that had escaped the trays. They had the mess under control in no time. Mel stooped to brush the stuff into a dustpan and toss it into a soil tub.

"Come on, darling, that's good enough. Now you're on school holidays for two weeks, no homework tonight." At the greenhouse door, she put an arm around Mel's shoulders. "Good job. Before we set up beds, come into the den for a quick debrief, eh? It's going to be fun tonight."

Mel galloped down the hall ahead of her and flopped on the couch. "I'm *so* looking forward to seeing Sarah. It's been *ages*."

"Only because her mum's been up north." Lorna sank into the other couch.

"What's brother Mikey doing tonight?"

"Tim's taking him prospecting somewhere around Coolgardie with his mates in a likely location that shall remain nameless. It's 'secret men's business,' so Tash said."

"Rad." Mel pulled a swathe of long hair from behind one shoulder and started plaiting it. "So, what's up, Mum?"

Lorna took a deep breath. "A couple of things that you need to know—"

"Oh, Mum…while I think of it, are you helping Nadeen on Sunday morning, again? It's just that everyone wants to go to Northam for tacos. If you don't need me, is it okay if I go, too? Jared would take me and a few of the guys."

"Hm. Do you know them well?"

"Sure, from school. They're in year twelve, like me. They're good guys. I wouldn't hang with them if they weren't."

"I know, darling. I trust your judgement. Just be careful of some of those Northam boys. Look, I have to ask. Is Jared as gay as I think he is?"

Mel stopped plaiting. "Why are you even asking? He's my bestie and a very private guy. What difference does it make?"

"For one, I'd be relieved if he was, simply because you spend so much time with him. And I don't want to…can't police your every move. I'm responsible for you until you turn eighteen."

With a short sigh, Mel said, "You needn't worry about him and me."

"Does he get bullied?"

Mel rolled her eyes. "Does he, *what*? All the time. It's painful. Two weedy science nerds cop it, too. And it's always the same brain-dead bogans mouthing off. *So* annoying. The teachers do nothing to stop it."

"Tricky. Does Jared answer them back?"

"No, but I do! Sometimes I tell them where to go. They just laugh cos they get away with it. That whole circus makes eating lunch in the quadrangle really uncomfortable, at times." Mel shrugged. "It's not forever. Another six months and it's goodbye, bogans, goodbye, school."

"Wow, already." Lorna hadn't thought that far ahead. "Time is flying by too fast. You'll be at uni next. But that's another conversation. What I have to tell you may make you a target at school, too. Just like Jared, but because of me, your mother. I'm involved with Nadeen, and we're more than 'just good friends.'" Head down and waiting, she knew better than to hurry her daughter.

Finally, Mel said, "Holy dooley, Mum." Silence dragged between them. "I think I sort of knew. You've been so different these last few months."

Lorna met her gaze. "How do you mean?"

"Lighter. Brighter." With a look so intense that Lorna blinked rapidly, Mel said, "Happier. You are happier than you were." She grabbed Lorna's hand and squeezed gently. "You're in love with her! That's rad, Mum. I didn't know you had it in you!" And she grinned, wild-eyed.

"Why not? You think I'm too old or something?"

Mel looked sheepish. "Well, yeah. I thought it would never happen after Dad died. A widow until death us do part, and all that."

"You cheeky girl!" But Lorna had to smile. "I just want to know how you feel about it."

Screwing up her nose, Mel said, "Y'know, I don't think I give a toss. As long as you're happy."

"Well, you might feel differently when I say I had to tell you now because people are already gossiping. And it's bound to get around the school. It could be awful."

"How awful? Because I sit with Jared, I get called a lezzo every second day."

"No way!"

"Yes, way. And you wouldn't believe all the stuff I've heard about you since Dad died. No, I'm *not* going to repeat it! But"—Mel frowned heavily—"don't think I don't give it back to them because I do. In spades. I call them every filthy name under the sun. And they call me every variation on 'lesbian' they can think up."

"What filthy names…what variations?"

"Uh, no. I'm not going there. What I'm saying is, I've heard it all before."

Lorna rubbed her cheeks. "Why don't you tell me these things?"

"Because. You'll just get upset, like now. And there's nothing you can do about it."

"Oh, can't I just! Those kids are brainless bullies. I can give the principal an earful."

"You wouldn't be the first. And it makes no difference. Let it go, Mum. I'm nearly eighteen and I can stand up for myself. You and Dad taught me that."

"Well, more your dad than me, but I'm glad you think so." Lorna rose to her feet. "No matter what happens, just remember you're my number one priority and I love you to bits, darling. Come on. Let's go make Sarah's bed before they turn up for dinner. Tash will have the spare room, as usual. You know what she's like. A few shots of schnapps and she's out like a light."

As they headed down the hall, Mel said, "What are we having?"

"Sarah's favourite. Hamburgers and chips."

"From the barbie? Yummo. Do they know about you and Nadeen?"

"Not from me, but I wouldn't be surprised. Good old Toodyay, a.k.a. Gossip Central."

# CHAPTER TWENTY-FIVE

"Thanks for the beetroot. It made all the difference," said Lorna.

"You're welcome." Tash stuffed a cushion behind her back and relaxed into the couch. She shoved up the sleeves of a long-sleeved green T-shirt and tucked auburn hair behind her ears. "It's nice and warm in here with the fire. You got some good grill-marks on those beef patties. Delicious burgers, especially with *my* beetroot." She smiled and cocked her head toward a distant bass beat. "What are our girls listening to?"

"Who knows? Spice Girls. Savage Garden. One of them." Lorna sipped her cider and waved the glass at her friend. "Cheers. It's been too long and I've missed you."

"Sorry about that. It couldn't be helped. But you heard the saga of my mum over dinner. Do you want to talk about where you're at?"

Lorna caught Tash's pointed look and blew air out of her cheeks. "Okay. Who told you?"

"Robyn. She thought I ought to know so I wouldn't get caught on the hop if Beth launched into a sermon. Not that it's any of her business, but that wouldn't stop her. To be blunt, I was gobsmacked. Never saw that one coming. You do realise there will be a whole swathe of Toodyay Shire's mature gentlemen sobbing into their beer when they hear about this." Tash started to chuckle. Cracking herself up, she said, "You've been their wet dream for donkey's years. Poor buggers!"

"Aw, stop it, Tash! What's with that? I have never worked out what's so fascinating about *me*!"

"Ah, you see it's the remote ice queen thing. Very intriguing, because other than Cormack, you've never really given any bloke the time of day. And now we all know why!"

Lorna gaped at her. "What are you talking about?"

"I mean, you've been sprung. Mystery over. Those fellas will dry their tears, their egos restored because they never stood a chance, anyway. See? Wrong gender."

"You reckon? Because I'm starting to feel like a goldfish in a very small bowl. I'm not enjoying the attention. At all."

"I figured that," said Tash. "It's not your style."

"You can say that again." Lorna stood up. "I'll go ask the girls if they want dessert. Do you want a slice? Spiced apple layer cake. With cream or ice cream."

"Let me help." Tash followed her out. "I'll go ask the girls."

In the kitchen, Lorna used a hot knife to cut neat wedges that went onto cake plates. Tash came back and squeezed Lorna's shoulders. "They both want some with cream. I don't think I've got room."

"Neither do I." She plopped thick cream onto each plate, added a cake fork and teaspoon. "If you'll take these to the girls, I'll dig out the schnapps. Do you want a coffee?"

Tash shook her head and, hands full, disappeared down the hall. Lorna found the schnapps and a couple of shot glasses. Just in case they got peckish, she emptied the last half of a packet of roasted pistachios into a wooden bowl and took it back to the den. She switched on the heavily shaded floor lamp and flicked off the overhead light, set up the shot glasses and was filling them when Tash returned.

"Here you go." Lorna slid across a shot glass. "And pistachios, if you fancy some salty crunch. Have to peel them yourself, I'm afraid. I like them that way so I don't eat too many at a time."

They clinked glasses and sipped. Tash said, "I care about you, you know. I'd really like to know how you're feeling about the whole thing. Please, Lorna? What you say to me goes no further. You know that. Just fill me in."

"Frankly?" Lorna chewed her lip. "I dunno, Tash. I'm a bit scared. It feels like it's going to blow up in my face. Which is alarming, to put it mildly. This 'thing' as you put it, is a feeling. A relationship that is very new, tender and vulnerable like a newborn. It's precious and fragile. And I don't know how to protect it. Or if I can, even. To be fair, Nadeen did try to warn me and I didn't quite believe her."

Tash had knocked back her glass, held it out to Lorna who couldn't help but smile and refill it.

"You see, we're only at the beginning of dancing around each other, in that 'getting to know you' way that couples do. You and Tim would have done exactly the same thing. Discreetly, privately. People would have left you alone while you courted, for want of a better word. They did for me and Cormack. It's just common courtesy and respect, you know?

"When it comes to Nadeen and me? It seems we're fair game. There's a lot wrong with that. Needless to say, I resent the intrusion." She sculled her glass and uncorked the schnapps bottle to refill it. "Not that it does me any good. How does that grab you?"

Tash had assembled a stash of peeled pistachios. She chewed them steadily, one at a time. "Best guess? It's a reaction to novelty that will pass. Yes, it's not fair, but trying to change that is a long road that rests on the shoulders of all of us as a society. Not your shoulders, my friend. What's difficult for you and her is the immediate pressure on your relationship. You're bound to experience a few stumbles."

Lorna cracked open pistachio shells. "How do I stop that from happening?"

"Like it or not, you're going to have to adapt. If you don't mind me saying, you've always experienced a great deal of deference from Toodyay folks. For them to criticise you, even if it's only a few folks, is disconcerting because you're not used to it. I would say, choose your battles. Don't let the naysayers get under your skin and make you jump in any direction before you're ready. If you're serious, hang in there. If it's just been a bit of fun, feel free to walk away."

"Huh? No, absolutely not. That thought appals me. Not happening."

"Another thing." Tash looked hard at Lorna. "Don't let a few very vocal people...or your resentment, for that matter...affect your relationship with the silent majority of Toodyay. Remember, for the most part, they love you dearly. There will be a few dipshits and drongos that mouth off. So what? It may be jarring but let it wash over you. In time, they'll bag their heads and crawl back under a rock. You're bigger than all this palaver. The people of Toodyay think so. Try to keep up!"

Lorna went from close to tears to tears of laughter in no time at all. She crunched nuts and grinned at Tash. "Oh, God, it's such hard work! I am *so* over this already. I mean, how dare I find love in the arms of another woman?"

"Ah, but you're held up as a role model for the community."

"Well, as far I'm concerned, I still am. Because if you're lucky enough to find love at my age, grab it with both hands, I say. And yes, I do get that there are those who can't help but disapprove. So annoying."

"It will all die down. Meanwhile, lighten up, kiddo. Tell me what I really want to know. What's it like?"

Lorna got the giggles and topped up their glasses. In the distance, they heard two voices warbling at the top of their lungs, "...if you wannabe my lover..." They looked at each other and said, "Spice Girls!"

"Yeah, okay," said Lorna. "Which bit?"

"The juicy bit."

"All of it…all the bits are juicy. Try to keep up!"

Tash threw pistachio shells at Lorna who threw some back. They kept giggling and sipping schnapps. Tash said, "Tell me what I don't know."

"Ah. What you don't know? Well, I don't know what you don't know, but I'll tell you what I didn't know and found out. Just how much of my body…my skin…is a landscape of sensation that I didn't know existed. It's sensitive to touch in the most unlikely places. My whole self joins in."

Lorna leaned back and examined a few peeled nuts in her palm with unseeing eyes. "She's like no one I've ever met. Gentle and strong, fearless and vulnerable. She allows me into some inner hallowed place, like a sanctuary. Gives me a feeling that both thrills and humbles. And yes, I'm aware I sound like a starry-eyed teenager. I love being with her…hate to leave her."

Waggling her eyebrows at Tash, she said, "Otherwise, it's not complicated. I just do what comes naturally and follow my instincts. No offense to Cory, but I've never had so much fun horizontally. And she's the best kisser that ever walked the planet!"

"Oh, no," said Tash. "That's Tim. He's the best, absolutely."

"I'm not about to test your theory."

"Nor me yours!"

More giggling. Lorna said, "I think we're all schnapped out, eh?"

"Yep. We fought the schnapps and the schnapps won. Time to hit the sack."

# CHAPTER TWENTY-SIX

"Can we do that again?"

Dewy, Nadeen murmured, "When I catch my breath." Lorna's mouth was between her breasts, lips wandering at will. "I'm not as young as I used to be."

"Piffle! You've no excuse. But I do so enjoy turning you into mush. Putty in my hands." Lorna chuckled and grazed a nipple with her teeth. "Breasts are so wonderfully sensitive. And taste so good."

"You're a very wicked woman."

"I try…getting the hang of it." Lorna shifted, laid her head on a pillow, and reached to touch Nadeen's shoulder. "I suppose you want to do something sensible like talk? Just when I'm attempting to make up for lost time. I'm happy to listen, but you're very distracting. Lovely with your clothes on, breathtaking with them off."

Nadeen grinned helplessly. "You incurable romantic. You say the sweetest utter nonsense."

"I have eyes that tell me otherwise. Better get used to it."

Nadeen studied her companion. "I think I'd like to get used to it. We need to take it slow and steady, don't we?"

"That would be sensible." Lorna clasped one of Nadeen's hands. "There's pressure to jump hard and fast in one way or another. I'd rather not have others dictate our decisions, but there's a lot going on around us. I prefer to just hang in and take each day as it comes. Are you okay with that?"

"For now, yes. Are you worried about what's going on?"

"No point. It's nothing I can control. Melanie will finish school in November and may go to university next year, depending on her results. Which would mean her finding accommodation nearer the city. It's all up in the air. I've told both her and Tash about us and they're perfectly fine with it." She kissed Nadeen's knuckles. "But I want to wake up with you. Sooner rather than later. When the time is right. It's all about divine timing, isn't it?"

"You mean, in the lap of the gods? That works for me."

"Settled," said Lorna. "Now, where were we?"


Nadeen was up to the eyeballs in paperwork. She kept manual ledgers, but her accountant in Melbourne had told her she would have to go digital eventually, which meant getting a computer and software. She'd resisted the inevitable so far. Helpfully, Melanie had said most of her friends were into computers, especially gaming. And she knew a few nerdy tech heads who could help get the shop's accounts set up. Maybe for next financial year?

The phone rang. On her precious Sunday afternoon, no less. She picked up.

Felix growled, "I want a word with you, my girl."

Distracted, she said, "Hi, Dad. What's up?"

"You may well ask. It's more like, what's up with you? Have you lost your mind? I mean, Lorna Chidlow?" He was spluttering.

"Oh. What have you heard? And from whom?"

"I've just had a call from my old mate Nick Heddon, that's who."

"Okay, that name rings a faint bell. What's his problem?"

"You're the problem!" Felix was breathing heavily. "You and her. It's all over Northam. He heard it from his wife, Felicity, the president of the Northam CWA. It's stirring up a wasp's nest over there."

"Why, Dad? What's it got to do with them?"

"Never you mind. It's complicated. You, my girl, are an embarrassment. What are you doing with a classy piece of arse like Cormack's wife? What the hell is with you? You *really* think you could pull a woman like that? Get real! You're batting *way* above your average! Making a complete fool of yourself. *And* me, by association. Just get over that nasty inclination, will you? *Nobody* thinks it's okay. Are you getting this? Grow up and get yourself a real man. Derek is right there, ready, willing and waiting. Wake up and—"

Nadeen eyed off the handset and dropped it in its cradle with a satisfying ker-thunk.

"Thanks for the vote of confidence." She went back to the ledgers.


It was just after eight p.m. when the phone rang again. She hesitated. Her father wouldn't be dumb enough to call again so soon, would he? He was many things, but he wasn't stupid. She picked up.

"G'day, Nadeen. It's Derek, just ringing you on the off chance."

"Oh. Hi. What's up, Derek? Is something wrong?"

"Heck, no. Your father gave me your number. Said you might be up for a drink, sometime. How about it?"

She was stunned into silence.

"Hello? Are you—?"

The temptation to hang up was nearly overpowering. "Sorry, Derek. You just caught me in the middle of something. Just a bit distracted. Look, I don't want to waste your time. I'm sure we've both changed a good deal in what is it, twenty-four years? It's nice of you to ask, but let's leave us in the past, eh? Good luck for the future. Bye." And she hung up.

Teeth clenched and arms crossed tight, she paced up and down the hall, back and forth. Back and forth. Her gut hurt. Her head hurt. Her heart hurt. Tears threatened.

It was cruel. Mean. Downright *mean*. Not just to her, but to Derek who, dork or not, did not deserve to be played. To be used to put her in an awkward position. To drop her in the proverbial manure and make her claw her way out.

Spitefully mean. The kind of mean a bloke might resort to when a girl got the girl. Very galling to those with a particularly delicate ego. Come to think of it, she knew one of those all too well.

"This time, father of mine, you've gone too far."

# CHAPTER TWENTY-SEVEN

At the other end of the phone, Tash asked, "Have you received the agenda for Friday's meeting?"

Lorna sucked in a breath. "I got it yesterday. Looks like I'm top of the list of items to be discussed."

"Beth's worded it very carefully with 'one member's unacceptable behaviour.' Are you going?"

"God, no. I don't think me being there will help matters, and I've no desire to be subjected to public humiliation by Her Righteousness. Besides, I'm a life member. Can she even do this to me?"

"I think she can if a member does something illegal or brings the CWA into disrepute. I vaguely remember wording like that in the Constitution. But listen up. I had a call from Felicity Heddon and she and a few others from the Northam branch plan to be there. On your side, as it were."

"Goodness, why would she get involved? Sure, I was born and raised in Northam, but I've lived here since I married Cory."

"Honestly? I don't know. This will be interesting. I'll put in a word for you if I get the chance and report back as soon as I can, okay?"

"Thanks, Tash. I won't hold my breath."

* * *

The Toodyay Memorial Hall had dominated the main street since the turn of last century, with the Town Hall tacked on out the back in 1910. Smaller meeting rooms were available for various community groups like the CWA where they gathered monthly.

When Felicity and two other Northam Branch ladies arrived, the meeting room was already packed, with standing room only in the corridor. Tall, strapping, and always stylishly dressed, Felicity could just see over most heads and into the room.

At the front, she recognised Beth—a bespectacled woman with a taut grey ponytail who bellowed, "Some of you may have to leave or you won't hear. Please leave if you don't have to be here. Or we'll have to move into the main hall, which is very inconvenient."

A murmur went around the room and nobody moved.

"This is most unusual. Very well, then. You people in the corridor. Go into the hall and the rest can follow."

Felicity nodded at the others and they all turned around, trudged into the musty hall, and found seats at the front near the podium. A motley mix of about thirty, mostly women with a few nonvoting blokes dragged along for moral support, rattled and banged chairs, muttered and grumbled, and made themselves comfortable.

Visibly flustered, Beth marched to the podium, shuffled papers and glared at the crowd. "Very peculiar. Our meetings have never seen such enthusiastic attendance. Let's get on with it." In quick time, she read out minutes from the previous meeting and had them accepted and seconded by a lightning show of hands.

"The first agenda item concerns the behaviour of one of our long-term members who has brought the branch into disrepute.

The motion that we will vote on is to confirm that, forthwith, Mrs Lorna Chidlow is barred from membership for life."

A rising murmur began and swept around the room. A bearded man rose and called out, "What is it she's supposed to have done?" Felicity couldn't think who he was for a moment. Ted Parmenter managed the Victoria Hotel.

Beth cleared her throat. "She has committed abominable acts against nature that reflect very poorly on the CWA. It won't be tolerated."

"Allegedly. Unless you were there too," said Ted. A ripple of laughter rose—petered out. "Has she done anything criminal in the eyes of the law?"

"In the eyes of God, she has. That's enough for us."

"You'll have to do better than that in the eyes of Toodyay. If she isn't a criminal, leave her alone!"

A chorus of "yeah" and "too right" echoed off the old walls.

Felicity took a deep breath and stood up. "If I may speak?" She scanned the audience, with silence its reply. "I'm president of the CWA Northam Branch, here with two of my colleagues. I went to school with Lorna, grew up with her where she was well-known as a very decent person who contributed to the community. This kind of groundless condemnation does not reflect well on the CWA at a national level." Shaking, she sat down.

"I disagree," said Beth. "We as a community have to maintain a standard of behaviour that we can be proud of. And not have our reputation sullied by such unnatural, perverted goings on as promoted by Mrs Chidlow!"

A male voice broke into sarcastic laughter. "What planet are you on? This is a farming community. Cows mount cows, bulls mount bulls. We've seen it all, haven't we, eh? Eh?" Guffaws swept around the room. "No one is out there giving the kelpies sex education. Or showing the ducks how to do what rhymes with 'duck.' It comes naturally, you silly old chook. Wake up and smell the silage!"

Beth leaned over the podium and hissed, "It's sick…disgusting! And if it isn't illegal, it should be, you heathens!"

Felicity shot to her feet and called out, voice rising above the protesting crowd, "I'll have you know I'm the mother of five children. Three sons, two daughters. Both my youngest son and my elder daughter are gay. And they are the most loving and decent human beings who deserve every bit as much respect as everyone else. It's out-of-touch people like you who bring the CWA into disrepute. Shame on you!"

Beth's jaw began bouncing off her double chins. Others called out muffled snarky remarks. A woman in the front row turned and shrilled out, "Shame on you lot, yourselves! We don't want her sort ruining the CWA's reputation!"

"You're entitled to voice your opinion, Martha," said Felicity. "As are those of us who don't share it."

An auburn-haired woman stood up—everyone knew Tash. "Hi, everybody." The muttering died down. "As you are probably aware, I've known Lorna for a very long time as well. We've always shared and shared alike with the Northam Branch and supported each other's efforts to improve the lot of our respective communities. I'd be very surprised if you weren't aware of how much time and effort, goodwill and generosity have been gifted to both communities by Lorna. Not to mention endless jars of apple jam! Herewith, I move that agenda item number one be struck off, because it's an embarrassment to the branch that it ever was proposed. All in favour?"

A sea of arms shot up. "All those opposed?" At the front, four nervous hands, plus Beth's popped up. "Motion carried." Clapping started, followed by wolf whistles and the stamping of shoes and boots on the wooden floorboards that quickly became a deafening din and raised an impressive cloud of dust.

Beth threw papers into the air, squealed, "Fornicators!" and stormed out.

Someone shouted, "Hands off our Lorna! Yeah, go on. Clear off, ya crabby ol' moll!"

* * *

"How was it?" asked Lorna.

Tash said, "A nonevent, really. The motion failed and everyone left and most went to the pub. Ted Parmenter shouted us a round, which was very generous of him. Nice bloke, that Ted. He spoke highly of you. Wished you were there."

"I've known him for yonks. Good bloke."

"Yep. Anyway, a nonevent. Rest easy and sleep well, my friend. You deserve it."

"Aw, thanks, Tash. You're an angel. See you round."

"Will do. Cheers." Grinning, Tash hung up. Word would spread in no time that Beth had copped a very public shellacking for having a go at "our Lorna." What really happened at the meeting would wend its way back to Lorna's ears eventually, and go down in Toodyay mythology as a bloody good show. As someone attempting to inflict public humiliation on another, Beth had experienced it for herself firsthand. And so deservedly.

# CHAPTER TWENTY-EIGHT

Fresh out of the shower, Nadeen was dripping wet when the phone rang. She shrugged on her dressing gown and roughly towelled her hair as she strode down the hall.

"Hi, Nadeen, it's Jodie." The woman's tone was cool and clipped.

"I'm sorry? Do I know you?"

"I'm Jodie, your father's partner. Sorry to ring so early, but I wanted to catch you before work."

"Oh. Hi. What can I do for you?"

"Well. He told me he spoke to you by phone and what he said. And I made it very clear to him how unimpressed I was. Not that it's any of my business. But…"

Nadeen flung the damp towel over a shoulder. "But what, exactly, do you hope to achieve by telling me this?"

"Sorry. This isn't the way I would have chosen for us to meet. In person would have been preferable. What I'm hoping for is to stage an intervention between you two."

Nadeen laughed mirthlessly. "An intervention…cute. Look, I appreciate your concern, but the issues between us are old and enduring. He's intractable, and I can't change who I am. I'm sure you can grasp the magnitude of that problem."

"But you can't give up on him!" Jodie's tone was tightly wound. "I know he loves you. You're his only child. And it's such a shame that you two have this ridiculous, troubling relationship."

Sighing heavily, Nadeen said, "I couldn't agree more. We have tried many times to come to some kind of neutrality, if nothing else. I know he took to heart your comments and opened up yet another conversation with me and seemed to have a fresh perspective for a while. Until that last phone call when he ranted and raved. Reverted to type, as it were. He leaves me with nowhere to go, if you get what I mean. I'm just supposed to suck it up."

Jodie took a while to reply. "That's frustrating. What if I acted as a mediator between you. Like the three of us sit down together and have a discussion. Would you come at that?"

"To be blunt, I can't see the point." Nadeen was suddenly tired before her workday had even begun. "It boils down to disappointment, which sounds like I'm trivialising, but it's accurate. I disappoint him and he disappoints me. It's painful for us both. I appreciate you'd like to fix it, Jodie. But I don't think anyone can."

"When you put it that way, I get it."

"Good. I have to get ready for work now. If you don't mind."

"Yeah, nah," Jodie drawled. "If I think of anything, do you mind if I call again?"

Tears welling up, Nadeen pulled the dressing gown closer. "Sure, whatever—"

"Thanks for your time. Sorry to disturb. Bye-bye—"

"Wait! Jodie…wait a minute!" Nadeen's throat contracted and she fought to draw breath.

"Are you still there?" said Jodie.

"Yes." Nadeen blew air out of her cheeks. "I don't know about you, but I find the strongest feelings are the hardest to find words for. To explain. To be honest, I've been a bit glib, because this is intensely personal. You just said that he loves me. Frankly, I don't believe that. Because if he did, he would accept me as I am. There, I've said it."

"Okay. I hear you. That's what really gets to you?"

"Uh-huh. Yet, from his point of view, he thinks I don't love him because I won't act straight. And that hurts at a very primal level. You'll have noticed he's a very proud man, and he wants to be proud of me. And he feels he can't be, especially not to his mates. He thinks the phrase 'gay pride' is the punchline of a bad joke."

Jodie chuckled drily. "I can believe that."

"The other thing is, he takes it personally. I figure it offends his masculinity, makes him feel like he failed somehow. I'm sure he and my mother would have argued at length over whose fault it was. Since it's not their fault, it must be mine, eh? And why won't I just change? From his point of view, I'm either being stupid or gratuitously difficult. And he knows I'm not stupid. You can see how this just goes around in circles, can't you?"

"I'm getting the picture. Thanks, Nadeen, you've been refreshingly honest, and it really helps me to understand where he's coming from."

"One last thing. I think that, in his heart of hearts, he knows it's him who has to change and it pisses him right off! He would rather it was me, yet he knows that, if we're to have a halfway decent relationship, he has to be the one to take a different view."

"Could be. He's your father…you must know him better than I do," said Jodie.

"Fine. I should add that all I've said is conjecture. He's never said any of this, so I would tread carefully if you were thinking of challenging him. For the record, I feel for him, I really do. But I got tired of being shot at and shouted down long ago. Just so you know, my tolerance has worn paper-thin."

"Gotcha. Okay, I won't keep you any longer. Leave it with me. I'll talk to him. Hope your day gets easier. Bye for now."

"Me too. Bye." Nadeen hung up the phone, towelling her eyes. And wished she could just go back to bed and curl up under the covers. More than anything, she needed a Lorna hug, but that wasn't going to happen any time soon. Meanwhile, the shop wouldn't open itself. Business was both a priority and a welcome diversion.

Nadeen drove down Morwood's driveway, thereby breaking their standing agreement not to see each other during the week, simply because it was too distracting. Yet, before she had shut up shop, she had weakened and phoned Lorna to ask if it was all right to drop in after everyone's evening meal, just for a while. Lorna agreed freely, but Nadeen didn't want to get in Mel's face, now that their involvement was public knowledge. It could be awkward.

Smoky eyes twinkling, Lorna opened the door. "Come in, honey-babe." She took Nadeen's hand and led her into the den. "Are you okay?"

"Not really. Can you spare a hug?"

Lorna held out her arms and Nadeen stepped into them, a long sigh escaping her aching chest. They rocked gently, Lorna's hands stroking her back rhythmically. "Hey, foxy lady. Lovely to see you. This is an unexpected, special treat. To what do I owe the pleasure?"

Nadeen loosened her hold and took a deep breath. "I needed a hug. And it had to be from you."

Lorna tipped Nadeen's head forward, kissed her between the eyes, then pecked her cheeks. "Do you want to talk about it?"

"Very astute of you," said Nadeen. "I don't, but it's best if you know what's going on."

They settled down on the couch. Lorna listened as Nadeen related a heavily censored version of the last conversation with her father, the abortive call from Derek, and the chat with Jodie. Nadeen had only briefly mentioned her father before, preferring to spare Lorna the difficulties in their relationship.

Nadeen said, "I don't think I've mentioned it, but he went to school with your husband. Which seems to have made him that much more reactive to you and me as a couple. That's just an observation. Honestly, I struggle to understand the way he thinks. We simply confuse each other." She rubbed her brow vigorously.

"Sorry about this. It just rattles me every time he goes off on a wild rant. Anyway, I thought you ought to know."

"You had me wondering. Painful and distressing. Has he met me? Because I don't remember him."

"He says not. But he knows *of* you, has seen a wedding photo apparently. Actually, I hope you never meet him, if this latest outburst is anything to go by."

"What's Jodie like?" said Lorna.

"I have yet to meet her, but she sounds remarkably sane, given she's with him."

"Well, whatever comes along, we'll deal with it."

Nadeen hesitated. "I was wondering if Mel is comfortable with me being here like this."

"Like what? We're just talking. Don't worry. She and I have discussed the situation, and she says she's cool with it. Even more than I expected, which is a huge relief. I really didn't know how she'd react."

"Excellent. Now, before it gets any later, I better shove off so we can all get a decent night's rest. I'll sleep easier, thanks."

Lorna stood up, took a step to the door and waited for Nadeen's arm to go around her waist. Outside under the veranda's security light, they shared another hug.

"Lorna?" Nadeen leaned away and looked at her intently. "I'm pretty sure I'm in love with you."

Lorna chuckled. "What, you've only just worked this out?" Then she was laughing. Then they both were. "Genius! Me too. I love you, too."

Nadeen hugged her hard, half-lifted her off her feet, both giggling and staggering about, ended with a deepening kiss. "Does this mean I'm more than just your Sunday morning bonk-buddy?"

Still catching her breath, Lorna said, "Eww! That really would be damning you with faint praise. Not a bit of it. Notably, I appreciate that you made this confession *not* in a moment of blind passion. When 'I love you' is said too much, and then not enough in the cold light of day."

"Is this a cold light?" Nadeen looked up. "Then let me tell you something you didn't know. I adore you." She quickly released Lorna and jumped down the stairs. "I absolutely adore you! Good night!" And she sprinted to the van, leapt in, started the engine, and drove off with a wave.

In the rear-vision mirror, Lorna blew kisses. Nadeen grinned all the way home.

# CHAPTER TWENTY-NINE

At the van's wheel, Lorna was twenty minutes down the road to the Papsom Medical facility when she missed the folder containing the carefully prepared consignment note that was essential for every delivery to their site. She was positive she dropped it beside her on the passenger seat as usual, but she couldn't see it anywhere. Swearing under her breath, she took the next side road of which there were few, did a hasty three-point turn, zoomed back onto the road home and pushed the speed limit more than she would usually dare. For security reasons, Papsom made appointments for every delivery, and they took a dim view of tardiness. Usually punctual, like it or not, she would be late this time.

Where had she put it, and how had she forgotten it? Too busy daydreaming about a certain woman? Last night's interlude had left her bouncing off the walls like a lovesick teenager. She'd slept well and floated through the morning's usually tedious van packing, smiling as she lifted trays of jiggling seedlings into place, strapping everything in securely. She had lithely leaped into the van with the usual fortifying thermos of coffee and the folder parked on the passenger seat. At least, she thought that's what happened. Yet, the folder wasn't there.

Was it in the back of the van? Definitely not. She'd put it down somewhere outside the house, gone back in to grab her wallet, then what? Biting her lips wasn't helping her memory.

She muttered, "You dozy…drongo." And swung off the main road into Morwood's driveway. Cruising down the drive, she spotted what looked like Murray's white Falcon station wagon parked with its rear facing the front door of the house, boot door ajar. A man wearing a black balaclava walked out of the new greenhouse. He started running and shouting. At the Falcon, he jumped in and started its engine with a roar and a belch of sooty smoke. That wasn't Murray, and that wasn't his car.

Lorna accelerated, then hit the brakes hard and slid the van to a halt. She flung open the van's door and raced over. "What the hell are you doing?"

Another hooded man marched out the front door with the old safe in his arms. Only, he was more mountain than man. He glanced at her, jumped off the top step and shoved the safe in the back of the Falcon.

By then she was beside him. "You thieving mongrel bastard!" She grabbed the hem of his hoodie and held on.

He growled, "Let go! I don't want to hurt you." He swung around and pushed her effortlessly back toward the steps. She flung out both arms, fell askew across the steps and slammed her skull into the edge of the veranda.

*Don't you love how people tell you they don't want to hurt you just before they hurt you?* Lorna peeled open her eyes, lifted a hand to the back of her head, winced and squinted at the fingers that came back bloodied. Lurching to sit up, she clutched at her left forearm and screamed, "Ouch! Ow…ow…ow! Manky…mangy…mingy… mongrel bastards." Its searing pain had her attention.

How long had she been out of it? All was quiet. The Falcon was gone. The back doors of the van were open.

Spooked, she struggled to her feet, arm held across her chest and warily made her way over to the back of the van. They'd tipped over the shelves of seedlings into an unholy heap, half-in, half-out of the back. Too numb to focus, she turned away and pulled the keys out of the ignition. The front door was still wide open, but she stopped and checked the swing and found the errant folder. In the office, she called the police. Then she called Murray.

"What did the cops say?" said Murray, shoving his hands in his pockets as he leaned against the kitchen doorjamb.

"The constable said it looked more like wilful damage than theft. They made a right mess of the office, maybe looking for something, used an angle grinder on the safe's bolts. And created more havoc in the greenhouses, wrecking seedling trays."

"Was anything important in the safe?"

"You mean my formulas? No way. I keep them well hidden. Cormack didn't trust that safe. He'd wedged two old house bricks inside. And a packet of expired condoms with a well-squeezed tube of lubricant." In answer to Murray's raised eyebrows, she said, "It tickled his sense of humour should anyone be dumb enough to steal it. We intended to get rid of it one day. I've no idea which decade it was installed, but I'll miss its rustic charm."

"You ought to get that arm seen to." Murray's gaze was tender. "I can take you to the medical centre. No trouble."

"That's kind of you, but Melanie will be home soon. And it really only hurts when I move it."

"You're one strong lady, Lorna." Beaming, Murray cocked his head.

"Ah, you men…the weaker sex. If you can handle childbirth, you can handle anything, don't you know? Your wife can back me up on that, eh?"

He looked at her blankly, cleared his throat. "Now, don't you worry your pretty head. I will report back to Papsom and discuss future strategies with their management people. Be assured, I'll get back to you. Better get going."

She walked him to the front door, stilled when he suddenly bent and scoured her cheek with thin lips fenced in by a five-o'clock shadow.

"If you need me for anything, just give me a buzz, okay?"

Alarmed, she waved him off. He had never acted this fresh with her—not a good sign. "Oh, Murray. Give it up, mate. This lady's not for turning."

With the bung arm in a snug black sling, Lorna used her right hand to pick up strewn papers that belonged in the three-door filing cabinet. They'd take a while to sort, but it was plainly a slow one-handed exercise—tedious, but doable. The medical centre team had plastered her arm down to and around the ball of her thumb so she couldn't twist the wrist. Six weeks of fun to come. Not.

With the floor clear, she tugged across the wheeled desk chair and sat before the pile on the desk. Were the intruders simply looking for cash and valuables? That would explain them stealing the safe, but not why they didn't touch resaleable electronics. Or why they searched through paperwork. Only her formulas held real value and she wasn't silly enough to leave them lying around the office or in an unlocked filing cabinet. And why make such a mess in the glasshouses so deliberately? What could those two blokes possibly gain from either action?

She'd had a painkiller, but the arm was still sore—severe bruising and a cracked ulna. There were bruises on her back and a nasty gash on her head, but it could have been worse. That mountain of a man could have killed her if he'd wanted to. What he did was probably his version of a gentle shove.

Clearly, he wasn't the murderous sort. It was more likely someone paid the two of them to do a dirty job, with instructions something like, "See if you can find Z but be sure to wreck X and Y first." Who would go to such lengths? She had a fair idea it was no one in Western Australia, let alone Toodyay. It all seemed far-fetched but, by the same token, there was more than small change at stake. Her livelihood, for a start. Murray would talk to Papsom, and they would immediately look to their other suppliers. They had no choice if they wanted to maintain continuous production.

She had to face reality—this latest assault could ruin her business. Permanently. If that was what someone intended, they may well have succeeded. Light-headed, she leaned over, rested her forehead on the edge of the pile of files and shut her eyes.

"Mum!" Hands on hips, Melanie stood at the door. "What are you doing? You're supposed be in bed resting."

"I can't lie around all the time—"

"Just for a day, or so, that's all. The doctor said you've got concussion, remember? She said your brain bounced around like a jellyfish in a coconut. It's *not* funny, Mum!"

"But it is very boring."

Melanie grabbed her mother's good arm and tugged. "Y'know, some days I'm glad I inherited Dad's smarts. Because some days, you have the IQ of a possum."

Lorna let herself be led. "Possums can be very clever."

"Not concussed ones. C'mon, possum-mum."

* * *

"Hi, Boss."

"Melanie?" Something in her voice made the hair on the back of Nadeen's neck buzz. "What's wrong?"

"I'm not supposed to bother you, but Mum isn't too good. And I was kinda hoping you might come over because I'm not sure what I'm supposed to do. I'm worried about her."

"Okay. What's wrong…what's happened?"

"She was taking a delivery to Papsom, forgot something, came home and found two guys had broken into the house. She tried to stop them and got hurt."

"What the hell?" Nadeen's stomach sank to her toes, while her mind raced. "Okay, got it. I'll come over now. Have you eaten?"

"No—"

"Don't worry, I'll bring food for all of us. Where is she now?"

"I managed to get her into bed." Sighing, Mel said, "The thing is, she's concussed and not making much sense. I don't know—"

"Mel, don't worry. I'm on my way. Hang up and go sit with her until I get there, okay?"

"Nah, yeah. Will do."

Nadeen drove as fast as she dared. Before she took off, she'd wedged the big pot of minestrone she made the evening before into a box, packed a few essentials into a bag, grabbed Bella and piled everything into the van. She climbed into the driver's seat and spotted a massive full moon that had just appeared at the horizon—a sight that only served to deepen her disquiet.

On the way, she berated herself to calm down and be ready for anything. She did not like the sound of Lorna's condition. Concussion could be dangerous. And it was just like Lorna to try and tackle burglars. For once, Nadeen wished her lover wasn't quite so feisty.

At Morwood, she found the front door ajar, took everything into the kitchen and put the minestrone on the cold hob. With Bella in tow, she trotted down to Lorna's darkened bedroom. From her perch on the edge of the bed, Melanie jumped up. Nadeen gave her a quick hug and peered at a sleeping Lorna. She steered Melanie out and they went back to the kitchen.

"There's minestrone that needs eating. Just nuke a bowl in the microwave and bung the pot in the fridge. Are you hungry?"

Mel peered in the pot. "What's in it?"

"Cannellini beans, beef and vegetables in a tomatoey stock with macaroni. Easy to eat. Help yourself. I'll just go take another look at her." Nadeen stopped at the door. "Are you okay?"

"Glad you're here," said Mel. "Can you stay over? Just for tonight, maybe?"

"Sure, no problem. Make sure you eat. You'll feel better for it." She strode back down the hall, an uncommon urgency at her back. In the bedroom's gloom, she switched on the bedside light, took off shoes and cords, and slid under the covers next to Lorna.

Lorna's eyes flew open. "Nadiyya? My honey-babe. You came!"

Nadeen froze as Lorna snuggled into her and draped a plastered forearm across her waist. "It's me, Nadeen."

"Nadiyya. I was dreaming of you." Lorna was barely coherent. Eyes closed again, she took a deep breath and exhaled softly, murmuring, "You came with me. Together in love. Forever us."

Bemused, Nadeen shut her eyes and relaxed. A silent shout-out to Queen Isis for healing couldn't do any harm—it could do a power of good. Her request found its way to the etheric realms and lay in the lap of the gods.

Safe in each other's arms, there was nothing else to be done. Nothing else that mattered. For now.

# CHAPTER THIRTY

*Thebes, Egypt 1108 BCE—Shomu (harvest)*

"Nadiyya! Where are you, child? Nadiyya!" The wabu was screaming like a whipped donkey. Nadiyya raced back into the house, found her father shoving medicines and implements into the medicine bag. He shot a glance at her, eyes wild. "Come on, we have to run. Now!" And he took off out of the house at a fast trot.

It was all she could do to keep up with him. He paused in a cloud of dust and handed her the bag. Alarmed, she struggled to get the strap over her shoulder. "Where are we going?"

"The palace. Hurry up!" And he took off again.

They raced up the stairs of the palace, past the guards and into the cool gloom of the interior. To Nadiyya's horror, a regal figure was waiting for them. Instantly, she fell to her knees and crawled forward to crouch behind her father who had dropped to kneel before Great Wife Tyti. As a peasant child, under no circumstances was she allowed to look upon so great a personage. The punishment was a brutal beating, if she were so lucky. If not so, she would be blinded. She kept her head down.

"There's no time to waste." Tyti's voice was distant, yet urgent. "This way."

Nadiyya jumped up and followed her father's heels, not daring to look left or right. They entered a chamber where netting hung all around a large sleeping platform. Someone was moaning.

"It has only just happened. You must heal the wound and ease her pain."

Haltingly, Akil asked, "If you please, what type of scorpion was it?"

"The fat-tailed one." Tyti turned to leave.

Her father began to shake, nearly lost his knees. He croaked, "I will try my best, Your Greatness."

Tyti spoke over her shoulder. "If my daughter dies, so does yours." Her soft footsteps faded away quickly.

Head still down, Nadiyya peeked around the room. The walls were painted with boats on the Nile and triumphant hunting scenes. On a series of low stools were small containers, odd trinkets, and shift dresses with long shawls dragging on the floor. At the door stood a bored guard, paying scant attention.

Akil drew aside the bed's drapes. "I need linen for a bandage. Bring the bag here."

Nadiyya did as she was bidden and took a sharp intake of breath at the sight of their patient. Laani's feverish gaze caught hers, rolled away, tossing from side to side erratically, her face beaded with sweat. Her white shift was crumpled and damp, left leg curled up, right leg jutting out like a lump of wood. Her right foot had swollen to become an extension of her calf. The ankle was an angry red, with just a small, blackish puncture wound at the outer heel.

Cheeks locked in a tight grimace, Nadiyya clutched the medicine bag. Her pounding heart set off a loud ringing in her burning ears. Dizzy, all she could do was stand and stare.

Her father said, "What's the matter with you? Make a mix of myrrh and cinnamon for the wound pad. We'll need two cubits of linen to wrap it in place. Get it ready while I give her the thebaine. Hurry up!"

Jerking the bag open with shaking hands, she thrust the thebaine pot at him, crouched down and laid out the makings on the floor, as per his instructions. She didn't dare let him see her mounting distress. And Laani needed her to be in control of herself. Jaws clenched, she went to work.

He unstoppered the little pot and, when he could, carefully dripped liquid from a tiny bone spoon between Laani's mobile lips.

"Shouldn't you dilute it, Father?" Before her, the blend of myrrh and cinnamon with oil had soaked into the pad evenly. The long piece of linen was ready for use.

"No time. She's delirious from the venom and pain. We can do more when it subsides."

In minutes, Laani's thrashing slowed. Together, they positioned the pad over the puncture wound and wrapped the length of linen behind the ankle, across, over and under the foot several times. Finally, he tore the end in two and knotted it in place.

"Give me the beer," said Akil.

She handed it to him, observing closely as he half-filled another pot with the beer and counted in drops of thebaine.

In a barely audible whisper, he said, "It's enough for them to give her for the pain. At least until tomorrow. If she lives that long."

Beneath her ribs, Nadiyya's heart lurched, then galloped on. "You think she will not?"

He took her elbow and moved out of hearing distance. "More likely she will not. Most don't. But there's a chance because it's her right foot, which is farthest from the heart. Come child. We've done as much as we can for her today."

She slung the bag's strap across her chest, stared back at a resting Laani for a few moments, then joined her father who was giving instructions to the guard. Keeping apace behind him, they left the palace and began the walk home.

She drew level with him and they continued sided by side. "The fat-tailed scorpion is the deadliest, isn't it?" He glanced down and gave a quick nod. "What the Great Wife said to you about if the princess dies was just a threat, no?"

He gave a hollow laugh. "My child, you must understand that what people say, what they do, and what they say they do are three different things. But when it comes to Her Greatness, she does not make threats. Her words were a promise."

She stumbled, swallowed hard and recovered herself to keep pace with him. Those interred as punishment were forced into the sarcophagus alive.

Abruptly, he halted. "Do not worry, Nadiyya. I am your father and I will not allow it."

Blinking at the dust that rose around them, she stalled and looked up into his kohl-rimmed almond eyes. "How could you possibly prevent it?"

A sudden gust kicked up a flurry of dust that made them both shut their eyes and cover their mouths. Both turned south toward the Sahara Desert.

She said, "Is that the Khamsin wind coming in?"

"Ahead of a sandstorm, likely. Let us hope not, for our crops' sake. The scorpions are on the march. Death and pestilence."

Hands clasped into a fist, he frowned at her. "I know you hate me many times, but I am strict with you for good reason. You *must* be the best to be a medical scribe, maybe even a physician. You are smart and diligent, a fast learner and have ability. I am nearly thirty-five years old. An old man. I want you to benefit from my knowledge, my legacy, to make a good life for yourself when I'm gone." Scuffing the track with one foot, he looked around. "Nadiyya, I am proud of you. Very proud. Your father loves you and will protect you. Do not worry, now. Tomorrow is another day." He shooed her forward and they walked home in silence.

Next morning, they changed the dressing on the puncture wound. Akil went to seek an audience with Tyti, while Nadiyya laboured through a conversation with Laani who was vaguely coherent.

Nadiyya said, "Is the thebaine strong enough to make the pain bearable?"

"Enough." Laani tried to smile. "I'm so happy to see you. I've missed you."

Taking her hand, Nadiyya said very softly, "I've missed you too...still adore you."

"Ah! When I'm with you, I don't need thebaine. You are my happiness."

Heart swelling beyond measure, Nadiyya hastily said, "When you're well enough, a harvest celebration accompanies you entering your cousin's house in marriage."

Laani closed her eyes, squeezed Nadiyya's hand and whispered, "There's something I want you to know. I was sitting by the wall at Horus's temple, thinking of us. I realised you really are my only one. My happiness." Her speech was becoming increasingly difficult to either hear or understand. Nadiyya leaned in to catch the words. "For many months now, you have been the shining light in my life. The only thing I ever looked forward to was to be with you. And I only asked you to get me thebaine to replace you when I marry. So, you see. When the scorpion showed me his stinger, I offered him my heel." She opened her eyes. "I don't want to be well if I can't be with you."

"Don't say that! I'm not worth it—"

"Life without you isn't worth it. The life they have planned for me is worse than death." Laani's feverish look drew Nadiyya's despairing eyes. "I'm dying now. Do you see that red line climbing my leg?"

"It's just some redness. Means nothing. You're delirious."

"Sweet Nadiyya, my honey-babe. I wish you could come with me into the afterlife. We could be together, forever us. Now, you deserve a good life. But that you cared for me at all is a priceless gift. I will treasure it for eternity. I can only thank you for you. For the all too brief joy. You have given me. May you live a long and happy life."

"Don't say such things. You'll be better soon."

Fumbling, Laani tugged at her wrists. "I want you to have my bracelets. Would you help me? Take them off."

"No! You can't do that. They'll think I stole them. Please stop. You need them to protect you from harm."

"Too late. If you can bear it, would you kiss me one last time?"

Nadiyya looked around, then quickly pressed her mouth against Laani's dry salty lips. "I'll see you tomorrow. Farewell, my love." Fighting tears, she turned and left the room, met her father waiting outside. He put a firm arm around her shoulders and steered her down the stairs to begin the walk home.

An ominous foreboding blanketed her thoughts, layering panic atop distress. A deepening terror about Laani's health threatened to overwhelm her. Around them, the painful brightness of the day belied the awful darkness descending upon her fearful heart.

A short distance from their house, Nadiyya asked, "Would drinking a whole pot of thebaine kill a person?"

Akil glared at her. "Don't be foolish. What a question!"

"Would it? I want to know."

He took a good while to reply. "Even the best medicine in extreme quantities is dangerous. It would render the person unconscious for a long time. Their heart could just stop dead. But I've never heard of such a thing. Truthfully, I do not know. Do not speak of this again. Do you understand?"

"Yes, Father. Thank you." She bowed her head.


An hour before dawn, Nadiyya awoke with a piercing cry. She had felt Laani's arms cradling her, her mouth tenderly upon her own.

She hugged herself and wailed. Wept and wailed until Akil stumbled in and clasped her to his chest, rocked her until she lay limp against him, whimpering. "She came to bid me farewell. She's gone, Father. Gone from this life."

"It is the way of all flesh." He released her, yet remained by her side in the pitch black that shrouded his usually brusque self. "I won't let them take you. I lost your mother too soon. I can't lose you too."

She sniffed and wiped away tears. "You plan to take my place."

Silence yawned like a merciless abyss.

"I am old and you are young. You have a life ahead of you. Without you…my daughter, I have nothing."

"But you could change that easily, Father. You could take a wife. I know you have denied yourself because of me, and your grief for my mother. There are women who would gladly wed you, the revered wabu who can provide a house and a comfortable home. A wife would look after you, and you would look after her. I will never have a husband, never have that with anyone, for the one I love has just died."

Akil cleared his throat. "You want to be with her?"

"I am frightened. But if we could be together in the afterlife, yes. That is why I asked about the thebaine. If you gave me a large amount, it would ease my passage."

"Oh, my daughter. You ask too much of me." She felt him shift away from her side. "No, I cannot do it. Do not speak of this again."

With her head in her hands, his fading footsteps served only to strengthen her resolve.

Great Wife Tyti perched upon a curved wooden stool covered in leopard skin atop a wide, high platform of the finest alabaster. An armed palace guard stood either side of her.

In front, Nadiyya was prone on the tiled floor. Akil stood to her right wearing his best skirt and tunic, head bowed as he spoke. "Your Greatness, I offer myself in my daughter's place. If it pleases you."

"It does not please me, wabu. Your daughter's life is forfeit with your failure. Why should I replace her with you?"

"My value is far greater than this child. I am more worthy of your daughter."

Nadiyya sat back on her heels, eyes diligently downcast. "I am *not* a child!"

He hissed, "Be quiet, foolish girl!"

"Your Greatness, I am fourteen years old and can bear children. I am a woman. I can speak for myself."

Tyti made a strange cackling sound. "I permit you to speak. Be quick about it."

Nadiyya took a deep breath. "My father has wide knowledge, experience and wisdom. He is the best physician in Thebes. Truly, he is more worthy than I could ever be. Yet despite this failure, he is vastly more valuable and useful to you alive than dead. Your

Greatness, I would be honoured to attend Princess Laani in the afterlife. Please allow me to do so."

"Well, well, well," said Tyti. "Young woman, you do yourself proud with your words. So be it." She called out to a robed figure in the shadows, "Have the last rites been given? Is the sarcophagus ready? Good. Take her away."

Choking, Akil said, "If you would permit me, Your Greatness, may I prepare my daughter for interment? A father's final act."

"Yes, yes…enough talk. Guards, escort them."


Underground, the tomb was large enough to contain at least ten sarcophagi. All had heavy stone lids that no one person could shift. Painted on the walls were pictures of daily life, wars, hunting, and excursions into foreign lands. At intervals, indented sconces housed oil lamps that gave off poor light and foul black smoke.

At the tomb entrance, two guards coolly watched Nadiyya standing patiently as her father slowly and methodically wiped down her exposed skin. After a short while, the guards disappeared into the entrance tunnel and talked too quietly to be heard clearly. Hastily, Akil pulled a small pot from under his skirt. He twisted out its rush stopper and handed it to Nadiyya.

"Drink as fast as you can. All of it."

Panicky, Nadiyya took the pot and downed the thick, bitter liquid, nausea rising the instant it hit her stomach. She swallowed and kept drinking until it was empty.

Barely audible, Akil said, "I am very angry with you. If I had my way, right now I would beat you to within a hair's breadth of your life for disobeying me. How dare you?"

She smiled wanly. "I love you, Father. Let us not quarrel now for I have accepted my fate. I trust you will find a good wife to cherish and be cherished by. You deserve it. You have given me so much more than other fathers would have…allowed far more than most. I am forever in your debt. We will meet again."

Tears streaming, he kissed her on both cheeks, just as she sagged at the knees. He caught her and picked her up as if she were nothing. Gently, he swung her over the edge of the sarcophagus and laid her out next to the wrapped figure within.

"Farewell, my dear child. Safe journey to the afterlife. May you find the happiness you seek."

From behind, the two guards pushed past him roughly, picked up the lid, grunting as they slid it noisily into position. The stockier one paused, put a hand on Akil's shoulder. "You took her life?" Akil could only bow his head. "We fathers salute you. Go now. Let us leave the dead to rest in peace."

# CHAPTER THIRTY-ONE

One hour before dawn, Nadeen slipped out of bed where her beloved remained, safe in the arms of Morpheus. From under a chair, Bella roused and stretched, then followed her mistress padding down the hall to the kitchen. Nadeen filled the kettle and switched it on to boil, then let the Cavalier outside. Bright-eyed in the moonlight, a lone magpie must have warbled a soft come-hither song all night long and was still at it, hopeful of a mate in time for this breeding season. Down by the river, kookaburras were laughing in the dark.

She took a mug of tea out to the front veranda where a chilly easterly blew in from the Great Victoria Desert. Low in the west, the huge full moon hovered, yet to set. The night had been more sleepless than not—restless concern left her red-eyed with fatigue. But it was peaceful outside in the fresh air, even if she should have put her cords on. Chilling out with a cuppa on the veranda swing was just what she needed. In the predawn gloom, her spirits lifted.

"Nadeen?" Lorna stood in pyjamas by the front door, a dressing gown slung across her shoulders.

"Here! Good morning. How are you feeling?"

"Remarkably well." Lorna perched on the swing next to Nadeen. "Almost human. Where are your pants? You must be freezing."

"I run hot." Nadeen shrugged. "Pants are optional."

Lorna giggled, peered intently into Nadeen's eyes. "Dear God, but I love you." She touched Nadeen's cheek. "How and when did you join me, because I only realised you were there in the wee hours."

"Mel rang me, very worried, so I turned up with food. Must have been about eight o'clock. You did talk to me, but none of it made any sense. I figured I'd best stay with you and must have dozed, on and off. You thrashed about a lot, nearly sconed me with that plaster cast a couple of times."

"Did I? So sorry, honey-babe. You realise this is the first time we've slept together? Not quite the romantic interlude I had in mind."

"Well, you can forget anything romantic for a while. Your head must have taken a fair hit. And, really, you should have been in hospital under observation for the night."

"If you say so. Still, I feel bright enough, even if this arm is a tad sore. You see, being with you is very healing. Pity about the romance, though. But I'll make it up to you."

"Promises, promises." Smiling, Nadeen stood up and held out a hand. "Come, dear heart, you must be famished."

"Now that you mention it, I could probably eat a horse."

Nadine snorted. "Minestrone will have to do."

"For breakfast? Why not."


They sat at the kitchen table, each devouring a bowl of soup reheated in the microwave. Nadeen had remembered to put on her cords, just in case Mel emerged and joined them.

Lorna said, "What's the cut of beef in this? It's very unctuous."

"You like? It's oxtail. Gelatinous, yummy stuff. It's in a homemade bone broth that's perfect for healing broken bone and the like. I'll leave most of it here so you two have backup for a few meals."

"Are you sure? You're spoiling me—"

"Nah, I'm being a friend because you're far from well. Speaking of, I can give you a hand with seedlings. What's your plan?"

"I haven't had a chance to come up with one. It's not looking good."

"Okay." Nadeen tilted the bowl and gulped down the last of the stewlike soup. "Talk it through with me. What are your options?"

Lorna put down the spoon and rested her forehead in her able hand. "Well, the easiest would be to bow out gracefully and tell Papsom to source their supply elsewhere. It amounts to shutting up shop."

"Let's call that Plan A. What's Plan B?"

"I persuade Papsom to source supply elsewhere and they grant me a sabbatical for six to eight weeks while I heal. Because I can't lift anything with this left arm."

"Right," said Nadeen. "Is there a Plan C?"

"I round up as many helpers as I can and shout encouragement while they work their arses off for me. I'm not comfortable with that."

"Fair enough. What would Papsom think of Plan B. The sabbatical?"

"I suspect they would be sadly unimpressed. While they are tolerant of unavoidable short-term problems, two months would really push the friendship. After all, they're running a business. Time is money. In fact, who am I kidding? It's not a viable option. Scrap Plan B." She finished the soup.

Nadeen took the empty bowls to the sink. "Who would you call in to help you with Plan C?" She leaned back against the sink, arms folded.

"Rocco has already cleaned out the mess in the back of the van. He will help when he has spare time. Then there's Tash who's the kind of friend who drops just about everything for me. She knows enough about how I operate and is a terrific help. Mel will help after school, but she's got pretty important exams not far away. I don't want to stress her." Lorna stroked the plaster cast and scratched an itch under her wrist. "Jared might help and I'd happily pay him for his time, no problem."

"So, you already pay Rocco and would pay Jared. What about Tash?"

Lorna laughed awkwardly. "She'd slap me around the head with a damp paper towel if I even suggested it. Toodyay friends don't pay friends. We just help each other, any way we can."

"Sure," said Nadeen. "I love that about the place. Anyone else? Apart from me, of course."

Lorna arose and came to stand, majestic, before Nadeen. "My right hand is fine now and I can do simple things with my left. Which means, even if I can't lift, I can seed." With the morning sunlight streaming through the kitchen window, her eyes glinted with flecks of gold like fiery embers in clouds of smoke.

Nadeen caught her breath and almost flinched. This woman had the power to completely unravel her socks. She swallowed and awaited her fate.

"I'm afraid you think I'm using you," said Lorna. Nadeen half-opened her mouth—Lorna put up a hand. "I feel I have to say this. Even though I've said that you mean far more to me than just a Sunday morning bonk-buddy, I suspect you don't really believe me. It's true, I could be lying. I've said that I love you, but we may have very different ideas what that word means. It's true, some people use the word to get what they want, however temporarily. I could be one of them. I could be playing a game, merely using you until I get bored and seek out the next unsuspecting fool. But that's not the way I work. While I love family and friends dearly, I've only ever been more involved with Cory and now you. No one else. I want you to know that I would never take you for granted, and I trust you implicitly. Now tell me what you really think."

Light-headed, Nadeen closed her eyes for a few seconds. "I'm sorry, but that's too complex for me to deal with right now. I appreciate your candour, but I need to get home, get ready for work and go open the shop. At the end of the day, a decent night's rest should clear my head. Don't get me wrong. It's just that I'd rather be well-rested because what we to say to each other is too important." She held up her hands defensively. "I'm just tired. Forgive me, but I promise to give you some answers. Just not now."

"Very well, then." Lorna cocked her head. "Right. Thanks for all you've done. We'll talk when you're ready. Do let me know. Take care."

Nadeen quickly pecked Lorna's cheek, rounded up Bella and strode out the front door.

* * *

It was hours later when Lorna took to her bed for a necessary rest that she went over what she'd said to Nadeen. What had she been thinking to put her on the spot like that? It really wasn't fair to start a deep-and-meaningful discussion out of the blue. And just after Nadeen had gone out of her way to step in to support Mel, lost precious sleep in the process, been there for her. Could she blame a nasty bump on the head for being thoughtless? Self-absorbed? She was way out of practice with the ins and outs of wrangling a close relationship. What had possessed her at that moment? Maybe Nadeen wouldn't get back to her any time soon? A sinking sensation had her wishing she'd held her tongue.

"Clumsy clod. Right now, I don't know much, but I do know you're far from perfect. Here's proof. Go do something useful." She had phone calls to make, especially one to Murray for an urgent top-up of poppy seeds, and another to Tash for help. She swung her legs off the bed. "Get on with it and try not to upset anyone else. Idiot."

# CHAPTER THIRTY-TWO

Nadeen had just walked out the front door to set off to work when the phone rang. Tempted to let it go through to the answering machine she hesitated, looked down at her patiently waiting pooch and went back inside to answer it.

"It's me, Jodie. Just getting back to you after discussing the situation with your father. Have you got a moment?"

Nadeen lowered herself onto an ancient jarrah three-legged stool she'd only just found in the garage and put next to the hall table. Bella lay down at her feet. "Yes, but I have to get to work soon."

"Got it. Look, I didn't get very far, but I was wondering if you might agree to an informal meeting in a public place?"

"Is that to shame us out of yelling at each other?"

"Er, not when you put it like that. Actually, I was thinking that you might bring along your partner to round out the points of view. Between the four of us, that is."

Partner? She'd not thought of Lorna that way—it sounded odd. Her breakfast was starting to curdle in her stomach. "I get the feeling this is some kind of proof-of-normalcy gig, like a show and tell. Folks, you see before you two normal-looking women doing abnormal things that you might deign to ignore, if you can stomach them. Please. I gave up trying to prove my worth to my father years ago. I have nothing to prove to him. Neither has the woman I'm seeing."

"Oh, sorry! I didn't mean it like that. I just thought we could be more open and receptive in a group."

"Speaking for myself, I'd find it restrictive having to be polite only until I get the chance to make myself scarce. Jodie, my private life is not a sideshow for others to pass judgement upon. And I'm not about to ask my lover to be Exhibit A, or whatever else you had in mind."

Jodie protested, "This isn't what I intended. Really, it isn't."

"I'll take your word for it. Quite frankly, I'm struggling to care anymore about him. About our relationship. I hate to break it to you, but I suspect you're the only one who gives a damn right now."

"Bugger it. I was hoping you might give it a go."

Nadeen guffawed. "Trust me, I've given it countless goes for too long. Over the last twenty-odd years, I've tried every which way to get him to accept me. I've begged and pleaded, wheedled and sucked up to him, trying to get his approval. Which only seemed to deepen his contempt. I'm not doing it anymore. It's his turn now. If *he* wants to be in *my* life, he has to convince *me* he's worth it!" She was almost shouting down the phone. "Sorry. I don't mean to shoot the messenger. Why do you care so much, anyway?"

"I'm starting to wonder," said Jodie. "It just seems so pointless when it's so easily remedied. Or so I thought. Okay, I'll let you go. I meant well. Really, I did."

"The road to hell is paved with good intentions, so they say. I'd best get on with it. Bye." She hung up, woke a sleeping dog and shut the front door behind her. This was turning out to be one heavy-duty day so far. It had to get better, didn't it?

After a light dinner of curried vegetables, Nadeen got stuck into the garage again. The little stool had been a real find amongst the remaining junk—a genuine antique treasure that had needed nothing more than a scrub and oiling. She was making good progress.

Shoved in the garage's back corner, a four-drawer chest that might have been presentable thirty years ago had yielded mouldering gardening magazines and planting tags and ties, some of which were worth keeping. Otherwise, she pulled each drawer right out, checked its contents, and emptied them summarily into the garbage bin.

The third drawer was a right mess. Boxes of long-expired packets of seed had been chewed open by mice, the seeds eaten, and the packets torn into tiny pieces then used for nesting. The gnawing mice had enlarged a splintered opening at the back of the drawer for easier access and, from the quantity of droppings, must have regularly returned to raise their young. The drawer stank to high heaven. Nadeen emptied it into the garbage bin and took it outside to hose it out, left it leaning up against the garage to dry.

For a breath of fresh air, she strolled through the garden checking the gerberas, especially those that had grown stronger in their fresh soil. Some had begun to flower, which was quite a buzz. She crouched down to examine a white one that featured a ring of red flecks. It reminded her of Lorna's eyes lit up by the rising sun that very morning. And her searingly honest words. They challenged Nadeen's expectations that mirrored her past experiences. Why would the trajectory of this relationship be any different from those in the past?

To decide it couldn't be was a self-fulfilling prophesy—a bias etched in her psyche by the scars of what had gone before. She had to face the fact that her experience with Greer had made a significant dent in her faith in any kind of happily partnered future, including her ability to embrace a relationship with Lorna fully. Which wasn't helped by the nagging feeling that they'd had a disastrous liaison back in the mists of time.

She got to her feet, hands on hips, and surveyed the greening gerberas that were responding so well. It was amazing what a decent dose of tender loving care could do for a living thing. She paced along the rows of plants, unseeing.

The onus was on her to find her faith. In herself, and in her and Lorna as a couple—as partners. An old saying came to mind: "Don't look back. It's not where you're going." She didn't know what she was going to say to Lorna, but she would try to explain herself. When the opportunity arose.

Energised, she strode back into the garage to finish what she'd started. The bottom drawer had practically nothing in it but, when she pulled it out, in the hollow plinth underneath were two bulging folders. The perfect hiding place.

She picked up one and rested it on the chest, flicked it open and leafed through a few pages. It was a tatty photo album with nothing but snaps of gerbera flowers, annotated below on small squares of paper in a schoolteacher's neat, round hand. Aunt Peggy's handywork? Each photo was named, dated, and described in detail—its origin and ancestry.

Adrenaline pumping, she heaved out the second folder. It was much the same, except with later dates. Was this Garry and Peggy's life work? Nadeen didn't know yet, but she dared to hope. If so, the folders were pure gold from a gerbera fancier's point of view.

She snatched them up, shut the garage door and took them inside to the sitting room where she pulled over the coffee table and set them down. Too excited, she sashayed to the kitchen and put on the kettle for a cuppa. Already seven thirty p.m. and dog-tired or not, she was going through them tonight. She did *not* want to be disturbed.

# CHAPTER THIRTY-THREE

The persistent knocking finally woke her. Peeling her lids open, she checked the wall clock. It was nearly ten p.m. and she had barely read through a third of the first folder. A half-full mug of stone-cold tea on the table told her she must have fallen asleep pretty quickly. Did the phone ring while she was out of it? The knocking came again, louder this time. Even Bella lifted her head.

She had pins and needles in one foot that had been at a funny angle as she slept askew on the couch. Wincing, she opened the front door.

"Lorna? What are you doing here? You shouldn't even be driving. Come in." She looked up and down the street. Lorna's van was parked in the driveway. Every house was as quiet as a pharaoh's tomb.

"Don't bother. They all know about us. I had to see you, couldn't bear thinking you might dump me for opening my big mouth this morning. I tried to phone but you didn't pick up, so I worried you might not want to know me. Not that I'd blame you. I'm so sorry. It was thoughtless of me."

"What are you on about? It's okay." She took Lorna in her arms. "It's quite late, you know."

"I do know and you need your sleep. And my being here is stopping you from getting that sleep. I was just frightened of losing you. I mean, why would you want an old lady with a half-broken arm, a gammy hand and a cracked skull? Why would you?"

"Shush. Settle down. Whatever ails you now is only temporary. You will heal from all that. As it happens, I was asleep on the couch when you knocked. I feel reasonably okay. Does Mel know where you are?"

"She looked at me as I was leaving like I'd lost my mind, of course. But guess what?"

"Okay, I'll bite. What?"

"She's got a boyfriend. A Northam lad. I warned her about them, but she took no notice. Proud of her."

Nadeen chuckled. "Then she'll understand us better, eh?"

"Eh, indeed." Lorna's bottom lip quivered. "Can we talk?"

"Mel's not expecting you back tonight?"

"Probably not."

"Then we can talk in bed. I have to put Bella out to do her business, brush my fangs, and we can hit the sheets."

"Fangs? Yes, Mrs Fox. Have you got a spare toothbrush?"

Nadeen lent Lorna an oversized cotton T-shirt that had seen many summers. She lit three scented votive candles and placed them on the dresser where they reflected light back into the bedroom. "Are you going to be warm enough?"

"With you as a hot water bottle? We could warm each other up in more ways than one."

"Not an option. Just talk and sleep," said Nadeen crisply.

"It's not like I'd have a heart attack."

"But you might have a stroke or an aneurism. Your brain is bruised and a clot is a remote possibility. Still, I'd rather not lose you for a moment's pleasure."

"You're *so* sensible."

"Right now, one of us has to be."

"If you say so." Lorna slid between the sheets and propped pillows behind her. "Have you thought about what I said this morning?"

"On and off. Something else got me to thinking, too. Jodie, my father's other half, rang this morning. She called you my partner, which shocked me. I haven't dared to think of you that way." Nadeen fluffed up pillows behind her, took Lorna's good hand in hers. "Are you okay if I just ramble on? Ask whatever you like. It makes it easier."

Lorna leaned right across and kissed her quickly. "All good, so far."

"Hm, that was nice. The problem I have is that I've broken all my rules with you. And that's scary. Rules like, us women of a particular ilk know to *never* get involved with a straight woman. The height of stupidity. My plan was to find a comfy spot in Toodyay, run my shop, hobnob with the locals, and live a quiet life until my dotage when I would discreetly pass away, no harm done. Also, should I happen upon a *passing* affair—note the emphasis on the 'passing'—all would be very discreet. No attracting attention from the neighbours. And none of that falling in love nonsense. Been there, done that, never again. You can see how well I've done at obeying my own rules."

"Very entertaining. You're not good at this, are you?"

"Truth be known…" She searched out Lorna's eyes. "I'm afraid to hope we can make a go of it. Afraid to risk it, probably because of Greer. Even though I'm already in love with you. I'm sorry…I'm not making much sense. It doesn't help that I've a god-awful feeling I've willingly died for you before in the distant past and might do it again."

Lorna said, "Sometimes you feel like a cornered, wounded animal to me. Love is always a risk, babe." She lifted their entwined hands and kissed Nadeen's knuckles. "If you once died for me, maybe I once died for want of you. Might we agree not to do that again?"

Light pierced whatever darkness harried Nadeen's most disturbing memories buried deep within her psyche. "Ha! That makes perfect sense. Could it be that simple?"

"Maybe. My mother always said the whole point of this life is to grow our capacity to love. The rest is just window dressing. It stands to reason that, if a lesson is learnt, there's no point in repeating it. Since the universe is infinite intelligence, it's not gratuitously bloody-minded. Humans, maybe. The universe? No."

"So, how do we do that?"

"We agree," said Lorna with a shrug. "We agree we are together, a couple, partners, you and me, us. Whatever words mean committed. And nobody and nothing is permitted to come between us. How does that grab you?"

Bright eyes reflecting the candlelight, Nadeen wrapped both hands around Lorna's. "Perfect. I can live with that. I might even sleep peacefully tonight."

"Promise not to bruise you with my cast. If I can help it."

Nadeen switched on the bedside lamp, slipped out to extinguish the candles, climbed back into bed, switched off the light, and shut her eyes. "I'm dead in the water. Do you think you'll sleep?"

"Positive. Nigh-night, sleep tight, don't let the bedbugs bite."


Barely whispered, "Are you awake?"

Nadeen rolled onto her back. A warm body snuggled into her side, head on her shoulder. She lifted an arm and put it around the culprit. "It's still dark."

"This is the second night in a row we've slept together."

"Uh-huh. Best alert the media."

"Ha, ha. I've let Bella out."

"Is this your usual waking up time or something?" mumbled Nadeen.

"More or less."

"Some of us need our beauty sleep. Wake me up when the sun's up."

Lorna moved away and slipped out of bed.


Nadeen roused to the sound of clinking in the kitchen. Bella was snoozing at the foot of the bed. It was only ever a cooler morning that lured the Cavalier to jump up and snuggle into the doona. Nadeen slid out of bed, gave the glossy black-and-tan dog a fond few pats, put on a dressing gown and went to catch the kitchen elf at whatever she was up to.

"Good morning. And what do you think you're doing?"

Lorna had her hands in the sink. "Morning, honey-babe. I found some rubber gloves, one of which actually fits over this plaster cast. Made myself useful." She fished out the last bowl and put it in the drainer, pulled the sink plug and peeled off the gloves. "And I've been snooping about. There's tea in the pot, if you fancy it."

Nadeen took out a mug and poured herself a brew. "Find anything interesting?"

"Those photo albums on the coffee table. I took one outside and compared the shots with some of your plants that are flowering. You've got some beauties."

"Hope so, but beauty is in the eye of the beholder." She took a sip of tea and put the mug on the table. "I've only just found those folders and not had a chance to look at them properly. Maybe we can do that together soon."

Lorna put an arm around her. "Have you had enough sleep?"

"I think so." Nadeen encircled her and they stood in the early-morning silence for a while—heads together, breathing, heart against heart.

"I still think I'm too old for you," said Lorna.

Nadeen frowned. "Really, it's not important."

"It might be one day."

"And that day may never come." Nadeen studied her beloved. "Most of what people worry about never happens. And we've committed to be together. Let's not allow fear and doubt to pull us apart."

"But you're an attractive girl, Nadeen."

"Thanks. And so are you, funny one."

Lorna sighed. "It's always mystified me how or why anyone finds me attractive."

"Are you kidding me? You are the most striking woman I've *ever* laid eyes on. When I first saw you, I opened my mouth to say hello and not a sound came out. I must have looked like a guppy. Then you walked up the street and townsfolk fell over themselves to win a glance…a glance from you, like you were royalty."

Lorna examined her palms, said nothing.

"Do you really not know the effect you have on people?"

Another sigh. "Sure, I've always known some fellas fancy me. Ho-hum. So what?"

"Ah, now I see. Lorna, it's not about your looks so much as the energy that you radiate. You're magnetic, which comes from inside…from the soul. Simply put, you have kind eyes that draw all sorts of people to you, not just fellas. You're on the inside looking out, so it doesn't make any sense to you." Nadeen squeezed her shoulders. "But the rest of us get it."

"Well, I still don't," Lorna said. "If I look back and think about it, it was Marissa who made me feel really desirable. That was exhilarating. To know that she wanted me, even if it was for only a moment in time. I remember running away from her, but I couldn't run away from myself. From how thrilled…excited I was to feel that way. And when I met you outside the shop, I think I just stared because you reminded me of her. It totally threw me."

She squeezed Nadeen's waist. "You make me feel desirable and very much alive. It's *you* who makes my heart race and skip a beat when you kiss me with your eyes. Oh, yes, that's what you do. I can't help it but I worry about losing you."

"No need. I don't easily change my mind once it's made up," said Nadeen. "Have a little faith in us. Maybe we've been separated for centuries, if not millennia, us two ancient souls. Who knows? Let's not waste time imagining the worst."

Lorna bit a lip. "I guess I'm not handling uncertainties too well."

"Hey, we've hardly had time to get to know each other. If we just keep talking, we'll work through the gnarly bits, eh? And that whole 'attractive' thing is so much personal taste. Some say beauty is only a light switch away and most of the best things are said in the dark." Nadeen leaned in and kissed her, whispering, "I secretly think of you as my 3D missus. Delicious. Delightful. Delectable!"

Lorna smirked, stepped away. "Is that right? We'll have to work on that 'getting to know you' thing some other time. Now I have to go home because I've a million things I should be doing. Tash will be there soon to help me prep trays and do seeding. Thanks for the sleepover. You have the best day, honey-babe."

"You too." Nadeen backed up into the hall. "Let yourself out. I'm in the shower."

"Wait up! There's something else we have to talk about. But another time will do. Next Sunday, maybe."

"Really? You do realise that for anyone in a relationship, those are the four most terrifying words in the English language."

"Which words?"

"We have to talk," said Nadeen.

Lorna smiled, turned on her heel, and waved over one shoulder. "Go make yourself nice!"

# CHAPTER THIRTY-FOUR

On a muggy Sunday morning in Nadeen's backyard, they compared photos in the albums with the plants that were in flower and matched up about a third of them. But it wasn't easy. Some of the photos had yellowed with age, while others had faded. Nadeen took photos as they went for closer comparison later. It helped that she had tagged every young plant with a number that matched the parent plant to avoid confusion.

Lorna stood over a large cream flower with bands of hot-pink petals. "Look at this stunner. Don't you love how plants throw everything into their flowers, no holding back, as if their lives depended on it? Which their progeny do. There's nothing half-hearted about them. And what about this red one which must be some kind of multiple."

"It's a multirayed triplex," said Nadeen. "I've got a match. It's called 'Radiance' according to this."

"Well, Radiance is blooming. More buds on the way. I'm sure there's an opium poppy called Radiance, too. A peony-style vivid red with a very large flower. It really does resemble peony flowers.

Could be why I like them so much. Actually, you know that ancient pink rose at the end of Morwood's veranda? The one with the powerful perfume. It's called Radiance too. I was told that Alice and Violet planted it around the turn of the century. Amazingly tough old thing, much like them. So, how are we doing?"

"We've exhausted the albums with the current blooms. There are more plants budding up. I'll have to document these results, otherwise I'll lose track of what's what. Thanks for your help. A second pair of eyes make it easier."

"You're welcome," said Lorna. "How many varieties do you think you've got?"

"Not as many as in the albums. Quite a few of the plants I found behind the garage had withered away. Damn shame. However, there still might be fifty or sixty. Only time will tell." She looked up at a swathe of gathering clouds. "Uh-oh. A mackerel sky. There's a change on the way. Let's go in."

Nadeen left the albums on the kitchen table and tapped the kettle on to boil.

"I brought fresh scones," said Lorna. She unwrapped the contents of a basket she'd left on the sideboard. "With whipped cream, plus a jar of apple jam for your larder."

"Thoughtful of you. There's an open apricot jam in the top cupboard. My all-time favourite." Nadeen rummaged for plates and cutlery. "What's so important that we have to talk about?"

"Oh, yes. That. It's more a matter of what I'd like to know about you. How you think and what's important to you in a relationship. I haven't any experience beyond me and Cory, which was pretty straightforward." Lorna found fresh mugs, set them on the bench by the kettle, and spooned coffee into each one. "You've mentioned your ex and her attempt to reconcile with you. I was wondering what went wrong between you two, if you don't mind me asking. Just a broad picture. I don't need to know the nitty-gritty."

Nadeen set the apricot jam on the table and pulled out a chair. "Okay, I get why you're asking, but it's tricky because it's just my point of view."

"I don't expect anything else. And I know you'll be fair. Simple." Lorna poured hot water into the mugs and topped them up with a little milk. She put a mug in front of Nadeen, sat herself down. In the centre of the table, the batch of six scones was wrapped in a tea towel. Still warmish from the oven, she loosened two and put them on plates.

"Let me think a while," said Nadeen. She sliced open the scone, slathered it with apricot jam and topped with the cream. They ate in silence. "You make a mean scone."

"One doesn't gain life membership of the CWA without passing the scone test. It's a rite of passage, trust me."

Nadeen chuckled. "I bet. Perfectly delicious." She brushed crumbs off her fingers and took a gulp of coffee. "Greer and I were both in our early thirties when we got together. I guess we just wanted different things. She wanted drama and excitement, while I wanted emotional connection with a reliable partner. A basic incompatibility. Over time, we drifted apart and her straying was a symptom of that. Maybe we just took each other for granted?"

"But it worked for a while, surely?" said Lorna. "Why didn't you want to reconcile?"

"Some people change but most don't. I've put it behind me and moved on. She said she would be a different person if I went back to Melbourne with her. I don't believe her, probably because I spent too many years wishing she'd wake up and smell the coffee. It's my experience that people may make an effort for a while, but they tend to default to living their lives exactly how it suits them, regardless of their significant other. I reckon compatibility in the beginning ensures a more likely compatibility long-term. And to me, going back to something that didn't work is no way to go forward. Does that make sense?"

"I suppose so." Lorna finished her coffee. "How does that compare to our relationship?"

Nadeen rubbed her cheeks with both hands. "Where do I begin? Fundamentally, I feel that you and I have a very strong emotional connection. On the one hand, you're so familiar, on another, extremely scary! The magnitude of my feeling for you boggles my rational mind, while my gut is perfectly comfortable with it, as is my heart. But I've never felt this way about anyone or anything before. I'm just going with it. Practically, I'm very comfortable around you and feel we get along just fine. You may feel otherwise?"

Lorna rose and held out a hand. "Come on, honey-babe. Cuddle time."

* * *

On the bed, she leaned over Nadeen and tucked soft dark curls behind one ear, her eyes sober with intent. "Did you love her?"

"In the beginning." Nadeen's voice was a mere whisper. "But love does not conquer all. It's all too easily eroded by carelessness and complacency. To me, it's not just a nice idea. Love is a verb and couples have to work at it. Both of us."

"I think so, too." Lorna took to kissing her, first slowly and gently, then with a deepening passion that drew their bodies together, wrapped tightly. Abruptly, she buried her face in Nadeen's pulsing throat, breath ragged.

"My lovely, are you all right?"

"Dammit. Just getting carried away. Wishing I didn't have to go home. Tash is coming this afternoon."

Nadeen reached down and tugged Lorna's hips against her. "A quickie?"

"Would be nice, but I know a five-minute quickie with you translates into a whole hour gone by. It's like entering a time warp." She dropped a light kiss on Nadeen's moist mouth, met her eyes. "I get lost in you."

"Hope you feel safe with me."

"I do...I *do* feel safe with you."

"Well then, a girl's gotta do what a girl's gotta do."

Lorna smiled ruefully. "Any chance you could spare an hour or so later to help move trays around in the glasshouse with Tash and me?"

"No problem. Actually, I'd like to meet her, your BFF."

"I'm sure she'd like to meet you too. It's about time."

# CHAPTER THIRTY-FIVE

Lorna had taken soil samples from each of the five planting mixes in individual tubs. She stirred them together and tested a teaspoonful for its pH that would indicate the soil's acidity. Behind her, the greenhouse door opened.

Tash shook herself and took off her spray jacket. "It's just starting to rain."

"We'll be dry enough in here. Have a look at this. About six point five?"

Peering at the shade of green gunk, Tash said, "Maybe nearer six. Is that too acidic?"

"Spot on, actually. Mel made up the mixes. I've asked Nadeen to come and help move trays. She should be here soon."

"Ah-ha!" said Tash, eyebrows waggling. "I get to meet the infamous woman herself. In the flesh."

"You're a tease. Be nice." Overhead, huge drops of rain started pelting the glass with a roar.

Tash shouted, "Aren't I always?"

The door opened and a hooded Nadeen swept in. "Struth! It's bucketing!" She glanced at Lorna and Tash as she peeled back the hood and stomped her Bogs boots, bellowing, "Hello! Lovely weather for ducks!"

With a cheeky smile, Tash took off her gloves and stuck out a hand. Nadeen shook it and returned the smile. All three looked up at water streaming down the glass in waves. As suddenly as it had started, the rain eased back to a steady pattering that might set in for hours.

Lorna said, "Have you got gloves?" Nadeen had just taken off her jacket, fished gloves out of a pocket and waved them at Lorna. "Let's start down the back."

Less than an hour later, they pulled out the folded plywood chairs and rested. It was still raining steadily. Tash asked, "What's happening with Papsom? Have they given you more time to restore supply, or what?"

"They have, but not because they're feeling generous," said Lorna. "Murray rang last night. Apparently, Adelaide Hills Nursery that they usually fall back on has gone bankrupt."

Nadeen said, "Whoa. How does that affect you?"

"It means, short of accessing supply from over east, they're waiting on me…us. He mentioned that mob might be bought out in a fire sale by a Victorian nursery who've been eyeing them off for some time. For the right price, of course. What it's done in the interim is provide breathing room for us to catch up, because Papsom is fresh out of options." Lorna shrugged. "To me, it sounds like dodgy goings-on. I suspect that break-in was to kneecap me, with the only people standing to benefit being the Adelaide Hills mob. Maybe they were getting desperate?"

"How so?" said Tash. "Just trying to slow us down as much as possible?"

"Maybe they figured me for a one-woman band and easily demoralised…deterred. No way did they count on Toodyay folks stepping in to prop me up. See, we've done extremely well to be where we are now. The next crucial part is up to Mother Nature, and in the lap of the gods. High germination, vigorous growth, happy seedlings, happy Papsom!"

"And happy Morwood," said Nadeen.

"Yep. So far so good."

Nadeen had excused herself to finish home chores, leaving Lorna and Tash to tidy up and faff about in the greenhouse which had grown steamy, the glass fogged with condensation.

Tash took a break from sweeping up remnant soil to lean on the broom, and looked down at Lorna collecting debris with a brush and pan. "How are things going between you two?"

"Steady as she goes, as they say. Come on, then. What do you think of her?"

"Not quite what I expected."

"What *did* you expect?"

"Someone more obvious. More high maintenance."

Lorna chuckled. "As if I'd be in that! I'm too old for dramas. Any of which, so far, are on the outside looking in. Not between us, thankfully."

"Yeah, nah. There must be something wrong with her. Nobody's perfect."

"She has her insecurities, but then so do I. The age difference, for one. I expect to cop some flak."

Tash snorted. "Oh, please. Folks are so fixated on the girl-on-girl action that they won't even notice."

"You think? If it helps, her father sounds like a tosser. A right pain in the arse." Lorna emptied the pan into a soil bin. "The controlling, disapproving type."

"Sounds like my father-in-law. A woman's place is in the home, preferably on her back."

"Eww! Is he trying to be funny?"

"Oh, yeah. He thinks he's hilarious. Old blokes are like that. And they hate changing their minds. Tim gets horribly embarrassed and skulks off, pretends the old bugger isn't his father." Tash propped the broom in a corner out of the way. "I can see you're comfortable with each other and she could be a keeper. Whatever makes you happy, my friend."

# CHAPTER THIRTY-SIX

Nadeen hadn't emptied the letterbox for a few days. She took the wad of envelopes inside and stopped to attend to the answering machine's blinking red light.

"Hi, Nadeen, it's Jodie. You should have received the invitation by now. Any questions, call me at work. I'm here until six most days."

Curiosity piqued and on her way to the kitchen, she shuffled through the envelopes, stopped at an ornate handwritten envelope. With the kettle on to boil, she sliced the envelope open with a paring knife. An embossed card announced that her father and Jodie were getting married by a celebrant at an address in City Beach. And she was invited. With partner.

"For the love of—?" She had to sit down and stare at it. What the hell did they think they were doing? They didn't actually want her there, obviously. A cruel joke. Temper rising, she bolted down the hall and rang Jodie's work number.

Two days later, Nadeen walked into the foyer of the upmarket leisure centre in Northbridge where Jodie worked. Her father's intended had her at a disadvantage because Jodie knew what she looked like, while the only thing Nadeen knew for sure was that the woman would have to look good in Lycra. And she did.

With a white towel slung around her neck, a square-shouldered, pleasant-looking, fairish woman in a shiny pink leotard over blue leggings came toward her, water bottle in hand.

"Hi, Nadeen. Good of you to meet me here." With a brief handshake, Jodie said, "I've just finished teaching a circuit class. Let's find a quiet spot for a chat, eh?"

On a black vinyl couch surrounded by scattered black ottomans, they perched uncomfortably.

Nadeen said, "Again, my apologies for getting the wrong end of the stick. But I really did want to meet you in person before the occasion. What's the date again?'

"Sunday the sixth of October." Jodie lifted her dark-blond ponytail and towelled the back of her neck. "Would you be able to come?"

"Yes, but I need to be a hundred percent confident that it's appropriate. I'm sure you understand. Things could be way too volatile otherwise."

"Of course. We've discussed the situation. He knows all about it, no surprises."

"Okay, but let's be very clear. Does he want me there?"

"You know him. And I've come to know that he's absolutely hopeless at apologies." Jodie leaned forward, rubbing her hands, and caught Nadeen's eye. "He knows he's in the doghouse with you because he went off at the mouth. And we all know he has much to be proud of in life, but he's also proud to the point of it being a fault. I don't think he's ever going to change, do you?"

In silence, Nadeen held Jodie's pale-blue eyes and shook her head.

"He wants you there. Definitely. With partner." Jodie grinned wryly. "Just quietly, he's dying to meet her."

Nadeen had to smile. "I haven't mentioned it. Yet. Since you think it's a good idea and everything is out in the open, I appreciate the invitation. Promise I'll be there." Nadeen stood up and held out a hand. "Nice to meet you at last. And I'll let you know if Lorna agrees to come."

Jodie clasped Nadeen's hand in both of hers. "Just to be clear, *I* want you there, too. With your partner." To Nadeen's surprise, she leaned in and gave her a quick peck. "You're about to become my stepdaughter!"

They both guffawed. Nadeen backed away with an easy smile and a quick wave, and took her leave.

* * *

With her cheek resting just above Lorna's hip, only a neighbour's lawnmower over the fence broke the Sunday morning's silence. An idle hand ran fingers through her hair and teased an ear.

"Hey, beautiful. Come talk to me. What's going on?"

Nadeen eased herself up the bed and curled into Lorna, one arm draped across her waist. "I've got a proposition for you. How would you like to trip the light fantastic in public? With me as your dance partner."

Eyes narrowed, Lorna said, "I haven't danced with anyone since forever ago."

"You could wear a frock."

"A frock? I haven't worn one of those since Cormack's funeral." Lorna turned to get a better view of Nadeen's expression. "What are you up to?"

Nadeen arched her brow. "My father is getting married. And we're invited."

"No! Really? This could be interesting." Lorna sat up and bolstered herself with pillows. "Nah, you're just pulling my leg. Come on, prove it."

Grinning, Nadeen hopped out of bed, opened a dressing table drawer and passed the stiff card to a sceptical Lorna. She read it, turned it over, read it again. "Right. Do we have to?"

"I've talked to Jodie and agreed to go. You don't have to. Totally optional, my lovely. No questions asked."

Lorna took a deep breath and exhaled heavily. "It is putting us out there, isn't it. And, by the look of that address, at a private residence in City Beach. Very flash. A bit pretentious for us Toodyay folks. Is that their place?"

"Nope. They've got an apartment in Cottesloe. Must belong to someone he knows. I'm not familiar with many of his friends."

"Uh-huh. Why did you bring up dancing?"

Pillows plumped behind her, Nadeen said, "Because my father loves ballroom. He and my mother used to go out dancing whenever they could. And I had to learn as a teen, like it or not. I guarantee there will be dancing. That said, it's not compulsory. I was just winding you up." She smiled shyly. "It could be fun or it could be excruciating. But I've committed myself to doing the daughterly thing by making an appearance, which is all Jodie asked of me. She wants you there, too. Have a think about it, eh?"

"All right. I'll run it past Tash who's better at these special occasions than me." Lorna folded her arms. "How good a dancer are you?"

"Passable. I can manage a decent waltz or foxtrot. Could even rustle up a cha-cha, if I had to. But I'm not too good at leading."

"Well, *I* am. In fact, I used to drive Cory mad. But he got to lead at everything else. Just not on the dance floor. Funnily enough, few noticed. Those who did said, 'there goes Mrs Chidlow again, leading her husband in a merry dance.' He got some sympathy, but it was largely a private joke between us." Lorna was silent for a while. "He was a good man."

"Would he and I have got along?"

"I'd say so. If I think about it, you're rather alike in character. How lucky am I?" She squeezed Nadeen's hand. "I'm so glad you're in my life. Especially since it's thousands of years overdue, allegedly. Fate, and all that."

"You're such an incurable romantic."

"You've said that before. Is it a problem?"

"No! God, no. I'm just trying to get used to it. So many people think it's cool to be cynical and very uncool to be romantic. I *want* to get used to it. Just quietly, I thank my lucky stars. Some days,

I'm just holding my breath in case it all crashes down. Enjoying it while I can."

Mute, Lorna pulled Nadeen into the tightest possible hug. Over the fence, the lawnmower fell silent. Almost quiet enough to hear two hearts beating in time.

# CHAPTER THIRTY-SEVEN

Tash draped the grey shift dress across Lorna's chest. "It's definitely a warm dove grey rather than a cool grey. Suits your colouring."

"I look like a corpse in black."

"Know what you mean. Most of us redheads can't wear it either." Tash rehung the dress and slid hangers along the rod. "You really don't have much to choose from, do you?"

"Apart from that dress and a jacket that I wore to Cory's funeral. After that, I couldn't see the point in keeping things I wouldn't have the occasion to wear again. It all went to the CWA opportunity shop." Lorna massaged her left arm. The plaster cast had been removed earlier in the day and it felt very strange to be able to move freely. "Besides, it was all out of fashion. And I couldn't see myself dating again."

Tash slid the wardrobe door shut and sat at the end of the bed. "Most women who say they have nothing to wear always have something. You? That little grey dress is it. This is an emergency."

"Hang on, Tash. I'm far from sure that I want to go to this do. Nadeen's perfectly capable of getting through whatever rigmarole is involved by herself."

"What did she say about you going?"

"That it was entirely up to me. No pressure."

Tash stood up and put an arm around Lorna's shoulders. "Let's go make a cuppa, eh? This needs sustenance."

Back in the kitchen, they found Mel munching an apple and flicking through a soapie magazine. She asked, "What's the verdict?"

"Your mother's in two minds about the wedding." Tash filled the kettle and put it on to boil. "Come on, Lorna. How do you *really* feel about it?"

"Really?" Lorna pulled out a chair and got comfortable. "Daunted. Very daunted. Fact is, I don't know any of those people, apart from Nadeen. Or what's expected at that social level. I don't want to make a fool of myself, or her."

"How likely is that, Mum?" piped up Mel. "They're no different from us. Just be yourself."

"Yet it's way outside your comfort zone," said Tash. "Those are the negatives. Any positives?"

Lorna looked askance. "I'm scrambling to think of one."

"Hobnobbing with the well-to-do," said Mel. "Dressing up. Free cocktails."

Tash winked at Mel. "All of the above. Except there's more to it than that. It's making a statement in front of a whole heap of strangers—you turning up on a woman's arm. Hell, I admit *I'd* be intimidated. If you don't go, no one will blame you, least of all Nadeen."

Steely-eyed, Lorna returned Tash's gaze. "In a nutshell, you're quite right. It's a challenge to put my money where my mouth is. And I'm not sure I'm up for it."

"There are no guarantees, apart from you arriving and leaving with Nadeen. You have each other. And it sounds like at least Jodie's on your side. Not to mention the spirit of Toodyay folks who will be barracking for you in absentia, because if you go, the whole town will be talking about this in no time at all. Word will get around."

Doubtfully, Lorna said, "You really think it's that big a deal?"

"Of course. You belong to Toodyay. Those people had better be nice to you. Or pay the price!" They both smirked.

"I don't know," said Lorna. "Let me think about it. No hurry, as yet."

"Fair enough. But if you change your mind, we could go frock shopping in the big smoke. One of the city department stores must have something that suits. In the meantime, I might make a few phone calls to ladies of a similar size and shape to you and ask what they've got hanging around that might be suitable. What do you think?"

"Sure. It's a special occasion item that I may never wear again."

"My thoughts, exactly. Give me some hints. What do you like?"

"Well, I've always preferred a simple shift, like that grey dress. It's a classic. You know the sort. A sleeveless number with a fairly high neck, semifitted for some shape, with a skirt more flared than that one, maybe, because it would be better for dancing. In a plain colour, nothing too leery. Not too long or too short."

"How short?"

"Just below the knee, maybe? I could wear a court shoe or a heeled sandal. Depends on the weather in October."

"Getting the picture. And we could get lucky," said Tash. 'Now, what happened to that cuppa? A soul could die of thirst around here."

At the front door, Lorna said, "Thanks for putting the word out for an outfit for me. I appreciate it. And thanks for listening."

"No worries. It's just in case. Whatever you decide, it's not an easy call. From what you've said, Jodie is trying to pour water on the burning bridge between Nadeen and her father. Maybe she thinks you being there will help?"

"I doubt that. Truth be known, he's the one who worries me the most. That he won't like me."

"Face it, Lorna. He doesn't seem to like his own daughter. Why would he like you?"

Lorna shook her head. "Best to have no expectations, eh? And most of the other people I'll probably never see again. No big deal. I may just have to do this, with no one holding my hand."

"Hey, that's not true. Nadeen will be. But maybe she needs you to hold hers just as much as you need her to hold yours? You're in this together and stronger as a couple. Remember that, old friend. You two are an item. It's up to you to make sure people get that, loud and clear."

"Hadn't thought of that. Good point." Lorna gave Tash a quick hug. "I'll think on it."

Laundry basket under one arm, Lorna had just come in the back door with the dry washing. The phone was ringing. She dropped the basket and jogged for it.

"Lorna? It's Felicity from the Northam branch. How are you?"

"Hello, Felicity. It's been a while between beers, hasn't it?"

"I'll say. I half expected you at that last meeting when Beth got her comeuppance."

"Pardon? I didn't think me being there would help matters. And Tash said it was a nonevent."

After a short silence, Felicity said, "Not quite how I remember it. Listen, Natasha phoned me about a dress for this wedding you're going to. Paula, my youngest, has moved to the city because she's going to uni. And there's one dress she doesn't want anymore that might suit you. It's only been worn once. She says it's too formal for the crowd she's hanging out with now."

"Kind of you. What's Paula doing at uni? I only ask because Melanie is looking at her options for next year."

"Environmental science at UWA Crawley campus. She loves it."

"Thanks, I'll mention it to Mel. Look, I haven't yet decided if I'm going. And I don't want to waste your time while it's up in the air. I'm just not sure about the whole thing."

"No problem," said Felicity. "If you don't mind me asking, what aren't you sure about?"

"Oh. Well. You can guess, can't you? I'd be very self-conscious."

"That's understandable, at least for the first five minutes. Then all the gawkers will get bored. And if you're wearing a great dress and look a million bucks, that will make them feel completely clueless."

Lorna giggled. "You have a way with words. Know anyone with that great dress?"

"I do, actually. Imagine a champagne-gold, matt-satin fabric, sleeveless fitted dress with a boat neck and fullish skirt. What size shoe are you?"

"Eight to eight and a half. Why?"

"Matching shoes await you. However, Paula must be taller than you, so you might have to take it up. And your bust might be a bit of a squeeze. Only one way to find out!"

"You're a hoot, Felicity. It sounds absolutely divine. I will get back to you, no matter what. Thank you so much for your thoughtfulness. You're a twenty-four-carat friend."

# CHAPTER THIRTY-EIGHT

Nadeen had an early dinner and drove over to Morwood where Lorna and Mel were just cleaning up after their meal. Lorna shooed Mel to her room to finish her homework and revise for a maths test. With the dishwasher suffering from an unknown fault and awaiting the repairman, Nadeen took to washing up. Lorna started drying as she related her conversation with Felicity.

"The dress she described sounds perfect, but I still don't know, honey-babe. What would you wear, if we went?"

"It depends," said Nadeen. "My father is used to how I usually present myself and that would be easiest for me. But you may not be comfortable with that. If I go alone, it doesn't matter. I'll just go as me. If I'm with you, something else might be better."

Lorna slid dried plates into an overhead cupboard and grabbed a bunch of damp cutlery with her tea towel. "Okay. Say you're going alone. What are you wearing?"

"A white pirate blouse over fitting black pants and Cuban-heeled ankle boots. More critically, I'll apply makeup to give me very Egyptian eyes, which I know will make my father smile. Also,

I'll wear a pair of Eye of Horus silver cuff bracelets that he had made in Egypt and gave me for my twenty-first birthday. And my Eye of Horus necklace. Yes, a bit over the top, but I'm dressing for him. It's his wedding."

"Right. You're in black and white and I'm in gold. Doesn't sound too bad, if you say it fast."

Nadeen pulled the plug in the sink. "You might want to up the bling for yourself. Necklace, rings, bracelets. Whatever. Or I can wear something else. Although I'd draw the line at matchy-matchy outfits, like 1980s ice skaters. The thing is, we have very different hair colour and complexions. What do you think?"

"Honestly? I think that combo on you sounds as sexy as all hell. But I'd like a preview, just to see. Assuming Felicity's dress is suitable, of course."

"And if it is?"

"I might be talking myself into this madness. Let me dash over to Northam and try it on. Dear Felicity will tell me bluntly if it's a goer or not." Lorna held out a hand. "Come into the den, babe. I could go a cuddle."

Nadeen took her hand and followed along to the low couch where they snuggled up.

Lorna barely whispered against an ear, "I ache for you. Every day. I miss you, long for your arms, your touch. The scent of you. Your mouthwatering desire. Your pulse against my fingers, my mouth. Your hot breath in my ear. Your heart hammering against mine. Your fierce strength. Your sweet gentleness. Know this—I love you, Nadeen Quin. Forever us."

Nadeen kissed her thoroughly and whispered, "Right now, I want you. More than I thought humanly possible. You really shouldn't say such things when I have to go home alone."

"Just sharing, babe. Wouldn't want you to think I don't appreciate you." Teasing and appeased, Lorna murmured, "Fact is, you'll just have to save yourself for Sunday, as will I. Anticipation is half the fun. Meanwhile, the other fun part is we're going to have to practise dancing together. Convincingly. Now, there's a challenge."

"Oh, I don't know…it'll be a blast. Any excuse to have you in my arms."

Nicholas and Felicity Heddon lived in a rambling country house in Northam that had been extended in various directions to cater for their larger-than-planned family. At the front door, Felicity ushered Lorna in and led her through a maze of corridors to an unoccupied south-facing bedroom.

"This was Paula's room," said Felicity, smiling ruefully. "She sometimes comes home for weekends but never often enough. I tell you, enjoy Melanie while you can."

"I do," said Lorna. "I love her to bits. I'm going to miss her like crazy when she leaves home."

Felicity slid back the wardrobe door and unhooked a hangar. "Come over here to the mirror." She held the dress in front of Lorna's figure, poised in reflection. They both fell silent.

Lorna pinched the dress at the waist and held it against her. "It's pretty close. Shall I try it on?"

"Please do." Felicity unzipped the back and took it off the hanger as Lorna stripped down to her underwear. Lorna put her hands up and Felicity slipped it over her head. Lorna wriggled and Felicity stepped behind her, held the waist while Lorna tugged and smoothed the fabric into position.

"I'll just zip you up slowly, see how we go," said Felicity. "Oh-kay…snug around the bust, but the hips and waist are fine. Paula is a bit up-and-down, with narrow hips and not much waist." She looked over Lorna's shoulder at her reflection. "I think you can get away with it."

Lorna smoothed the skirt out and half-twirled on the spot. "It's a gorgeous fabric that drapes beautifully. Very expensive."

"I'll say. I had it made for her to a pattern I chose. And my kind daughter humoured me by wearing it, just the once. It's a timeless classic that's worlds away from the trendy little number she would have preferred. Not that she said as much, but us mothers work it out, don't we? Eventually."

Lorna caught Felicity's poignant look in the mirror. "It's like that, isn't it? The joys and sorrows of parenting." She turned to look at the back of the dress in the mirror. "Fits well, but I'll need a more supportive bra to look my best. What do you think?"

Felicity beamed. "Could have been made for you. If you don't mind me saying, you look really good in it. This relationship has put a fresh spring in your step, I reckon. In fact, some might say you're positively radiant."

"Aw, thank you. But that's a bit of a stretch." Lorna patted warming cheeks.

"Is it?" Felicity twinkled at her reflection and leaned into the wardrobe to pick up a pair of plain, burnished court shoes. "While we're on a roll, try these."

Lorna slipped off her wedges and wriggled into the shoes. "They'll do just fine. I'm sure I can dance in them. Let's give it a go, eh?"

Felicity unzipped her, lifted the dress up and free of her body and patted her shoulders. "I'm delighted beyond words. Just thrilled to be part of what you're doing. You and Nadeen."

Getting dressed again, Lorna said, "How do you mean?"

"Two of my five kids are gay. You may not understand just how important it is for our young ones to have role models. To see other same-sex couples visible in the community. You two are a breath of fresh air and more well-known than you might care to be. But I for one, as a parent, am so glad you're around." She shook her head. "Sorry. I sound like I'm making a big deal of it. But it is a big deal on a local level."

"It's all right." Lorna slipped on her wedges. "I'm humbled by what you've said, because I hardly think of myself as a poster child for same-sex folks. It's all very new to me."

"But everybody knows you, Lorna. Because of your work with the CWA. You're very country—normal and relatable. And now you're something more layered, shall we say?"

"I can assure you that where I find myself was never even remotely a plan," said Lorna. "But I do understand about your kids. Or at least I'm beginning to. A whole lot better than I did once upon a time. Still, I hope all the interest dies down for the sake of our privacy. The irony is Nadeen planned to ease herself into the Toodyay community and discreetly fly under the radar while enjoying a quiet life. You have to laugh, don't you?"

"I'm glad we can. Nick and I talked about you and wondered how many other couples might be in the area, keeping a low profile. My kids have copped a heap of very hurtful abuse."

"Hate to say it, but I'm not surprised. Melanie has told me a story or two. She said most kids seem to leave town as soon as they can and head for the city where there's more acceptance. The problem there is a lack of family support, potential homelessness, plus the danger of drug, alcohol and mental health problems. It's such a shame, because rural communities like ours lose out on all those talented young ones."

"And it's all so unnecessary." Felicity sighed heavily.

Lorna reached over and touched Felicity's forearm. "I'm very sorry people are so determinedly one-eyed. To be honest, I have quite the trepidation about meeting Nadeen's father. He still doesn't accept her. Really, the only reason we're going is because his bride-to-be wants to pour oil on troubled waters. Do you know him?"

"You mean Felix? Yes, of course. He and Nick go way back. He's perfectly charming when he wants to be. But a dyed-in-the-wool old-school hard arse about what he calls 'politically correct' nonsense. Like homosexuality."

"Why is he so hung up about it? She's his daughter, for pity's sake. What is his problem?"

Felicity looked doubtful. "Well. A little bird who shall remain nameless told me some time ago that he feels robbed. What sticks in his craw is the absence of grandchildren. He has only one child. A girl. And a gay girl, to boot. He blames and resents Nadeen for that. Big time."

"Oh, no." Lorna grimaced. "There's no fixing *that* problem. Oddly, she hasn't mentioned it as an issue at all. Maybe he hasn't said as much?"

"Blokes can be funny like that. They skirt around the real issue because it hurts. And moan about everything else except the one thing that cuts them to the core. I suggest you tread carefully, even keep it to yourself." Felicity expertly rolled up the dress. "Listen, please go ahead and take the dress and shoes with you now. If you change your mind, no problem."

"Felicity, it's near perfect. Maybe a little long, but that I can adjust myself. I can't thank you enough. And do thank Paula for me, please? Tell her it's gone to a good home!"

# CHAPTER THIRTY-NINE

Handpiece clapped to her ear, Nadeen said, "What are you up to?"

"Plaiting," said Lorna. "I'm holed up in the den with a mug of hot chocolate and a roaring fire. Not that it's cold. Just makes me feel better when it's bucketing down outside."

"What are you making?"

"A new belt for Tash's son, Mikey. He's outgrown the one I made for him a few years ago. Kids these days seem to grow like wildfire."

"Well, I have to go down to Freo again for a pickup on Monday. It occurred to me that you might like to come with me. We could do lunch or something."

"This *is* a surprise," said Lorna. "Things are fairly quiet at the moment. Have to say, I've heard worse ideas for this miserable weather."

"Okay. As a plus, there's an Aussie film called *Love and Other Catastrophes* playing at the Luna cinema which might be fun. I could buy you a choc top. We could walk along the waterfront. Look at the boats. Inhale the fresh sea air. Am I selling it to you?"

"You know what this sounds like, don't you? A date. Are you trying to chat me up?"

Nadeen hooted. "Sprung. We've not had one of those. A date, that is."

"Still haven't convinced me," said Lorna. "It could lead to all sorts of unmentionable goings-on. What's a girl to do?"

"Say yes and I'll pick you up at ten o'clock on Monday."

"Oh, have it your way. Yes, it's a date. And thank you, my gorgeous hunk of womanhood."

* * *

Tentatively, Lorna said, "May I ask you a very personal question?"

At the van's wheel, Nadeen risked a quick glance at her passenger. "If it's something you really want to know. Ask away."

"Did you ever want children?"

"That's a curly one. I did think about it in my early twenties, then again when I got together with Greer. We discussed it and decided it wasn't a good idea. To put that in a context, it was a time when society preferred we didn't exist, let alone thought we'd make suitable parents. Has it changed that much since, I ask myself?" Raising an eyebrow, she glanced at Lorna. "Also, any child would have had to run the gauntlet of being bullied or ostracised because of us. And assumed to be somehow guilty by association. Not to mention that Greer's parents would have disapproved, as would mine. My mother would have been outraged and gone off the deep end completely. She could be persistently vicious, starting yet more shouting matches. In other words, there would have been zero support from either society or family."

Lorna studied her. "Good grief. That's very off-putting."

"Yep. It really wasn't worth the protracted angst. Those women with a husband and kids and who came out later in life, stood to lose custody. Again, the unsuitable parent bias. It happened all too often, which was extremely traumatising for both mother and kids. One read about such things in the papers and saw it on film. It's just how it was, and continues to be, albeit to a lesser extent than twenty years ago. Anyway, does that tell you everything you wanted to know?"

"Yes, thank you." Lorna grasped Nadeen's free left hand and kissed the back of it. "So sorry, babe. It can be a tough old world."

"Ain't that the truth? Having said all that, I know of some couples who did have kids, usually by way of a gay friend as sperm donor. How that worked out for everyone, I don't know because we lost contact over time. The thing is, no matter how much kids might be loved by their parents, they need to feel 'normal' and fit in." Nadeen slowed for traffic lights in the distance. "Apologies, my lovely. I'll get off my soapbox before you regret ever asking me."

"No, no, it's okay. I guess I needed to hear it. I was just wondering."

Nadeen cruised behind traffic that was beginning to pick up speed with a green light ahead. "As a matter of interest, if I haven't mentioned it of late, I adore you."

"Duly noted." Lorna's luminous smile made Nadeen tighten her grip on the steering wheel because swooning and swerving could have proved fatal.

* * *

Careful not to make too much noise, Lorna unwrapped her choc top and whispered, "Why are there just a few white-haired wrinklies and us?"

Nadeen leaned over. "Because only retirees and the less gainfully employed watch films during the day. Even then, it's only because it's a warm and comfortable place out of the rain."

The prefilm ads had just finished rolling. As the main feature started, Lorna bit into the chocolate coating and savoured the ice-cold sweetness. Lively music and madcap action grabbed her attention, the ice cream gone in no time.

In the cosy darkness, Nadeen dropped a hand in Lorna's lap. She glanced down and took it in both hands, shifting to more easily let it rest there, comfortably warm. The film was quirky and engaging with awkward university students displaying endearingly flawed characters. She couldn't help but get involved, even if some scenes were very silly. It made her smile and laugh out loud in places. Good Aussie self-deprecating humour.

Somewhere in the depths of the film, Lorna grew unnervingly aware of where she found herself—sitting in a cinema holding hands with this woman she loved beyond reason yet didn't know existed less than a year ago. Not meaning to, she squeezed Nadeen's nesting hand.

Nadeen's dark eyes gleamed with light from the big screen, and she turned to Lorna. She looked at her with such naked affection that Lorna's heart plummeted, then soared. Helplessly, she just shook her head. Nadeen's brows knitted fleetingly, then she smiled and went back to watching the action.


Well rugged up in hooded jackets, they each nibbled the remains of a shawarma from a busy Lebanese takeaway on Marine Parade. The rain had stopped, but it was far from warm.

Lorna said, "Did you know there was a female couple in that film?"

"Yep. I read a review that made it sound a bit different and possibly amusing. Typical Luna arthouse fare. Did you enjoy it?"

"Oh, it didn't take itself too seriously. Very entertaining and the acting was surprisingly good."

Shawarma wrapping in hand, Nadeen stopped at a street waste bin. "Have you had enough of that?" Lorna passed the remains of her wrap and both were tossed.

"I haven't done anything like this since I don't know when," said Lorna, tucking her hand through Nadeen's arm. "The sea smells amazing. A world away from Morwood. I guess we should be getting back, eh?"

"Let's enjoy a few more minutes." Nadeen put her other hand over Lorna's and steered them toward the beach. "A quick gawk at the Indian Ocean is a must. Then we'll be on our way."

At the turnoff onto Toodyay Road, Lorna asked, "What about your mother?"

"What about her?"

"I mean, where is she and what sort of life is she having without your father."

"Last I heard from Dad, Carla's camping with friends in Cairo and searching for tombs in Thebes, or thereabouts. It's all second- or third-hand information, I'm afraid. In fact, she could be anywhere. But she is an archaeologist and Egypt is a passion. That's where they met and how they ended up together. A mutual obsession with all things Egyptian. If anything, she's crazier about the place than he is. Going back and living there was always her dream, not his. Now she's living the dream."

"Is she in a relationship?"

"No idea." Now off the highway, Nadeen reduced speed. "A lack of interest in what she gets up to is one of the few things Dad and I are in total agreement about."

"Does she work by herself?"

"Oh, no. Definitely not. She has a knack for persuading entrepreneurs with more money than sense to sponsor digs with the promise of unearthing untold fame and fortune. Works for her."

"It's sounds like you don't approve of her."

Nadeen snorted. "That's ironic, given what she thinks of me. I suppose I don't. It's always mystified me how archaeologists justify digging up people who died thousands of years ago purely to steal their possessions and desecrate their bodies. Then they put everything on display and sell tickets. Can you imagine the outcry if they started doing that in the Old Sydney Burial Ground?"

"The what? Never heard of it."

"It's Sydney's oldest cemetery that houses the very first deceased colonials. It's under Sydney Town Hall. Imagine them digging up coffins, rummaging about inside, looting clothes and jewellery, poking about in corpses. All in the name of what... curiosity? Selling tickets? The public would protest mightily, but no one makes a murmur about disturbed ancient Egyptians. I don't see the difference, myself. It's digging up the dead and thereby desecrating each person's sacred interment. By whose authority, do they dig? How insultingly entitled is the whole circus?"

"I guess you have a very good point. Can't say I ever had reason to think about it that hard," said Lorna.

"That's okay. Call me crazy…you wouldn't be the first. Maybe it's because, somewhere in the back of my skull, I sense that a body that once was mine, thousands of years ago, is buried in Egypt where it deserves to be left alone to crumble into dust undisturbed. Maybe yours is, too. All too often, my life has been turned into a sideshow. I'd hate for her, that earlier version of me, to undergo similar disrespect. I just wish people would leave the dead alone."

"It must seem like a cruel twist of fate to be the daughter of an archaeologist."

"Doesn't it? Sorry, ignore me. I may be merely perverse because it's my mother's sole reason for being." Ahead, the road began to wind through deepening valleys that signalled the Avon River was close. "We'll be home soon." They continued in silence for a few minutes.

Lorna said, "This year is going so fast, I can't believe your father's wedding is only six weeks away. I told Melanie that we were thinking of scrubbing up our dancing for it. She mentioned her boyfriend's mother might be able to give us some private coaching. Apparently, she used to teach ballroom in the States."

"Have you met whatshisname?"

"Conrad. With a surname something like Bettlemans. I haven't met him yet."

"Sounds very American."

"Sure does. I'm not sure how serious those two are. Early days. Anyway, what do you think of us having a few lessons?"

"Well, I'm very rusty," said Nadeen. "Could be good. If she doesn't mind coaching a same-sex couple."

"I know it's an issue. We're going to mess with people's heads, anyway. Me in a frock leading and you in pants following. It will be entertaining, won't it?"

Nadeen grinned at her and slowed the van right down for the turn into Morwood's driveway. "You bet. Let's have fun with it."

She peered through the windscreen. "Hello. Looks like you've got company."

"That's Murray from Papsom. What's he doing here?"

Nadeen swung the van around in a semicircle to bring Lorna's side toward the house. Lorna leaned across and gave Nadeen a quick peck and said, "See you soon." Nadeen circled back and drove away down the driveway. In the rear-vision mirror, a man got out of a station wagon and tipped his hat at Lorna. Had he seen that kiss?

# CHAPTER FORTY

"Hi, Murray. How are things?" Lorna unlocked the front door, a precaution she'd felt necessary only since the safe stealing incident. "Come in. Make yourself at home."

Unsmiling, he took his hat off and followed her. "I couldn't raise you on the blower, so I thought I'd drop in with some special news that you ought to hear. When you didn't answer the door, I was just about to leave. Saw you coming with your lady friend."

Lorna caught his flinty stare. "I'll put the kettle on."

"Thanks, but I won't stay." He hovered like a redundant house guest.

She filled the kettle and turned it on to boil. "As you wish. Take a seat and I'll be with you in a minute."

Down the hall in the bathroom, she washed her hands, wary of Murray's unexpected presence. What had brought him here? She hurried back to the kitchen and pulled out a chair. "What's this news you have for me?"

Murray leaned elbows on the table and looked at her over laced fingers. "You remember the Adelaide Hills mob went bust?

GreenRWe Limited, that big Victorian nursery, *did* buy them out in a fire sale. In the process of their due diligence, they discovered the Adelaide Hills's financial records had been fudged. They'd been in dire financial straits for quite some time. They also found blowout expenses and substantial payments to nonexistent contractors. It seems that, as a competitor, you were a thorn in their side. You can bet those two clowns were sent in to nick your seeding protocol and slow down production. They must have decided to help themselves to your safe while they were at it."

"Sounds like a raw deal. I hope the Victorians didn't pay too much."

"Just a commercial property and equipment. There was no goodwill to speak of."

"These things happen." Lorna made as if to get up. "Is that it?"

With a smug smile, he said, "It gets better. GreenRWe want to buy you out. That is, they want to take over supplying Papsom with seedlings using the Adelaide Hills Nursery's location and equipment, for now, with a plan to set up a nursery like yours locally so they can do what you do."

"This is confusing. Do they want my equipment, or what?"

"They want your secrets, Lorna. They want to know exactly what you do to produce superior seedlings so they can replicate that process anywhere. And they're willing to pay top dollar for your knowledge and expertise. Providing, of course, that you cease production."

Lorna sniffed, took to chuckling mirthlessly. "I bet. Tell them they're wasting my time."

"I think we're talking big money, here," Murray cautioned. "You might want to seriously consider your future in this business. As a matter of interest, do you have a patent?"

She sat back and studied him. "It's an ancient process. Simple, but little known. Not patentable, as far as I'm aware. What do they call 'big money'?"

"They haven't said, but they very much want you to sell to them. Me talking to you is only a fishing expedition because I advised them it's your passion and your primary income. And that their chances were slim. I'm merely asking the question."

"I see. What does Papsom think of all this?"

"It's business." He shrugged and shook his head. "Papsom has limited loyalty to their suppliers. It can't afford to have. Whoever can supply the best product at the best price consistently will win the order. It's just how it is." He pushed back the chair and stood up. "Give it some thought. Better go."

"I'll see you out."

On the front veranda, he said, "Will you at least consider meeting with them to discuss it?"

She nodded. "Of course, Murray. And you're quite right about me needing to consider my future. I'll think on it."

He touched her shoulder. "As a matter of fact, I'm very concerned for your future—positive a nasty rumour is just that. A rumour."

With a pasty smile, she stepped back into the house and held the door ajar. "Please do give my warmest regards to your wife." She shut the door on him, more certain than ever that he never passed on her regards to his wife. Never, ever.

From the kitchen, Lorna leaned into the hall and called out to Mel, "Dinner's on the table." She pulled up a chair.

"What's for dinner?"

"Veal schnitzel. While you're up, I forgot the water."

Mel filled two small glasses and put them on the table, sat herself down. "We haven't had this for a while."

"They don't often stock it. People seem to prefer precrumbed frozen mysteries in boxes, these days. I'd rather do it myself so I know what I'm eating."

"Bet it doesn't taste as good as this. Yummo."

In silence, they ate the greater part of the meal.

Mel said, "How was that film?"

"Quirky. Good fun." Lorna finished her plate and laid cutlery across it. "Murray was here when we got back. He had an unexpected proposition for me. From a Victorian nursery. They want to take over our seedling business."

"For real?" Mel sipped water. "Did you tell them where to go?"

Lorna smiled gently. "I was tempted. But I told Murray I'd think about it."

"Why, Mum? You love what you do."

"True. As is the fact that your mother isn't getting any younger. I think you were a ten-year-old when I started this game. Maybe it's time I did something else."

Mel stacked their plates and cutlery. "Like what?"

"Well, those peonies down the gully are calling to me. I'd love to produce *the* most marvellous blooms and send them to exotic places like Tokyo and Beijing. Asian people have great taste and will pay top dollar. But it's not all about the bucks. It's the pleasure of growing something so beautiful that grabs me. A new goal to aspire to. What do you think, my darling girl?"

"I dunno. Sounds like you've thought about it already. What does Nadeen think?"

"I will run it past her. But I want to know what you think, first. Seriously."

Scratching an ear, Mel leaned her elbows on the table. "Won't it take a big bunch of money to set up a flower business? And what's your age got to do with anything?"

"First off, handling the seedling trays is getting quite physically demanding and only likely to become more so with increased production. That's never-ending. Peony growing is in the ground and easily managed with machinery. Secondly, the Victorian nursery would compensate me with a lump sum. How much is moot. But you know I can drive a hard bargain when pushed. How does that grab you? Come on, my girl. Ask the obvious."

Crockery in hand, Mel rose, placed it in the sink and ran water to soak. With her back to her mother, she said, "Where does Nadeen fit into the picture?"

"Short answer, she doesn't have to. I can do it all myself."

Mel turned and sat down again. "Aren't you two serious?"

"She's got this theory." Lorna tented her hands. "Psychologists assert the first nine months are the honeymoon period. Best not to make any firm commitment until time's up. Plus, she said lesbians are notorious for cohabiting way too quickly. She knows more about that than I do, obviously. We both need to be comfortable with how things develop. But yes, we are serious."

"Glad to hear it." Across the table, she squeezed her mother's hand. "I think she's good for you. And you're kinda interested in the same things, y'know? Like growing things."

"Quite right. Did you know that gerberas make terrific cut flowers because they last for weeks? And they can flower twice a year. And sell well as potted plants in flower. You can see where I'm going with this, eh?"

"Yeah, a sideline for your peonies." Mel stood up and started stacking the dishwasher. "I'm sure she'll be up for it."

"I think so, too. I'm excited!"

After they'd tidied up, Mel was about to head back to her room to study when Lorna said, "When you next talk to Conrad, please ask him if I may phone his mother. Nadeen and I think a few dance lessons would be good."

"I'm sure she'd be fine with it."

"Maybe so, but I'd like to have a chat with her. I hate putting people on the spot so they feel they have no choice. It's only polite."

"Okay, will do." And Mel disappeared.

Lorna wiped down the frying pan and put it away. She would have liked to have taken Mel's word for it, but while Conrad might think all would be well, his mother was an unknown quantity. And after Murray's snide remark, she was a touch more wary of the unknown.

# CHAPTER FORTY-ONE

"Hi, Mrs Bettlemans. I'm Lorna, Melanie's mother. I believe Conrad mentioned to you that I was looking for refresher dancing lessons?"

"Hello, Lorna." The woman on the other end of the phone spoke with a twangy soft drawl. "Yes, he has. And my name is Estelle, but everyone calls me Stella. How can I help you?"

"Well, I'm just wondering how an American ended up in Western Australia. You're a long way from home, Stella."

"You bet. It's Conrad's father's fault. I was dancing at a nightclub in New York in 1972 when I met Laurence. He was a bass player in a jazz trio playing at the club. Swept me off my feet and took me home for a short visit to meet his parents." Stella laughed gaily. "Talk about a short visit. Twenty-four years later and we're still here."

"You must really like it," said Lorna. "Anyway, you may be aware that my partner is woman. Are you willing to give us a few lessons?"

"Oh, sweetheart, don't you worry none. I worked for years in the entertainment industry, which wouldn't exist without gay guys. Believe me, I've seen it all, and lost two sweet friends to that AIDS epidemic. If a couple of dames want to brush up a soft-shoe shuffle, it's fine with me. Happy to oblige."

"Wonderful. If you don't mind me saying, I love your rolling R's."

"I'm a New Yorker, sweetheart. And I'm happy where we live. But believe me, my accent is going nowhere!"

* * *

Barefoot and wearing the gold dress inside out, Lorna stood on the marri timber coffee table. A vintage wooden skirt marker was set at the preferred height, just below her knees. Mel knelt on the den's floor, folding up the hem to the right height and securing it with pins from a dish on the table.

"Turn, Mum."

Lorna rotated a little. "When are you going out?"

"Kelly's picking me up about five thirty. We'll meet the guys outside the Northam Hoyts cinema at six. Will you hand-sew this?"

"I think so. Felicity said the fabric could easily pull with machine stitching. I'll have to do my best invisible needlework, preferably in daylight. What time will you be back?"

"We're going to the YMCA dance after the movie. Turn again."

Lorna swivelled around and glanced down. "Are we there yet?"

"Just about. Yeah, that's it. Do a three-sixty while I check."

She shuffled around slowly, made a full turn. "How's it looking?"

"Pretty good, I reckon." Mel got to her feet and held out a hand to help Lorna step down from the table.

"Please unzip me, darling." She held up her arms as Mel carefully lifted the pinned dress off her. "Did you hear me ask what time you're coming home?" Dressing gown on, she sank to the couch. "Look at me, darling. Sit down."

Mel found the coat hanger, slipped it through the dress and draped it on a chair. Only when she sat did she met her mother's gaze.

"I don't need to know everything that's going on in your life, but I do know a thing or two about boys. And they're always in a hurry."

"Mum, I'm eighteen now."

Lorna held up her hands. "I know, I know. In my mind, you'll always be my little girl, even though you're a young woman. All I want to say is girls like you and Kelly face a mountain of pressure to get explicitly sexual, often well before you're ready. There's no harm in taking your time, despite what the guys may say about that. Moderate your alcohol intake, and don't be nagged into doing anything you may regret later."

Mel squeaked, "Conrad's not like that. He's very gentlemanly."

"Good!" said Lorna. "In that case, he'll have you home by midnight, won't he? If not, his mother will hear about it. And while Stella may be as sweet as apple pie to your face, if there's any trouble, there will be hell to pay from that very streetwise New Yorker. Guaranteed."

"All righty. I have to get ready." Mel got up and started for the door.

"Melanie! Believe it not, us old dragons are merely looking out for you. If you get any pushback, feel free to blame me. Say your mother laid down the law. No worries. I can take it."

Half out the door, Mel paused. "Got it." And set off down the hall.

Lorna jumped up, stuck her head out and bellowed, "And if things go pear-shaped, phone me. No matter how late. Okay?"

Striding away, Melanie had her fingers in her ears. "La, la, la… not listening! Whatever. Okay!"

Lorna grinned gleefully. Sometimes this lone parenting gig sucked, but she wouldn't miss it for the world.

# CHAPTER FORTY-TWO

Late Sunday morning, Lorna pulled into the Ellery Place driveway. "That's the last lesson done and dusted, but I haven't seen your outfit yet. Have you got time to do a quick show and tell?"

Nadeen said, "I've heaps to do, but I can spare a few moments. Come on in." She clambered out of the van and unlocked the front door. "I'm glad we got to learn the jive. Not too hard and a bunch of fun. Although I think you do all the work while I get to twirl about."

Lorna shut the door and followed her to the bedroom. "If you think it's not too tricky, we could swap roles middance, just to confuse ourselves."

Bella was asleep on the bed, no doubt missing her human. She raised her head, then stood, tail wagging. Nadeen picked her up, kissed an ear and put her on the floor from where she wandered out and into the hall.

From the wardrobe, Nadeen drew out a white blouse and black pants. Lorna sat on the edge of the bed while Nadeen undressed.

"You wear some really lovely lingerie."

"I *like* lovely lingerie. It makes me feel good. Say…we could go lingerie shopping. Showcase your assets in something that says, 'get it while it's hot.' How's that for togetherness?"

Lorna chuckled. "I'll be in that. When you're ready."

Nadeen put on the outfit. Getting into the pants was a wriggle, the blouse easily shucked on. Lorna stroked the white sleeve. "So soft. Is it pure silk?"

"A cotton and silk blend. Silk alone tends to drape and cling too much. This fabric holds its shape well. I'll wear my black boots that should be fine to dance in. And the pants are cotton elastin so I can move better than you might expect."

"Babe, they leave nothing to the imagination. And the plunging neckline on that blouse is going to be very distracting."

Hands on hips, Nadeen said, "That's the idea. It's a wedding, not a funeral." Smiling, she wriggled her eyebrows. "Will I do?"

"Oh, I think so." Lorna looked her up and down, swallowed. "You said you've got heaps of things to do right now. Might I be one of them?"

"Let's see. Since it's Sunday." Nadeen took a big step closer. "I'm sure I can…fit you in. But I'll need help getting out of these pants."

"Why am I not surprised?" Lorna unbuttoned and unzipped, lifted the blouse and blew a raspberry in Nadeen's navel. Nadeen wriggled and pushed Lorna back on the bed.

"Now you're in trouble."

"At last. Oh, yes."


They lay facing each other, at ease with a deepening intimacy. Nadeen lifted a shock of ash-blond hair from Lorna's forehead, exposing its widow's peak. Then she tapped her own lips.

"More kisses?" Lorna moved closer, the back of her fingers first brushing Nadeen's cheek, then the palm as she spread her fingers to clasp her head. A light kiss grew hotter and hungrier until Nadeen's arms tightened, allowing no space between them. Released, Lorna kissed her cheeks, eyebrows and eyes, gently, damply—thoroughly.

Dark eyes glittering fiercely, Nadeen said, "I love you. Forever us."

Lorna kissed her between the eyes, then buried her face in Nadeen's throat. "Forever us."

Silence pillowed them from things unimportant, at least for a time.

"Honey-babe? The wedding is only next weekend. We've cut it a bit fine. Are we good to go?"

Nadeen said, "Ready enough. In the scheme of things, it doesn't really matter. Let's do what we're comfortable doing. And if it's not, we won't. Simple."

"I like your style."

# CHAPTER FORTY-THREE

Late afternoon, the broad City Beach streets allowed Nadeen to park just around the corner. In passing, she had counted twelve cars, which might mean a similar number of couples—a very select invitation list for a celebrant wedding at a private house. She parked and unbuckled her seatbelt. Lorna didn't move.

"I'm not too sure about this. Sorry, babe. Just nerves."

Nadeen glanced up and down the street. "It's okay. We don't have to do this." She leaned back and fiddled with the rings she rarely wore—a fine silver ankh on her right middle finger and a heavy silver scarab beetle on her left. Freshly polished, they chimed perfectly with the ornate silver cuff bracelets inset with a turquoise cabochon Eye of Horus on each wrist. At her throat, hung the Eye of Horus silver pendant.

"Or we try to make it easier. I could walk in by myself and you follow a few minutes later."

"And who's that going to fool?"

"Just you." Nadeen put up her hands. "I'm not judging. I've done this many times. You haven't, and I get it. People will judge you if you walk in with me. At least initially. So what if they think something unsavoury? That's their problem. Don't make it yours."

Lorna grimaced. "Easier said than done."

"Perfectly true." Nadeen let out a soft sigh and peered out the windscreen. "My lovely, we've been invited. And by the look of things, my father and Jodie have invited only those they really want to be here. It's not a free-for-all." She swivelled in her seat. "I would be enormously proud to walk in with you at my side. Let's do this together, eh?"

"Well, you look stunning, dripping in silver. And that eye makeup is something else."

Nadeen grinned. "Just some shadow and a whole lot of eyeliner. And you look utterly gorgeous in that frock. I suggest we walk in there like we own the place. No guts, no glory."

Lorna's eyes narrowed to blades of steel. "I *am* letting them get to me, aren't I? What a wuss. And what a crying waste of Stella's lessons. Enough said. Let's go!" She jumped out of the van and met Nadeen, hand outstretched. They whizzed around the corner, hand in hand.

Too busy taking in the magnitude of the mansion, they were halfway up the driveway bordered by a riot of flowering colour before Nadeen ground to a sudden halt. "Will you look at these garden beds? They're all gerberas, going gangbusters. Wow, what a display. Someone's a gerbera fancier, that's for sure."

The massive front door opened and an elegantly dressed older woman smiled wickedly. "Nadeen Quin. And her lady friend." She showed them in and shook Nadeen's hand. "Delighted to see you again. And you must be Lorna. How do you do?"

Lorna beamed and shook her hand. "Very well, thanks."

Nadeen took a moment to recall where she had seen the woman before. The Gerbera Society. "Irma? Of course. Lorna, Irma kindly came and advised me about Uncle Garry's gerberas."

Irma purred, "Nice to be remembered. Come with me, ladies." She led them down a long wide hall. "Everyone is out in the garden awaiting any stragglers before the ceremony starts. As you know, it's champagne and canapes thereafter. Nothing too complicated.

Now, I must check the caterers have everything under control. I'll leave you to mingle."

They went to walk away. Irma called out, "Nadeen? Just to warn you that your father is bunny-in-the-headlights nervous. He's up the back with a bunch of fellas, including my husband, Errol. Best left well alone until after the ceremony."

"Sure thing. Where's Jodie?" said Nadeen.

"Upstairs making herself perfect. I suggest you find the women congregating in the wisteria arbour. Your safest bet."

Nadeen raised her eyebrows at Lorna, and they went looking. On the other side of an arch covered in climbing roses, they spotted a group of women milling about in groups by two rows of tables and chairs next to a large black-and-white tiled area, very much like a checkerboard. They introduced themselves to a smaller group dominated by a statuesque woman wearing a white robe over a long purple shift. With a broad face and a booming voice, she introduced herself as the celebrant.

Nadeen asked, "Where is the ceremony taking place?"

With a glance at her watch, the celebrant said, "At the end of the wisteria arbour. We're just waiting for Jodie and we'll all go up to assemble. Since it will only be a short service, it's a stand-up-and-watch affair. Hang about, here she comes."

The groups parted to let through Irma and a shyly smiling Jodie in a fitting sky-blue dress. They joined the celebrant and headed into the arbour.

Lorna whispered to Nadeen, "This is different."

"You can say that again. Very minimalist." In a corner at the end of the checkerboard floor stood a conspicuous jukebox plugged into a disappearing extension cord. It looked promising.

Up ahead, the celebrant had taken to a rostrum and faced the congregating crowd. Felix and Jodie stood side by side, backs to their guests. Nadeen took Lorna's hand and eased them through the crowd around to one side to see her father without him seeing her. He wore a double-breasted black jacket with a snow-white shirt and sky-blue tie, his dark hair neatly trimmed, as was his salt-and-pepper moustache. Even from a distance, his tanned hands were shaking. She pressed her own hands together and felt for him.

The celebrant spoke well—loud and clear. Felix and Jodie, not so much. A small aircraft flying low overhead at a crucial moment didn't help at all. But it didn't matter. The pair kissed and turned their relieved, dazzled faces toward the clapping and cheering crowd.

Three younger women surged forward to congratulate Jodie with hugs and air kisses, while the guys slapped Felix on the back, leering and laughing, everyone heading back toward the tables.

Nadeen stopped to read some of the jukebox's titles. "By the look of it, my father has had a hand in its playlist. This could be good."

One table had been converted into a temporary bar with a lineup of full champagne flutes. Waistcoated catering staff handed them out as people went past. Irma handed one to an older man and whispered in his ear. He took it and called out, "Listen up, everyone! Hey, you lot. Quieten down!" The murmuring crowd fell silent.

"My wife and I would like to thank you for coming to witness Felix and Jodie's nuptials. On this momentous occasion, let's make a toast to the happy couple." He raised the flute. "To Felix and Jodie!" The crowd repeated the sentiment, accompanied by clinking glasses. "Long may they live and love!" A chorus of "ayes" and "yeahs" rang out. Someone turned on the jukebox and Neil Diamond began a familiar song. Irma and Errol herded Felix and Jodie back into the house for the formal signing of the register.

Lorna said, "Are we there yet?"

"Heading that way," said Nadeen. "Let's see how long it takes for the women to find the perfect spot to sit and hover, while the men take up residence around the bar. Sheilas and blokes, take your corners. Don't you love Aussie get-togethers?"

"Let's go find a seat and schmooze with the girls."

Waitstaff appeared with trays of finger food and meandered through the throng. The very hungry swooped with gusto.

Lorna and Nadeen found a spot near the checkerboard. Nadeen said, "I always feel at a disadvantage at these things, simply because I can't bang on about my hubby and kids. If I'm lucky, I find a fellow gardener. So far, that's Irma, but she's busy playing the hostess with the mostest." A tray of food drifted past and she took a small quiche.

"It's tough when you don't know many of the guests," said Lorna. "Not a problem in Toodyay." A pair of highly polished men's dress shoes appeared in front of her. She looked up.

Felix was staring intently. He turned and kissed Nadeen on both cheeks, squeezed her shoulders. "Please introduce us."

"Sorry. May I introduce Lorna Chidlow? Lorna, this is my father, Felix."

Lorna stood up and copped a bolt of shock from Felix's dark eyes, the mirror image of Nadeen's. "A pleasure to meet you, Felix. We've both known of each other but not actually met for way too long. Congratulations. I'm honoured to be here on this special day."

Felix took her hand and pressed his lips lightly to her knuckles. "Thank you, and the pleasure is all mine." He batted eyelashes at her, as insanely long as Nadeen's. "Perhaps we can have a conversation later. But please excuse me. I must attend to my guests." He dropped his chin in a slight bow and stepped away, touched Nadeen's shoulder. "Talk soon."

He easily moved from person to person, couple to couple, group to group—courteous and engaging, in turn.

"Impressive," said Lorna. "He can certainly turn on the charm, can't he."

"Oh, yes. He's a past master." Nadeen glanced at her, batting her eyelashes.

Lorna smirked. "You didn't put on mascara, did you? Of course not. You don't need it. Neither does he."

Felix was waylaid by Errol whispering in his ear. Errol called out, "Hey, everyone. The bridal waltz is coming up, and the bride and groom would like you to join them on the dance floor." With its volume cranked up, the jukebox sent out a classic tune. Felix beckoned Jodie and they steadied themselves, then flowed into a waltz. The loitering crowd stepped back to give them room to move. Errol worked his way around, encouraging others to venture out. Couple after couple followed Felix and Jodie until the checkerboard was quite crowded.

Lorna jumped up and offered a hand to Nadeen. "Come on. Let's not miss out!" They managed to squeeze in and keep up. A change of tune brought another waltz and, after an awkward pause, they began again. Felix and Jodie had escaped to the sidelines where he took off his jacket and tie, loosened his collar, and returned with a laughing Jodie. Expertly, Lorna lead Nadeen away from the newlyweds with a decorous distance between them, despite the swelling number of dancers. When the tune ended, Lorna led Nadeen back to their seats.

"That went better than expected," said Nadeen.

"Aw, we're not that bad. Everyone's enthusiastic, which might be a different story in no time. It was getting tricky to move at all. But, hey. We got in there with the bride and groom. That's the main thing."

"Do you want a drink?'

"Lime and soda. Or similar, please." She smiled as Nadeen walked away, admiring her form as she stood at the bar. That Nadeen and her father were both wearing black and white was a little disturbing, if not surprising. Olive-skinned, they both looked good in the combination. She rubbed her bare arms, the approaching evening air casting a chill.

Nadeen passed her a tumbler. "Are you getting cold?"

"Just a little. I should be okay."

"You left your shawl in the van, didn't you? I'll fetch it. Back in a tick." Nadeen strode off toward the house.

# CHAPTER FORTY-FOUR

Lorna was sipping her drink when the black dress shoes reappeared.

Felix said, "Have we lost Nadeen?"

"She's gone to get my shawl. Won't be long."

A slow foxtrot started playing on the jukebox. He held out a hand. "Madam, may I have this dance?"

Lorna stalled. "If your wife doesn't mind."

Gaze locked on her, he smiled and tilted his head, hand outstretched. There was no getting out of dancing with the most important man of the moment. Lorna stood and allowed herself to be led. He held her confidently as they took the first step together, him moving in a flowing, loose-hipped Latino way. She was rather glad she'd had recent practice. Light on his feet and clearly fit, despite being the other side of sixty, she was very aware of his lean physique. Jodie had been busy.

He said, "You're a competent dancer. A pleasant surprise."

Trusting silence would make the experience end sooner, she nodded with a polite smile. The music stopped and they ground to a halt. He clasped her hand and led her to a peripheral table with two chairs.

"May we sit down for a short while? I'd like to at least get to know you better."

It would have been churlish to refuse. "As you wish." Scanning the crowd for Nadeen, Lorna took a seat. "You dance like a pro. It's good to have the opportunity in these days of boppy pop music."

Felix sat back in his chair. "Music always has a beat, regardless of style. But yes." He locked his fingers together in his lap. "If I may say, you look very fine in that dress. It suits an attractive woman."

"Thank you...I think." She raised her eyebrows.

He laughed abruptly, then stopped. "Do you have children, Lorna?"

"A daughter." Relieved to be in safer territory, Lorna said, "Melanie has just turned eighteen. She's doing her final exams soon. Might be off to uni next year."

"And what do you do with yourself?"

Lorna relaxed into answering whatever he chose to ask. At least he cared enough about his daughter to make an effort. And so could she.

* * *

When Nadeen returned, she spotted Felix and Lorna in plain sight. She sat down and sipped her drink. A sky-blue dress appeared beside her.

Jodie said, "May I join you?" She sat and followed Nadeen's gaze. "Oh, I get it."

"I think your brand-new husband is chatting up my sweetheart."

"See, you *do* have something in common," said Jodie. "Good taste." They shared a smile. She leaned in and whispered, "I have something to tell you that you really ought to know."

Nadeen looked askance. "But do I *want* to know?"

"Oh, yeah, you do. Because early next year, you're going to become someone's big sister."

Eyes wider than an owl's, Nadeen said, "What? You're not. Really?"

Jodie nodded. "I'm about seventeen weeks."

"Wow. Congratulations, I hope. Was this planned?"

"Um, no. Not right now. But I'm very excited."

"And my father?"

"He's stoked. I've never seen him so thrilled!" Jodie laughed. "Honestly, it's like he's won Olympic gold."

Nadeen peered at her. "But still, are you okay with it at this stage of life?"

"Very much so. Before, I was in a relationship with a super guy for thirteen years, but he didn't want children. We ended up arguing all the time until I packed up and left, two years ago now. To be honest, I'd given up. Then I met Felix at the gym and fell for him. For me, it's a dream come true."

"Well, I'm delighted for you. And I'm sure it helps that you're fit and healthy. May you have a breeze of a pregnancy. For sure, between you and him, this baby's going to be gorgeous."

"I'll be happy enough with healthy," said Jodie.

Nadeen touched Jodie's forearm. "I'm sure it will be. Just so you know, when I was a child, Dad was a thoughtful and generous father. Gentle and loving. I'm so glad you found each other."

Unexpectedly teary, Jodie covered Nadeen's hand with her own. "And I'm so glad you and Lorna found each other. She's simply lovely. Well done, you."

"Why, thank you, Jodie. I appreciate it."

Felix and Lorna made their way through the hovering guests toward them. Nadeen got up and draped the shawl around Lorna's shoulders. Rubbing her arms vigorously, Lorna said, "That's better, thanks."

"Your turn." Felix grabbed Nadeen's hand, led her to the dance area and into his arms. "Let's waltz, my girl. Do you remember how?"

She stepped into the dance, his hand in the small of her back guiding her expertly. "You make it easy."

With a pleased smile, he steered her around the other couples. "Have you and Lorna had a good time?"

"It's been great. And I must congratulate you on two counts. Your marriage and that you are expecting. Jodie just told me. A welcome surprise, eh?"

"Can you believe it?" He swung her around fast, grinning wildly. She couldn't help but crack a brilliant smile back at him. "Your old man is the luckiest guy alive!" He drew them to a sudden stop and wrapped his arms around her, more tightly than she could remember him doing since forever ago. Damp-eyed, she hugged him back and kissed him on both cheeks. With an arm around her shoulders, he started to walk her back to where Lorna and Jodie were sitting, deep in conversation.

Midwalk, Felix slowed and said out of the corner of his mouth, "Just between you and me, that other girl never measured up. This one is worthy of you." He followed it up with a blokey grin. When he took off again, Nadeen gaped and hurried to catch up.

At least half the guests had drifted inside the house or left for the evening. Others stood around in groups, chatting and making their farewells.

Jodie said, "I presume you're driving back tonight. You'll be off soon?"

With a quick glance at Nadeen, Lorna said, "Actually, we're booked at the Rendezvous Hotel in Scarborough for the night. Just so we can chill out, go for walk on the beach and drive back tomorrow sometime. We thought that would be nice for a change, eh, babe?"

"It'll be a treat. And we might catch a full moon rising soon."

The jukebox struck up a tune that had played earlier. "Oh, quick, it's a foxtrot." Lorna grabbed Nadeen's hand. "One last dance, come on!" In passing, she tossed the shawl on a chair and pulled Nadeen into her arms on the dance floor.

"Come closer. And closer, still. I want your right hip joined to my right hip. I step between your legs. You step between mine. This isn't too fast. Let's go." She steered Nadeen across the floor in a gradual curve. "Just look at me. Trust me, babe. Step in, step back, step in…that's it." Cheeks almost touching, they flowed around the floor, in the groove. Around and around.

Nadeen murmured, "We're being watched."

"No harm done."

# CHAPTER FORTY-FIVE

Nadeen unlocked their hotel room and dropped her overnight bag on the luggage stand. Following, Lorna did the same with hers. "Your father was full-on," said Lorna. "Oh, wow. Will you look at this view over the ocean? That is something, isn't it?" She did a pirouette. "Seriously. It was like an interview for the job of being your husband."

"I'm not surprised. Did he stay polite?" said Nadeen.

"He was perfectly civil. But otherwise?" Lorna shook her head. "He just couldn't conceive how this…us, might work. Poor man." She shrugged. "So, what's the plan, darling honey-babe?"

"How about a walk along the beach at sunset? Room service for a light meal. Maybe washed down with a local summer ale? Whatever you fancy, my lovely."

"Excellent. I'll just phone Melanie to see that she's okay."

"And I might run through the shower to get this makeup off and freshen up," said Nadeen. "Would you check she's fed Bella? Sometimes the old girl needs to be woken up to toilet and eat."

"I'll remind her."

Dressed down into jeans, they made their way through avenues of Norfolk pines to the sea's edge and wandered barefoot through the shallows. Quite a few people had the same idea, with a couple of hardy souls still swimming. On the horizon, an orange sun peeked through clouds as it hovered over the ocean, and they stopped to admire it.

Nadeen said, "I just remembered…Jodie is pregnant."

"She told me while you were dancing with Felix. At their age, it's challenging. Explains his good humour, eh?"

"Doesn't it, just? I couldn't be happier for them. Even if that's partly selfish on my part because I'm hoping he'll get over the missing offspring thing."

"You knew about that?"

"He only raised it once, umpteen years ago. Yeah, I knew. Disappointment can wound terribly. This news gives me solid hope."

Lorna cuddled Nadeen's arm and gave it a squeeze.

Caesar salad nearly finished, Nadeen said, "What did you mean when you asked if I knew? The thing about my father."

Lorna put down her glass and addressed the ceiling. "You know when I went to Felicity's to try on the dress? I blundered in and casually asked her, only because he's friends with her husband, if she knew what your father's problem was. And she told me. As soon as she said it, I wished I hadn't asked. Because if it was something you weren't aware of, then it wasn't for me to say anything. I'm sorry if I put my foot in it."

Nadeen set the empty bowl aside. "In the scheme of things, it doesn't matter. He's not easy, but I can't help but love him, flaws and all. I'm betting this marriage will make him happy."

"And maybe take the strain off your relationship with him?"

"For sure. That baby could make a difference. To some extent, I think it already has. Bring it on, I say." She took a sip of beer. "It doesn't hurt that he likes you."

"Oh, I'm not so sure—"

"I am! He's never been one to conceal his feelings. He and Greer couldn't stand each other. Mutual loathing at first sight. He said as much."

"In that case, lucky me, I guess."

"Lorna, you're simply likeable and good at wrangling difficult types. You radiate majesty without being a princess, in wild contrast to himself…a bit of a prince!" They looked at each other and giggled. "But that's enough about him. When are you signing that agreement with the Victorian nursery?"

"Tuesday arvo. Murray and my solicitor are acting as go-betweens with the paperwork. Then it will be a matter of handing over formulas, seedlings, and equipment. Should be all done and dusted by month's end." Lorna waved a forefinger. "And I get to keep the glasshouse. Papsom aren't interested in dismantling it. Could prove useful in the future."

"You must be a bit sad about no longer raising poppies."

"Even so, I think it's the right time to change things up and do something different. This year has had its turning points and share of complete surprises. First there was you, out of the blue." Lorna smiled and snapped her fingers. "Just like that. And here we are, in this beautiful spot with its amazing view and a promising future."

"Speaking of which, I've been thinking about that future," said Nadeen. "And us living together. There are all sorts of long-term legal, financial, and inheritance ramifications for both of us. Actually, I think we'd need legal advice. Federal marriage laws are immediate, more comprehensive and protective, but we can't marry. De facto laws apply after a year of cohabitation for same-sex couples, with variations from state to state. It can be complicated."

"All important considerations. But do the pluses outweigh the minuses?"

"Dear heart, I want to wake up with you…live my life with you. Even so, we need to ensure Melanie's inheritance remains certain. Should I cark it unexpectedly, my father is my sole heir. Therefore, when it comes to ownership issues, we need all eventualities covered. For my part, I don't care who inherits my belongings, but Morwood is a big deal because Mel is Violet's only direct descendant. Also, to me, Mel feels like a bonus daughter, if you would allow me that."

"A bonus daughter. Why not? So, we have to get paperwork organised before we do anything substantive. Makes sense to me. Otherwise?"

"I confess I've got my eye on your glasshouses for gerbera cultivation. Big plus."

"Oh, have you, now? Great minds think alike." Lorna lifted her glass and clinked it against Nadeen's. "Here's to us."

Nadeen emptied her glass and stood up. "How about a boogie around the balcony? Just because we can."

"Without music?"

"Oh, I don't know." Nadeen slid open the glass door and took Lorna's hand. They stepped outside and into a snug hold, swaying gently. "Waves breaking in time with our beating hearts…will that do?"

Lorna flashed an impish grin. "Sounds good to me." She kissed Nadeen's willing mouth.

While Lorna showered, Nadeen hunkered down in the king-sized bed, gratifyingly tired. Keeping her eyes open was a struggle. Sleep won. She didn't stir when Lorna slid between the sheets, spooned against her back, reached a hand around her waist to cradle her belly, and kissed the nape of her neck, ever so lightly. With a contented hum in her throat, she laid a hand over Lorna's and slept on.

* * *

"Wakey, wakey. Come on, it's nearly dawn."

"Huh? It's still dark."

"Yes but look. Look out the window."

Nadeen peeled open an eyelid. The moon shone straight into the room, its eerie shaft wincingly bright. "If the moon's still up, it's night. Go back to sleep."

"No, no. We have to go down to the beach and watch the moon set over the ocean. Then we'll have seen both sunset and moonset, one after the other. Isn't that something?"

"Can't you just watch through the window?"

"Nope. Has to be on the beach…the real thing. Oh, come on. When are we going to get the chance again? I want to see this. Just this once. With you."

"When you put it that way."

"Fantastic. Put some warm clothes on. Let's go!"

Alone apart from a meagre flock of dozing seagulls, they sat on a grassy dune facing the ocean with Nadeen in front and Lorna sitting higher up behind her, legs astride, arms around Nadeen's shoulders. A light, salty breeze came off the sea. The surf's waves were unusually subdued, breaking wistfully on the shore. The moon hung half above, half below the horizon, sinking fast. Behind them, a faint first light was spreading.

Lorna whispered, "Isn't this romantic?"

Chuckling, Nadeen muttered, "Very. Loony, but romantic."

"Just think. The sun and moon have been doing this tandem dance for millions of years. All those years, we've missed out. Until now."

"No more missing out for us."

The moon threw the last of its brilliant light toward them, like a wake across the black ocean. A container ship passed by, on its way to safe anchorage in Gage Roads outside Fremantle Port. Navigation lights ablaze, the ship left its own frothing wake as it crossed the moon's dying path of light.

All too soon, the moon surrendered to the sea.

"What a buzz." Lorna gave Nadeen a quick squeeze. "That was mega special. Let's go home."

# CHAPTER FORTY-SIX

Nadeen waited as Lorna unlocked Morwood's front door. She followed her in with the overnight bag and was met by an old dog whose whole back end and tail wagged furiously. She knelt down and cuddled Bella, kissed her ears and, when the dog flopped and offered up her belly, rubbed it and her chest until her tongue lolled out in bliss.

"You tart," said Nadeen, getting to her feet.

Lorna had disappeared into the kitchen. She called out, "Would you like a cuppa?"

"I'd better get on. I'm sure you've got things to do. And Mel will be home soon."

At the kitchen door, Lorna cocked her head. "So? We can sit out on the veranda with a cuppa and wait for her. Please stay."

"Okay, just for a while. Since I'm tempted to stay forever." Nadeen smiled wryly. "One day…just not yet, eh?"

"Eh. I'll bring the tea out. Go sit."

Nadeen trotted out the front with Bella in tow. It was a warm afternoon and the swing was inviting. She made herself comfortable and inhaled the fresh air heavily tinged with the scent of spring's first roses. Bella bailed up a sluggish bobtail lizard and let out her legendary cough-bark. In reply, the lizard flashed its blue tongue and hurried off to safety. Bella sniffed out a more intriguing beastie odour and made it her mission to track it down.

Lorna sat on the swing and passed over a brimming mug. "It's good to be home."

Nadeen sipped in silence for a while. "I love coming home with you. And I *love* dancing with you. So much fun. We need to do more of that."

"Anytime. With or without music. So. How are we going to cope when Mel leaves town?"

"Ouch. I'll miss my trusty sidekick. She's a credit to you."

"Noted. And she wants you to live with me, if and when she goes. She doesn't want me out here alone, but I figure I'd be fine."

Nadeen said, "Of course you would, but all things being well, it's going to be you and me."

"Alice and Violet will be pleased."

"Maybe they'll blow angelic trumpets when it happens?"

"Honey-babe, they started bugling the moment you walked through Morwood's front door."

Nadeen grinned and they snuggled closer, sitting in silence, all eyes on the driveway. Bella trotted up the stairs with strands of dry grass hanging off her ears and stood in front of Nadeen, looking hopeful. "Where have you been, ding-a-ling?" Nadeen scooped her up, plonked her on the swing beside her and picked off the grass. "Scruff bag." Bella did a pirouette and settled down, laid her head in Nadeen's lap. Smoothing Bella's silky mane with one hand and holding Lorna's sure hand with the other, things couldn't get any better.

Lorna glanced at the big old rose at the end of the veranda, laden with pungent pink flowers. "Radiance is blooming. Blooming her heart out."

A lone figure appeared in the distance. "There's our girl, now."

www.ingramcontent.com/pod-product-compliance
Lightning Source LLC
Chambersburg PA
CBHW061736310726
48969CB00002BA/543